[handwritten] ~~~~~ ~ to be centre stage!

Lust & Lyrics

Hanleigh Bradley
Author of Romance

[signature] Hanleigh Bradley ♡

Copyright © 2020 by Hanleigh Bradley

www.hanleighbradley.com

hanleigh@hanleighbradley.com

First Edition

All rights reserved. No part of this book may be reproduced in any form or by any electronic or mechanical means, including information storage and retrieval systems, without permission in writing from the publisher, except by a reviewer who may quote brief passages in a review.

This book is licensed for your personal use only. Please respect the author's work and refrain from sharing it with others. If you would like to share this book with another person, please purchase an additional copy for each recipient.

The characters, organisations and events in this book are fictitious. Any similarity to real persons, living or dead, is coincidental and not intended by the author.

To be the first to hear when Hanleigh Bradley releases a new book, join her subscribers at

http://bit.ly/34IL3J3

Dear Reader,

Love doesn't always come to us the way we want it to.

But when it comes, we should definitely embrace it.

Hanleigh

His, His Or His?

CLOVER

My mum's addiction to plants went overboard the day she named me. *I mean seriously, who names their daughter Clover?*

Fortunately, she didn't name my twin brother. That responsibility had fallen to my dad and he'd called him Creed.

I blame the drugs.

They've told us countless times that they haven't "done drugs" but *who are they kidding?* I've heard the stories. I've seen the articles.

Having a pair of rock stars for parents definitely gave Creed and I cool points in school but to us they were just like every other set of parents on the planet, except maybe slightly more absent. They got pissed if we didn't do well in class, they grounded us if we spoke back to them and all the rest of the usual shit that parents do.

They'd pushed us to succeed but their idea of success looked a little different to my friends' parents. My friends' parents wanted them to become lawyers or doctors… professionals.

Adults.

But my parents?

They wanted me to become the princess of rock. No exaggeration – those were their very words. Even now, that's their goal for my life.

Fame, fortune… and all that.

Everything I've never wanted.

It's not that I don't like music; I bloody love it. I just don't want to be famous. I don't want to stand on a stage and be gawked at by strangers. I don't want to be chased down the street by my supposed fans aka crazy stalkers.

Creed loves all that stuff. He's a complete attention whore.

Me? Not so much.

If my parents had actually asked me what I wanted to do when I was growing up, I'd have told them I wanted to write music for film. I'd always had a bit of an odd celebrity crush on Hans Zimmer. I mean seriously, that guy isn't on my most attractive list and he's like a zillion years too old for me but if I could compose the way he can… I'd lose myself.

Instead of asking what I wanted to do, my parents had pretty much guaranteed that I had every possible opportunity… or at least where it came to music. If I'd wanted to spend my time playing a sport, they'd have lost their shits but if I wanted to play an instrument, they never said no.

I'd learnt the piano, violin, guitar and bass guitar before I even knew all my times tables and that was not because I was shit at math. The teachers said I was a fricking genius but what would they know.

They called it genius. I called it hard work.

"Clo, aren't you going to answer that?" the barista asks me as she hands me a fresh coffee.

I've been coming here a lot in the last few weeks. I managed to wrangle a deal with my parents that has allowed me to take a year out traveling before becoming their perfect daughter. One year of freedom before locking myself into the cage that my loving parents have crafted for me.

Her voice breaks into the fog that's currently taking up residence inside my mind and I divert my eyes from the window I'm staring out of to look at her. It's only then that I hear the screeching of my phone.

The ominous word MUM lights up the screen and I find myself begging the universe that I'm not being called back three months early.

It's not like she'd be ringing just to check up on me. My parents don't do that. Out of sight, out of mind. Just the way I like it.

I take a breath and swipe the screen before bringing it to my ear.

"Hi mum."

"I've booked you a flight. You need to come home."

"What? Why? I've still got three months." I shouldn't have answered the phone.

"It's your brother. He's in the hospital." Those aren't the words I was expecting, and they leave me a little lost for how to respond.

"Er… what happened? Is he okay?" The questions are barrelling out of my mouth as I gather my things together and drop some cash onto the table.

"He was in a car accident."

"Is he…" I'm too scared to ask.

What if he's dead? She sounds insanely panicked and fear grips my heart. He can't be dead. *Twins know that sort of shit, right? They say that twins have some crazy assed bond, right?* Where they can sense stuff… I've never felt like that but if it was ever going to kick in, this would be the moment… *wouldn't it?*

"He's in theatre. They're operating. You need to come home."

I'm nodding my head as I practically run down the road, pushing people out of my way. This is no time for a leisurely stroll through the Parisian streets.

"I'm on my way," I say before preparing to hang up the phone.

I stop dead, finger hovering over the call button, feet firm on the ground when she says, "you know your brother's songs, right?"

Huh? Why the fuck does that matter, right now?

This is a perfect example of one of those moments when I wonder if my parents are perhaps still on crack.

"His band! Clover? You know their songs, right?"

"Yeah…" I say hesitantly. *What the hell is she up to?*

"Good. Rush back. Your flight leaves in two hours. It's only an hour's flight so I should see you at Heathrow at five. That will give us two and a half hours to get you ready."

"Ready for what?"

"The concert!" She's exasperated. I can hear it in her tone. I don't have a clue why she expects me to be following her delusional ramblings. Surely the concert is cancelled…

"Concert?"

"Your brother's concert." Now she sounds like she thinks I'm the one on drugs. "Just hurry up."

I'm tempted to refuse but I'm not daft. She'll have someone on the next flight here if I don't come home right away.

She can't seriously expect me to take my brother's place though, can she?

Fuck! Of course, she can. *My mum's mental.*

If I Was Your Boyfriend

Faded Love (#1)

You know you love me, just bleed whenever

And I'll be there. I know you care

You are my girlfriend, the only one I want

And I can't let you go

If I was your boyfriend, I'd never let you run

Keep you in my arms, you'd never be alone

I can be your heart, anything you want

If I was your boyfriend, I'd never let you run, I'd never let you run

Darling. Darling. Darling. Don't run.

My heart. My heart. We can't be apart.

Darling. Darling. Darling. Hold on.

Your heart. Your heart. Beats inside my chest.

Darling. Darling. Darling. You're mine.

If you need me, I'll come running

From a thousand miles away

Hanleigh Bradley

When you call me, I'll come running

Faster than a high speed train

If I was your boyfriend, I'd never let you run

Keep you in my arms, you'd never be alone

I can be your heart, anything you want

If I was your boyfriend, I'd never let you run, I'd never let you run

Darling. Darling. Darling. Don't run.

My heart. My heart. We can't be apart.

Darling. Darling. Darling. Hold on.

Your heart. Your heart. Beats inside my chest.

Darling. Darling. Darling. You're mine.

Na na na, na na na, na na na na.

If I was your boyfriend.

Na na na, na na na, na na na na.

If I was your boyfriend.

My friends say I'm a fool to think

That you're the one for me but

Lust & Lyrics

You know you love me, Just bleed whenever

And I'll be there, I know you care

You are my girlfriend, the only one I want

Don't leave me

Don't go

I said, don't leave me

Don't go

RIGBY

"What do you mean, he's not answering his phone?"

They have got to be joshing. *This is a fucking joke.*

We've got just a handful of hours before tonight's gig and our bloody lead singer and guitarist is fucking AWOL.

Nash looks up from his phone.

"But he wasn't at rehearsal earlier, either… He better be fucking coming."

Then he's looking back at his phone as Nona, our stylist tries to attack his face with makeup. He's batting her away as best he can as he texts whatever girl he plans to fuck tonight.

"You can do my face if you like, Nona," Ziggy says bashfully, causing me to shake my head with disdain. That lad has it bad. I get it. She's fit. But I don't mix lust and lyrics.

I have this whole philosophy going; *it's a fucking way of life.*

Lust & Lyrics

My lyrics are for my fans. I don't write songs for girlfriends, not ever and I don't fuck or date anyone I work with. I don't have a lot of rules, just those two and so far, things are working out pretty well.

Point is, that for me, Nona is off limits.

She's fit but she falls into the category of lyrics… she's work. But Ziggy doesn't have the same rules as me and so right now, he's on a mission to win over the pretty little stylist at all costs. Except he's completely missed the fact that's she's lost in lust over Creed and has been since the day she met him.

"I'm going to murder Creed," I mumble more to myself than anyone else.

"He'll be here," Nona says softly, a hint of protectiveness in her tone.

"Why tonight?" Nash complains. "It's the bloody O2."

He's right. Creed has a habit of choosing his fucking moments and if he's going to fuck up, he'll fuck up royally. I guess that's what happens when you're rock royalty. His parents own our fucking label. He probably won't even get pulled up on this shit.

I try ringing him again but there's still no answer. Giving up, I fling my phone down on the table.

"I'm going to fucking have him!"

"Do you think he's alright?" Ziggy asks. He's too soft. The baby face of the group.

"He better be fucking dead, because he will be when I get my hands on him."

Nona tuts disapprovingly but doesn't look my way. The door practically falls off its hinges as Jett bursts into the dressing room.

"Creed is on his way," he says in a lacklustre voice that doesn't match the urgency of his pace.

"Where the hell was he?" I ask.

He ignores me until he's sat in front of the mirror, ready to get his face done.

"He was in a car accident."

Shit. Now I feel like a dick.

"Is he okay?" Nona is the first to speak, fear dripping from her words.

"I guess so," he doesn't sound convinced, "or we would have cancelled."

Creed and Jett are best buds. They have been for fuck knows how long. The expression on his face doesn't reassure me one bit.

"Have you seen him?" Nash asks.

"No. They wouldn't let me."

I open my mouth to ask more but close it when our manager walks into the room, calling us to attention.

"Nona, just get these four sorted. Creed will arrive ready and head straight on stage. We've got thirty minutes before you're up. Break a leg, kids."

Then the middle-aged man is walking back out of the room as if the world hasn't fallen off its hinges.

"What the fuck?" I ask before collapsing into my own chair.

We're a new band. We've only been together for nine months, but I thought we'd all become pretty tight. But right now, one of us has been in a car crash and our manager is saying jack shit about it.

Shouldn't we be cancelling? Logic says he can't be that fucking hurt if he's still going to actually play.

I stick my earphones in and try to switch off my brain for a little while, turning up the music and closing my eyes. It wouldn't be so bad if Creed wasn't the fucking front man... who am I kidding, if it was Ziggy we'd be without a drummer and if it was Nash, we'd lose the base. Without Jett we'd have no keys and without me... well you'd lose your second guitar and vocals.

Point is we all have a job to do. *This shit is a mess.*

We didn't even have a proper rehearsal and it's the fucking London O2. Why couldn't he have been late when we played in that bloody dive in Aberdeen.

No, it has to be the O2!

I've got to calm my shit. It's not like it's Creed's fault. Accidents happen. What matters is that he's alive and well enough to play. He's on his way and everything is going to be fine. It feels like saying it out loud will jinx it though.

Stretching my arms, I take a yawn. Then Nona is sorting my hair before sending me off to change my clothes. She might be fit but she's damn bossy. She flips her blonde hair and makes her way towards Jett.

There's a bang on the door a few moments later.

"Ten minutes to show time," a squeaky voiced kid says as he darts his head round the door. Then we're all barrelling out of the dressing room as Nona wishes us luck.

I don't get nervous. I was born for this shit. I fucking love it. But tonight, I'm shit scared that Creed won't make it here in time. I'm silently berating the label for not cancelling. It's his fucking parents' label. You'd think they'd cancel.

Walking towards the stage, I can hear the buzz of the crowd. I thrive off that sound. The place is packed. I can tell without peeking through the curtains, it's a full house. Tonight is either going to be bloody brilliant or we're going to fall flat on our arses. I guess it really depends if Creed shows up or not.

"He'll show," Ziggy is saying from somewhere behind me and no one bothers to contradict him so perhaps I'm the only one wondering if he will.

"He has to show," Nash says in a voice that says he's less than impressed.

Our manager, Switch – that's what he has us call him. Daft nickname if you ask me – is patting us on the back and pushing us onto the stage. The lights are down so I can barely see as I make my way towards where my guitar is waiting for me.

I stop the moment I see him, causing Ziggy to walk right into the back of me.

Creed is stood centre stage, checking his guitar is tuned, larger than life. Not a mark on him that I can see. *I'm going to fucking kill that lad.*

Oh Darling Violet

Faded Love (#2)

Oh darling Violet

My love for you runs deep

Your face reminds me

Of pretty words that keep

Roses are red

But Violets are blue

I like drinking tequila

Especially with you

Oh darling Violet

I love your elbows, your pretty elbows

Oh darling Violet

I love your elbows, your pretty elbows

Oh darling Violet

Your loving face lights up. Your sweet soul calls me back

Oh darling Violet

Lust & Lyrics

My love for you won't quit

Your face reminds me

Of promises yet to be made

Roses are red

But Violets are blue

I like drinking tequila

Especially with you

CLOVER

Waiting for me when I make my way through the arrivals terminal is my mother's assistant, Jasper. If anyone knows how mental my parents are, it's him.

You wouldn't know it from the benign look on his face as he waits for me though. From that expression, you'd think that today was just any other day. And maybe it is.

Maybe I've just forgotten how ridiculous things get because I've been away for nine long months. Nine months of no parents, no expectations. Just me and my guitar.

Maybe I'm the only one in complete shock at my parents utter audacity.

They seriously can't expect this to work, can they?

Except knowing my parents, of course they expect this to work. They are about as obnoxious as it's possible to be.

I love them to bits, but they really have no concept of reality. Then again why would they? Their lives have been a dream. They've had it all. Fame. Fortune. A fairy tale love story.

"They aren't serious?" I ask as soon as I reach him.

He takes my case from me before answering. He's just trying to buy time to school his face into hiding his amusement. He's been working with my mum for decades so for him, it really is just a usual day at the office. It's not like this is the most absurd request he's ever received from her.

"As serious as a heart attack," he says as he drops his hand to my shoulder, patting it gently.

Jasper has been more of a parent to me and Creed than either of our real parents. Whenever they went on tour, it had been Jasper that took care of us. It was Jasper that helped us with our homework growing up. It was Jasper who took us to school and who attended our parent teacher conferences.

I nod my head because as angry as I am with my parents, it's not Jasper's fault.

"I've got a stylist waiting in the car," he tells me. "She's going to get you ready on the way. We haven't got much time."

Again, I'm nodding my head mutely because I'm at a complete loss for what else I'm supposed to do.

My parents expect me just to go along with this so what else can I do?

"Is my brother okay?" I ask as I follow Jasper out of the airport, towards the place where the limo is waiting. I wish I could tell him to take me to the hospital to see Creed rather than to go to the concert.

"He's still in surgery."

He glances my way and I see concern in his eyes. Opening the door for me, he offers me a sad smile.

"I know that this probably all seems a bit crazy," he says softly, "but remember this is your brother's dream."

Those words catch me. My parents might have asked me to do something completely ridiculous but actually this isn't for them. Not really. Sure, they're doing it, so they don't lose coinage. They don't want to have to return the ticket money. I get it. But I won't do it for them. I'll do it for my brother. *It's for Creed.*

"Okay," I reply. "I'll do it but I'm not cutting off my hair."

There's no way in hell I'm cutting my hair. Not for my mum. Not for my dad. Not for the fucking label. Not for Saving Creed. Not even for my brother.

That gets a chuckle from Jasper.

"Don't worry. Crimson has a wig for you."

He nods his head towards the car.

I breathe in deeply before climbing into the backseat of the limo. Maybe insanity runs in the family. I'm clearly losing my marbles if I'm agreeing to do this. I nod my head at the stylist that's now sat opposite me.

"Wow," she whistles, "you really do look just like Creed."

"Except the colour of our eyes," I say absent-mindedly.

Creed's eyes are a deep blue, almost cobalt. Growing up I'd been jealous as hell of those eyes. As pretty as mine are, they can't compare. I don't actually know what colour my eyes are, if I'm honest. They're neither blue or green or grey. They change depending on the lighting and my clothes. I suppose they're more green than anything else.

"I've got you a blue shirt," Crimson says. "It should bring out the blue in your eyes."

She's quiet as she holds up the shirt in front of me.

"If worse comes to worse, I also have contacts."

I'm nodding my head again. This is why I don't want to be here. Whenever I'm around my family, I find myself jumping through hoops just so they're expectations are met, their dreams are kept.

You're doing this for Creed, I tell myself again. *It's all for Creed.*

"We need to put this on your head," she says as she flings what appears to be a swim cap at me. She must realise I'm not impressed because she says, "it's the only way to save your hair."

The idea of hiding my rose gold curls under a wig causes me to pout. *It's for Creed. You can do it for Creed.*

You owe him, I remind myself. *You have to protect his dream.*

Crimson leans towards me as she begins to plaster my face in stage makeup. I should be grateful she's not overly talkative.

"Who knows?" I ask Jasper.

"Knows?"

"That I'm back… about Creed… everything."

"Your parents, me, Crimson, Saving Creed's manager and you."

It's a relief that the list isn't crazy long. As if this isn't embarrassing enough, the idea of the band knowing would be too much to bear.

"Good," I reply, "let's keep it that way. That's my second condition."

"I didn't realise we were negotiating," Jasper retorts good humouredly.

"Everything in life is a negotiation."

"If you're negotiating, you should do it properly."

"Properly?"

"You could ask for an extension on your gap year," he suggests, "or you could demand that you won't sign with the label."

Ironically, like a fool I haven't even considered placing those sorts of demands. The reality is that I don't want to gamble with my brother's dream.

When Your Life Is Full Of Boring Bills And Dishes

Faded Love (#4)

Day one, I wash my face

I go to work, I stay late, overtime

I cook, I wash the dishes

I sleep, This life is mundane

My guitar is dusting over in the corner

There's no living when you're skint

All I want to do is drink beer with you

And sing this song for you to hear

But instead I'm falling apart

Day two, I wake up late

Rushing around, going to work late again

I eat on the go

I don't see your face once

My piano goes unplayed for another night

There's no living when you're skint

All I want to do is drink beer with you

And sing this song for you to hear

Lust & Lyrics

But instead I'm falling apart

Day three, life's on repeat
I think I'm coming down with a cold
But I can't stop, need to work
Living in my overdraft
At this rate I'll forget how to sing
There's no living when you're skint
All I want to do is drink beer with you
And sing this song for you to hear
But instead I'm falling apart

Day four, wake up early
Go to work, stay late
I need the money to pay the bills
Need to at least cover the rent
Music is my life
But there's no living when you're skint
All I want to do is drink beer with you
And sing this song for you to hear
But instead I'm falling apart

Hanleigh Bradley

Day five, finally finished with work
The weekend is on its way
I'll be able to live
Even if its just for two days
The song is calling my name
There's no living when you're skint
All I want to do is drink beer with you
But instead I'm falling apart

Day six, goes too fast
We sing, we live, we play
For one day I forget
And it's the perfect day
Me and you and my guitar
But there's no living when you're skint
All I want to do is drink beer with you
But instead I'm falling apart

Day seven, trying to ignore
I'll be back at work tomorrow

Lust & Lyrics

This reprieve isn't real

Love is only for the weekend

Music is only for the weekend

Coz, there's no living when you're skint

All I want to do is drink beer with you

But instead I'm falling apart

There's nothing in this world that makes me smile like you do

But you'll never look at me and my guitar

Because I'm just a skint musician

I could tell you you're my muse but what would that do

I'd still have to pay the bills and wash the dishes

Because I'm just a skint musician

JETT

I know it the moment I see him. *That's not Creed.*

It's all in the posture. Creed holds himself with an arrogance that can't be replicated. But that doesn't make sense.

If it's not Creed, then who is it? Who could possibly have the balls to try to pass themselves off as Creed Levon?

They're about the same height. Creed could be an inch taller. The person on the stage has a slighter frame... definitely less muscle.

If I didn't know any better, I'd say it was Clo but she's currently in Paris. I know because I saw her Instagram post just a few hours ago about drinking an iced cappuccino under the Eifel Tower.

Also, there is no way in hell that Clover would come back early. She's got another three months and at least two more places she plans to visit. Not that I'm tracking her whereabouts or anything.

I stride the distance between us and turn him to face me. He looks me dead in the eye, his eyes wide, scared, a deer in the headlights.

Clover.

I don't know what I'm supposed to do. Act like I don't know it's her? Give her a hug and welcome her back? Ask after Creed? *Fuck, what about Creed?*

"How was the iced cappuccino?" I ask the first thing that pops into my head.

She licks her lips in a motion that is pure Clover. It's an action that is so not Creed. Although if that boy pulled that look off as well as his sister, it would definitely win him some more fans.

"Tasty," is all she says in response.

Considering she's definitely nervous, you wouldn't know. Her voice is an octave higher than Creed's and her eyes are not quite right.

"Clo," I try to ask her, but I can't bring myself to ask the question that most needs answering.

She blinks a few times and I'm reminded that she's far prettier than her brother. The girls fall all over Creed but it's nothing compared to the effect Clover has on... *Men? Women? Anyone who breathes?*

The woman is sex on legs. She's twenty-two and as hot as sin. Green eyes. Long coppery pink hair. Although that seems to be missing right about now. I find myself cringing at the idea that she's chopped it off.

"He's okay." Her voice breaks the trance I've found myself in, as she tries to soothe my concern. "He's still in theatre but they say it's going well."

"You've not seen him?" I ask bluntly.

I'm clinging to her, my hands clamped down on her shoulders. We haven't exactly got time for a reunion. I glance towards Rigs and the others but they're not paying us any attention.

"No. I came straight from the airport."

"What are your parents thinking?" I knew they were mental but they can't seriously expect this to work…

She shakes her head, looking down to her guitar before looking back at me.

"It's the drugs, Jett. I'm telling you, it's the drugs."

Her words cause me to burst out laughing. In typical Clover fashion, she's eased my concern and brought a smile to my face.

"Can you do this?"

It's not that I don't believe she can. I know she can. But I also know she doesn't want to. She doesn't want the fame.

I've seen her on stage more times than I can count and every time she's owned it.

She performs like she was born for it and yet, she hates it. Ironically, I think that she'd see it differently if she hadn't been pushed into it by her parents.

"How hard can it be?" She offers me a wink. "My brother sings like a girl anyway."

"Don't let him hear you say that."

I drop my hands from her shoulders, preparing to walk away. I glance back towards the others. They look oblivious. As far as they know Creed has arrived just in time. They don't know that we've just had our arses rescued by the future princess of rock herself.

They know she exists.

Everyone at the label knows all about Clover, the illusive daughter of the Levon family. But they don't know her; they've never met her. They've just heard stories. Most of which do nothing to describe her. They know that she's supposed to be a musical genius. They know that she's abroad.

They probably think she's a spoilt rich kid but that's not Clover. Musical genius, sure. If you ask me, limiting her genius to music is underestimating her though.

Rich, sure.

Spoilt, never. I've known her since primary two and I like to believe I know her pretty well. She's anything but spoilt.

"You know what you're doing?" I ask softly.

She smirks at me, before licking her lower lip subconsciously, causing my stomach to flip. Her green eyes are bright, and I almost wonder if she's excited.

"I wrote at least a few of these songs."

She's right. I've seen her name on the manuscript paper often enough. She probably knows our sound better than we do.

Even so, its funny hearing her brag. She's not the cocky twin. That's Creed.

I nod my head, chuckling under my breath before walking away. I don't like leaving her there, exposed, vulnerable and alone. She's not like her brother. He digs this shit. Clover's different, softer, shy… She hates being centre stage and yet I'm convinced it's where she belongs.

Making my way towards my keyboard, my eyes drift towards the other guys. Ziggy is already behind his kit, drumsticks in hand. His usually happy expression is clouded over with anticipation. Nash is leaning against an amp as he pretends to look bored. He's far from bored. He's wired, buzzing with the energy of the crowd that we can't see.

Lust & Lyrics

Rigby is adjusting the height of his mic stand. It's a nervous habit that we rarely see from him. Rigs doesn't usually get nervous. He's like Creed in that way. But he likes it when things go to plan and tonight nothing has gone right. Including the fact that right now in the place where our lead vocalist should be stood is his twin sister.

Only the fucking Levon family would do something as batshit crazy as this. Perhaps Clover is right, and her parents are on drugs…

I Want You Naked

Faded Love (#5)

I want you naked

I want you naked

I want you naked

I don't care what you're saying

I don't care what you're doing

I don't care so long as you're naked

I want you naked

I want you naked

I want you naked

Laying on my bed, in my arms

Sitting in my lap, right here with me

I don't care so long as you're naked

I want you naked

I want you naked

I want you naked

I'm not going to tell you I love you

Lust & Lyrics

I'm not going to ask you to dance

I'll never be your boyfriend, I just want

I want you naked

I want you naked

I want you naked

CLOVER

It's practically pitch black and I'm alone. Sort of. The rest of Saving Creed is behind me, messing around with their instruments. The lights are about to go up, but I can barely breathe.

My heart is skipping in my chest and my palms are sweaty. I need to calm the fuck down.

I need to be ready for the moment when the lights go up. I have to play the first song. It's one I wrote but that doesn't make me any less nervous. We're meant to be playing this song first to ease my nerves but it's doing nothing of the sort.

I feel the heat of the spotlight as it hits me. I play an E minor and hope against all logic that I don't fuck up. For a split second it's just me and my guitar and then I open my eyes and see the sea of faces before me.

"You know you love me. Just bleed whenever," the words fall from my mouth easily, "and I'll be there. I know you care."

Lust & Lyrics

The lights are still low, the rest of the guys in the dark as I sing the first verse.

"You are my girlfriend, the only one I want. And I can't let you go."

I almost jump out of my skin when I hear Rigby join me singing, "If I was your boyfriend, I'd never let you run."

Focusing on the chords I'm playing, I try not to look at the crowds of people in front of me. Instead I stare at the sound desk at the very back. I put a smirk on my face that hopefully resembles my brother's and sing my lungs out.

Somehow, I manage not to fuck up our first song which if you ask me is a minor miracle since I've never played with Creed's band mates before.

When I sing the final line of the song my nerves are slightly less frayed, but I'm still convinced that I'm going to mess up. I take a breath and glance behind me at the drummer, Ziggy. Giving him the nod, I let him lead us into the second song.

I'm overheating already. There's sweat on my forehead. The wig I'm wearing is itchy, but I try to ignore it.

The second song is one my brother wrote, and I don't know it as well. My brother has never been one for serious lyrics and this song is no exception. Together Jett, Rigby and I sing the chorus.

Hanleigh Bradley

Roses are red

But Violets are blue

I like drinking tequila

Especially with you

The song almost causes me to giggle at the idea of my brother having a girlfriend. If there's one thing I know about Creed, it's that he loves being loved. There's no world in which he'd settle down and have only one girlfriend.

I make my way through the rest of the set without much issue. But then it hits me that I have to sing the final song. It's one I wrote a long time ago about a person I'd rather forget.

I huff gently, closing my eyes for a split second in an attempt to prepare myself. When I gave this song to Creed, I'd promised myself that I'd never sing it again. Not for him. Not for anyone.

The lights are swirling around me, a blue colour that almost blinds me before they settle on me. The whole auditorium is silent with anticipation.

I begin to pluck at my guitar softly.

I can't play this the way Creed plays it. I know I should but I can't. If I'm going to play it, I'm going to play it right, the way it was written. I glance towards Jett and he offers me a nod, giving me the go ahead to follow my heart. He's heard it played this way countless times back when we were in school.

"I don't know how many times," I sing softly into the mic, "I can say these words."

It's just me and my guitar. There's no one else here. Or at least that's what I tell myself.

"Before they set in, before you believe." I wait a beat and glance towards Jett, inviting him to add the keys. "Why won't you believe."

"I'm so sorry that I love you," I sing the chorus, twisting my neck to look at Rigby, hoping he'll add a harmony. I shouldn't be messing up their usual routine, but I can't sing this song if I don't sing it my way. "I'm so sorry I hurt you." I'm relieved when I hear Rigby's voice merging with mine in my ear. "I'm sorry, I'm sorry."

I nod my head towards Ziggy, silently asking for a gently beat. "I broke my word. I broke your soul." He joins us just as the chorus ends and I feel something that I've not felt in the longest time. I can't describe it, the way this song affects me.

I nod for Rigby to sing the second verse and take a breather. He adds his own guitar to the sound, strumming gently. "For every time I made you smile, with those three words. For making you dream, for making you believe. But why don't you see."

My breath catches in my throat as I listen to him sing the words someone else once sang to me and I'm not ready when the chorus comes. Fortunately, Rigby and Jett carry it well, giving me a chance to add a harmony ad hock. This time Nash adds the bass guitar, adding a depth to the chorus that brings butterflies to my gut.

"Every hurt that I've caused," I begin the third verse, "your dream that I cursed."

Rigby joins me for the next line. "For all I have done to you and everything I failed to do."

"I'm sorry but don't you know," I finish alone.

We blitz through the chorus once more and then Jett sings the bridge, "Did I hold you too tightly? Did I forget to let you fly high? Did my love hold you back? Did love make me blind?"

I struggle to control my emotions. I hate this song as much as I love it. Then Rigby and I are joining Jett for the chorus once again.

Leaving the last verse to Rigby, I just listen to the sound we're making together. It's so completely different to the way Saving Creed usually play this song but I don't regret it.

"I didn't even realise that I was falling for you," Rigby sings. "I was so lost in you that I didn't even see you."

I join him for the last line. "I can't make this right now."

Then all the sound drops out again and it's just me in the spotlight with my guitar. I pluck the strings softly.

"I'm so sorry. I'm so sorry. I'm so sorry that I love you."

I focus on the movement of my fingers, taking a deep breath before continuing to sing, "I'm sorry, I'm sorry. I'm so sorry. I'm so sorry. I'm so sorry that I love you. I'm sorry, I'm sorry.

I don't see the crowds before me, for the first time in years I see his face in my mind.

"Words mean nothing at all. An apology can't turn back time." I pause even though I know I must continue.

Jett picks up the slack. "Words mean nothing at all."

Then together we sing, "an apology can't turn back time."

Jett continues to repeat those two lines over and over again as the other instruments join back in and I sing, "I'm so sorry. I'm so sorry."

"I hurt you. I put you through hell," Rigby follows after me with the next line.

"I didn't even realise that I was falling for you," I sing softly as all the music fades out. "I'm so sorry, I'm so sorry."

For the last time, it's just me and my guitar. "But words mean nothing at all. An apology can't turn back time."

I close my eyes as I hear the crowd erupt with applause.

I'm So Sorry That I Love You

Faded Love (#7)

I don't know how many times

I can say these words

Before they set in

Before you believe

Why won't you believe

I'm so sorry that I love you

I'm sorry I hurt you

I'm sorry, I'm sorry

I broke my word. I broke your soul

For every time I made you smile

With those three words

For making you dream

For making you believe

But why don't you see

Hanleigh Bradley

I'm so sorry that I love you
I'm sorry I hurt you
I'm sorry, I'm sorry
I broke my word. I broke your soul

Every hurt that I've caused
Your dream that I cursed
For all I have done to you
And everything I failed to do
I'm sorry but don't you know

I'm so sorry that I love you
I'm sorry I hurt you
I'm sorry, I'm sorry
I broke my word. I broke your soul

Did I hold you too tightly?
Did I forget to let you fly high?
Did my love hold you back?
Did love make me blind?

Lust & Lyrics

I'm so sorry that I love you

I'm sorry I hurt you

I'm sorry, I'm sorry

I broke my word. I broke your soul

I didn't even realise

That I was falling for you

I was so lost in you

That I didn't even see you

I can't make this right now

I'm so sorry

I'm so sorry

I'm so sorry that I love you

I'm sorry, I'm sorry

I'm so sorry

I'm so sorry

I'm so sorry that I love you

I'm sorry, I'm sorry

Hanleigh Bradley

Words mean nothing at all

An apology can't turn back time

Words mean nothing at all

An apology can't turn back time

I'm so sorry

I'm so sorry

I hurt you

I put you through hell

I didn't even realise that I was falling for you

I'm so sorry, I'm so sorry

But

Words mean nothing at all

An apology can't turn back time

NASH

The crowd is going crazy. I don't understand why we've never played it that way before.

Rigby is clearly pissed. He doesn't like it when we deviate from the plan. He puts down his guitar in its stand and then storms off stage.

The rest of us follow after him before the lights go up.

Back in the dressing room, the atmosphere is tense. Creed looks unsettled as he takes a seat. He pulls out a phone that I don't recognise. The cover is wrong. Instead of the cobalt blue one that he insists matches his eyes, it's a rose gold colour. He raises the phone to his ear, completely oblivious to the daggers he's receiving from Rigs.

"How is he?" he says into the handset. His voice is slightly hoarse, higher than usual.

He's quiet as he listens to the person on the other end of the call. Jett is watching him closely. After a moment's pause, he's jumping out of his seat.

"Is he awake?" Creed asks.

His face drops. I guess he didn't get the answer he wanted. "Bring the car around," he demands. "I want to see him."

"Fuck sake," he says gruffly, running a hand through his hair as he bites down on his bottom lip. "Tell her to fuck herself."

"I don't think I can get away with telling your mother that," Jasper replies as he enters the room, lowering the phone that is held to his ear at the same time.

Creed sighs as he gathers his stuff together.

"I want to see him."

"Your mother…" Jasper begins before sideways glancing around the room. "Not tonight." Jasper leaves the room without waiting for a reply.

"Creed," Jett begins, "I can take you."

But Creed shakes his head.

"No. Thanks. There's no point. I'll go first thing tomorrow."

Jett looks ready to argue but anything he plans on saying gets cut across by Rigby.

"What the hell was that in there?"

Creed looks up at Rigby. It's funny. I never realised how short Creed is. Right now, he's a full head shorter than Rigby.

"What?" Creed sighs.

"You changed the order of the songs and then completely fucked around with 'I'm Sorry That I Love You.'"

Creed nods his head, not disagreeing.

"Technically, management changed the set list. As for Sorry, actually I just played it according to the sheet music."

"We've never played it like that before!" Rigby argues.

"That's because we weren't allowed." Jett steps forward.

"Says who?" Ziggy asks, his interest peeked.

"The composer," Creed replies.

"Then why were we allowed to this time?" I ask.

Creed shrugs his shoulders and I'm not sure if he can't answer the question or if he doesn't want to answer it.

"I thought your sister wrote Sorry…" Ziggy remarks.

Creed nods his head once.

"Anyway, I'm sorry for changing it without practicing it first with you all… but you played it well so… no harm no foul."

Rig's eyes look like they're about to pop from their sockets.

"No harm no foul? You've got to be fucking joshing."

I try to defuse the situation before it gets out of hand.

"Are you alright, Creed? We heard about the crash."

Creed looks stricken for a second before he says, "I'm all good."

He sounds nonchalant enough but it's clear from the way he's holding himself, much of his arrogance gone, that he's far from okay.

Rigby opens his mouth, but I pat him on the back.

"Come on man. Let's just drop it now."

"Yeah," Ziggy agrees, "I really liked the way Sorry sounded tonight and the fans definitely liked it."

Jett pushes us all towards the door.

"Should we order in tonight? I'm dying for a slice of pizza," he says.

Rigby still doesn't look impressed but at least he's holding in whatever it is he wants to say to Creed.

He's watching him closely as if he's just biding his time.

"I'm not really in the mood for pizza," he says as we make our way through the corridors that will take us to the carpark, where our car is waiting.

As we enter the carpark, we pass Nona and Crimson. Creed stops for a second and I think he's going to speak to Nona, but he doesn't. Instead, he turns to Crimson.

"Thanks for your help today, Crimson."

"You're welcome, Creed," she replies.

I've never known Creed and Crimson to get along. He's called her every name under the sun, but I've never seen him thank her. She could save his mother's life and he'd probably still not say thank you. After that, he's quiet as he makes his way towards the car. He seems oblivious to the chaos he's stirring around him with his odd behaviour, but all the guys have noticed it.

Rigby has an eyebrow raised and Ziggy look like he's just eaten something that didn't quite taste the way he expected it to. The only person who looks unphased is Jett.

CLOVER

They didn't say anything about spending the night at my brother's house!

I consider phoning my mum and demanding that I spend the night at home but actually that's the last thing I want to do. The idea of living under my parents' roof is terrifying.

Even so, the idea of living with four men who don't know I'm a woman… that's pretty scary too. Sitting in the car with my brother's best friends, I try to covertly check them out. I only really know what Creed has told me about them and that isn't much.

Ziggy is a bit of a blonde cutie. His hair is not quite short but not long either. It's just long enough for it to curl. He has his drumsticks in hand and is drumming the headrest in front of him, annoying a tired Nash.

Nash looks broody. His hair is dark and shoulder length, pulled into a man bun. He has stubble on his chin.

Jett is everything he's always been; mature, handsome… black hair that's gelled to sit exactly the way he wants it to.

Then Rigby is something else altogether.

If Ziggy is the pretty boy, then Rigby is the bad boy of the group. He looks downright pissed, with a frown that seems to storm across his face. His hair is a chestnut colour and his eyes are blue. He's the sort of guy that I have a habit of falling hard for. The sort of guy I write songs about. The sort that breaks my heart.

I remind myself not to take Rigby's current mood to heart. One thing Creed has definitely told me about Rigby is that he's a moody shit.

The London traffic is awful as always and I find myself wishing that I could escape the car and its inhabitants – especially Rigby.

"Snap out of it, Rigs," Nash says after ten minutes of awkward silence.

"Yeah! He said sorry," Ziggy adds. "Although I still think it sounds better the way we played it tonight."

"That's not the point," Rigby complains. "He can't go around messing with our songs without talking about it first."

"Technically it's not our song," I respond irritably, causing Jett to chuckle from somewhere behind me.

"We have the rights to it."

"Not exclusively."

He's beginning to piss me off. It's my fucking song and I'll play it how I fucking want.

I flew home early to save their arses and he can't even be fucking polite. Maybe I'll just take the rights back and stop them singing the song altogether. Except I couldn't take my brother's number one away from him. I'd have to be a seriously shitty sister to do that.

Rigby doesn't reply, instead he puts his earphones in so that he can ignore us. As much as I don't want to admit it, he's got the right idea with that one. I copy him, putting my earphones in so I can listen to the track I'm currently working on. I have the music but still no lyrics and it's driving me nuts that I don't have the words yet. I begin to hum along with it as I try to clear my thoughts, in an attempt to see if anything comes to mind.

It doesn't. Instead, I just seem to piss Rigby off even more if his grumbling is anything to go by. Apparently that lad has super hearing because he can hear my humming over his own music.

This better only be for one night. If I have to put up with Rigby Nicklen for more than one day, I might do something that will land me in jail.

Hopefully my brother will wake up and I'll be able to get on a plane and return to Paris.

***

When we arrive, I realise I've never been to my brother's place before. I have no idea how I'm supposed to pretend to be Creed when I don't even know where his bedroom is.

Fortunately, Jett comes to my rescue, guiding me through the house, saying in a loud voice, "you must be proper tired after your crash."

I almost tell him that tired doesn't cut it, but I can't be bothered to enter into a conversation about it. All I want to do is sleep.

When it's just the two of us in my brother's bedroom, he smiles at me. It's a smile that could melt a girl's panties.

"Thank you, Clover," he says softly. "We really owe you."

I shake my head. There's not much I wouldn't do for Creed or Jett for that matter.

"It's all good," I say as I begin to pull the wig from my head.

"Don't forget to lock the door," he says softly, "so the guys don't see your hair." He takes a lock of my rose hair between his fingers. "I really am glad you didn't chop it off."

"Do you really think they'd ever be able to convince me to do that?"

"Not bloody likely," he replies with a smirk. "Hopefully, Creed will wake up tomorrow and you won't have to put that wig back on."

"A girl can wish."

The truth is, it feels a little bit too much like wishful thinking. It's a bit odd that my parents haven't allowed me to see Creed. I don't say it to Jett. I don't want to worry him, but I can't help but wonder if things are worse than they've told me.

I wouldn't put it past them.

I lock the door behind him as he leaves and then I begin to undress, removing everything that is Creed, gradually revealing Clover underneath. I unwrap the bandage that is currently restricting my boobs before pulling one of my brother's t-shirts on to sleep in. Perhaps, this is all just a crazy assed dream and I'll wake up in the morning back in my hotel in Paris.

Kissed Her Over And Over

Faded Love (#3)

This was never the way I planned it

I got so brave, Lost my mind

No, I don't even know her name

It doesn't matter

I see her soul and that's enough

I kissed her over and over

I liked it more than I can say

I kissed her over and over

Her soul calling my name

I kissed her over and over

I liked it more than I can say

I kissed her over and over

Her soul calling my name

She's kissable, so magical

This is not the way it's supposed to go

I still want her, Too good to deny

Hanleigh Bradley

She's too good by far
I see her soul and that's enough

I want her over and over
I liked it more than I can say
I want her over and over
Her soul calling my name
I want her over and over
I liked it more than I can say
I want her over and over
Her soul calling my name.

ZIGGY

For the first time since our very first gig, Creed breaks his warm down routine. Rigby has settled onto the sofa, x-box controller in hand but Creed has vanished upstairs with Jett.

We all have our own routine that we follow.

Jett always winds down with a book while Nash goes out and fucks whatever girl he's currently seeing. I tend to just head to my room and listen to music and Creed and Rigby play x-box together.

Even when Creed and Rigby fall out, they still play video games together after a gig. It's like a tradition or something. So, the fact that Creed hasn't sat his arse down next to Rigby is beyond weird.

There are only two possible reasons; he's actually really hurt, or he's not just pissed with Rigs, he's livid.

Looking at Rigby, it's clear to see that he's beginning to feel guilty.

"Is he actually hurt?" he asks absent-mindedly.

I shrug because I don't know any more than he does. Creed is behaving weird but if I was him, I wouldn't want to spend time with Rigs either. Rigby has been a fucking bastard all night.

When Jett returns alone, Rigby pretends to be oblivious but he's definitely listening when Nash asks, "Creed alright?"

"Just needs some sleep, I think."

Rigby doesn't say anything. Instead, he just flings the second controller at Nash. Shaking his head, Nash passes it to me.

"Sorry man. I'm heading out."

Of course, he is. There's no world in which he'd stop in to play x-box with us. We don't ask where he's going or who he's seeing. Whoever it is, she won't last the week.

I take a seat on the sofa, ignoring Rigs grumbling. As much as he won't admit it, he's worried that Creed is pissed with him. We play for about an hour, but Rigs is unsettled and keeps changing the game. One minute we're racing cars, then we're in a boxing ring, then before you know it, we're in a bloody war zone.

Abruptly, Rigby drops the controller on the table. Jett looks up from the book he's reading, glancing at me with a silent question written on his face.

Lust & Lyrics

What's wrong with him?

I shrug my shoulders again. Rigby has been a total shit all night so it's probably better not to say anything. I really don't like him so much when he's like this. Sighing, I watch him leave the room, slamming the door behind him.

"He just feels like a dick," Jett says.

"Still. He should just apologise and be done with it."

"Have you ever seen Rigs rush to apologise?" Jett chuckles at the idea.

"Is Creed alright?"

Jett doesn't respond immediately.

"He should be. I'm not really sure. We'll find out tomorrow, I suppose."

I watch him closely, trying to process what he just said. It doesn't make a heck of a lot of sense.

"Did he tell you what happened?" I want more details.

"Not yet."

"I guess we're not playing anymore. I can go to bed," I say.

There's no point asking Jett any more questions. It doesn't look like I'm going to get a straight answer. It's weird though. It's not like Creed not to tell us when something happens. That boy loves spinning a story. He's pretty overdramatic, a bit of a joker. He usually sees the funny side in everything so for him to be so serious that he's headed to bed early… well words don't explain how weird he's being.

Turning off the tv, I say good night to Jett. On my way up the stairs, I see Rigby stood leaning against Creed's door.

"Since when do you lock the door, man?" he's saying. "Are you still awake?"

I might be too far away to hear anything, but I don't think Creed responds.

"I just wanted to say that I'm sorry."

Rigby looks awkward as fuck as he rubs the back of his neck with his palm.

I try to avoid eye contact as I walk past him but I can't resist adding my six pence.

"Come on, Creed. You know Rigs is an arsehole."

Rigby lunges for me, pulling me into a headlock.

"You little shit!"

Relieved to see him smiling again, I manage to escape his grip.

"Night dick face."

NONA

He didn't even look at me. *Not once.*

Usually he at least gives me a smile. Instead, he smiled at Crimson. I thought he hated Crimson.

I consider sending him a text but really what am I supposed to say… I'm just his stylist. We're not friends and I'm definitely not his girlfriend. As much as I like him, he's never given me a reason to think he might like me that way.

I type out several possible messages, but I delete each of them. I want to know that he's okay, at least. He didn't look like he'd been in a car accident but from what I heard from the rest of the team, the accident was pretty nasty. He was definitely hurt. He'd spent the best part of the day in the hospital and yet when I saw him, he looked perfectly fine. Better than fine, he looked great.

Creed, are you okay?

I don't know what else to write so I press send.

For the next fifteen minutes I wait for a reply that doesn't come. It's eight am. He might still be asleep.

I'm lying in my bed. I haven't slept much at all, but I've got to get to work. Perhaps I'll get to see Creed today and he might actually smile at me, instead of Crimson. I'm not usually the jealous sort, especially when it comes to Crimson. She's my best friend. I feel like a total bitch for being so irritated over something as small as a thank you.

I'm totally over-reacting and I'm fully aware of it.

Rushing around, I get ready for work. I've got to get my shit sorted if I'm not going to be late. I take extra care doing my makeup just in case I do get to see Creed today. I know it's silly. He won't notice anyway. He never notices.

Everyone else knows I like him, except him.

I check my phone every few minutes, hoping that he will have replied but he hasn't.

***

He's already at the label when I get there. He walks right past me, still no smile. Talking to Jasper, he looks cross.

Jasper hands him his phone and I feel a tiny bit of hope that maybe he hasn't seen my text yet. He doesn't even glance at the screen before placing it in his pocket. Then he's pushing past Jasper and into his father's office without so much as a knock.

Jasper looks exasperated.

I want to ask him what's going on but it's really none of my business. It's not like Creed is my boyfriend or anything. I turn to walk away when I spot the other guys walking towards me. Ziggy has a big grin on his face when he spots me. I return it.

"Hi Nona," he says. He's a bit of a cutie. "What you up to?"

"Not much. You?"

"Just looking for Creed."

There's a weird atmosphere around the lads like they've all fallen out or something.

"He's in with his dad," I tell them.

A flash of concern passes over Jett's face but then it's gone.

"We're meant to be recording the new album today," Jett says.

"You mean the one we still haven't written yet," Rigby retorts. "This is a joke. We haven't got time for this. Nona if you see him again, tell him to get his ass to the studio."

I nod but he doesn't see it because he's already storming away.

"What's got into him?"

Ziggy just shrugs his shoulders before following after him and the other two look at each other as if hoping the other one will answer for them.

I giggle softly as I walk away from them, going in search of Crimson.

I Hate This

Faded Love (#6)

I hate this love song

Have I told you

I hate this love song

It's pointless to say

I love you

I love you

I've been trying

To win your heart

For too long now

I didn't give up

But now I know

There's nothing I

Can do, nothing

I can do

I've been working

Over time so I can

Hanleigh Bradley

Take you out

But dating you is

A waste of time

There's nothing I

Can do, nothing

I can do

Because you don't

Even see me

You don't even

Know my name

You're blind to my heart

You're deaf to my love

And there's nothing I

Can do, nothing

I can do

Don't you know, there's nothing

Nothing I can do

That's why…

CLOVER

"So, when am I going to be allowed to see Creed?" I ask.

My dad is sat behind his desk, sleeves rolled up, tie loose. To look at him you'd never guess his son is in the hospital.

"Not today, Clover."

"Why?" I press.

"He's still not awake." Even if he doesn't look concerned, he sounds exhausted.

"What?" I'm floored. How can he not be awake?

"Your mum is with him. The doctors said it could take a few days."

"But…"

"Please Clover," he glances up at me, his elbows on the desk and his face in his hands, "just go with it."

"Go with it? Are you insane?"

"I haven't got time for this, Clover."

He climbs to his feet, pulling some papers together. Then he's walking around the desk. As far as he's concerned this conversation is over and I'm supposed to just do as I'm told.

I follow him out the door.

"What do you expect me to do?" I sound petty but I can't keep pretending to be my brother. One concert should have been more than enough. "You should cancel…"

"There will be no cancelling." He stops dead, turning to face me. "You will do everything he would be doing."

"But…"

He groans.

"Christ sake. Is it too much to ask? One thing. I'm asking one thing."

"No, you're demanding and it's not one thing. It's about a thousand."

"Just use it as an opportunity to get ready to go solo."

His words remind me that my dad doesn't know me at all.

I stop following him because there really is no point. My parents decided how my life would go years ago and there's no way in hell they'll let me stand in the way of their dream.

I lean against the railings as I watch my father make his way down the stairs. Resting my head on the cool metal, I try to gain at least a shred of composure.

Why the hell won't they tell me anything?

I don't even know if my brother is okay or how badly he was injured in the accident. All I know is that he's asleep. For all I know he could be in a coma or on death's door, but they have no intention of telling me jack shit.

The stylist who helped me yesterday and another girl I don't recognise are making their way towards me, carrying coffees.

"We got you a cappuccino, Creed," the girl I don't know says.

"Thanks," I reply, accepting the coffee from her.

She looks at me expectantly and I'm at a complete loss because I don't even know her name. Fortunately, Crimson comes to my rescue.

"Nona and I are going to find the others. Wanna come? Apparently, Rigs is looking for you."

So, this is Nona.

I've heard a lot about her. I look her over as stealthily as possible. This is the girl my brother likes.

She's pretty, I'll give him that. She's definitely his type. Shy. He's always had a thing for quiet girls.

I want to get to know her, find out more about her but I'm scared that I'll fuck it up for my brother by not knowing something he's supposed to know. It would be far too easily done.

"How are you feeling?" she asks.

I'm not really sure how I'm supposed to respond. I don't like the idea of lying to anyone, but it feels especially bad lying to her.

"I'm alright."

"That's good."

I try to think of something else to say, preferably about something else entirely but my mind is a complete blank. I'm grateful when we arrive at the studio where the rest of the band are waiting for us. The girls make quick work of handing out the coffees.

"Where's Rigby?" Crimson asks.

Ziggy is the first to respond. "Went looking for Creed." He's lounging against the wall lazily.

I'm not really sure what I'm supposed to be doing. It's all a bit daunting, one tiny mistake and the whole lie could crumble. Me and Creed might look alike but personality wise, there's no similarity at all.

Jumping out of my skin, I turn towards the door when Rigby thunders into the room. He barks for the girls to leave, completely ignoring the coffee they offer him. He gives me a look of pure thunder and I wonder what the fuck I've done now.

"Does anyone have anything?" Rigby asks. "Anything at all that could possibly go on the next album?"

The lads are all quiet and for the most part they're looking at me. Rigby and Creed write most of the songs. The problem is I have no idea if Creed has been writing anything. I feel like screaming at the top of my lungs that I'm not Creed but really, what would that achieve.

"Er, do you?" I go for a counterattack instead of defence.

"I have a few songs but they're not ready for the album," he admits, barely looking at me, his eyes angry.

"Well, why don't we work on one of those today?" I suggest.

I'm not sure what I've done to piss him off this time. Sighing, I take a seat. We're going to achieve jack shit like this.

"Perhaps we should all just work alone for today?" I ask when he doesn't reply.

Apparently, that's a mistake.

"You'd like that wouldn't you?"

Rigby's eyes are seriously staring daggers right at me but no matter how much I'm intimidated, I can't react because today I'm not Clover, I'm Creed and Creed doesn't get intimidated by dickheads.

"What the fuck, Rigs?" Jett cuts in, coming to my defence.

"Yeah, come on man. This isn't cool."

Nash pats Rigby on the back.

Rigby pulls away, making his way towards me. I'm backing up, trying to work out what the hell is happening. I have no idea what's wrong with him.

"You bastard!"

He prods his finger into my shoulder. It fucking hurts but I don't flinch. I can't flinch because Creed wouldn't flinch. I'll be guaranteed to bruise.

"I heard you talking to your dad."

Panic grips me and I think I'm going to throw up. He knows I'm a girl. There's no other explanation. I look towards Jett, silently begging him to help although I'm not sure what I want him to do exactly.

"You're going solo," Rigby grits out.

"What?"

"You heard me," he replies angrily. "You're planning a solo album."

"Creed wouldn't do that."

Nash's expression is a mixture of disbelief and betrayal. Ziggy is nodding his head in agreement with Nash.

Coming to stand beside me, Jett says, "Creed has no intentions of leaving the group."

"Shows what you know."

Rigby squares his shoulders, crossing his arms. He doesn't even glance at the others, just stares right at me.

There's no way for me to win this. He's right. He heard what he heard. Instead of trying to defend myself, I push past him and out the door. I've only been doing this for a day and already things are well and truly fucked up. I have no idea how my parents expect this to work.

Running down the corridor, I lock myself in a second studio room. Leaning against the door, I try once more to call my mum, but she doesn't answer.

Disappointed as usual, I take a seat at the piano.

I begin to play the melody that has been in my head for the last few days, the one I've yet to write lyrics for. I try my best to forget the situation with Saving Creed, forget my irresponsible parents, forget that I still don't know if Creed is okay.

Focusing all my attention on the notes my fingers touch, I lose myself in the sound that gentle touch can create.

At some indeterminable point, I start singing. I don't know where the words come from, they just do.

"I'm caged in, confined. Restricted by words."

I allow my fingers to move seamlessly across the keyboard.

"Wrapped in someone else's dream, I'm caged in, confined," I jot the words down before continuing, "Restricted by words, wrapped in someone else's dream."

"You leave the cage door open. It's an illusion, mocking me." The music sounds more mournful than it had when I first wrote it, as if I'm putting all my emotions into it. "Telling me that I am free. Telling me that I can escape."

Glancing up, I notice Rigby just beyond the glass. He's leaning against the far wall. I can't tell if he's still angry. I'd be livid if I was him.

I continue to sing, trying my best not to faulter even though I'm daunted by him watching me.

"But I'm caged in, confined, restricted by words, wrapped in someone else's dream."

I breathe, not taking my eyes of him, almost wishing that this song could tell him everything that I'm unable to.

"I'm caged in, confined, restricted by words, wrapped in someone else's dream."

I glance up and notice that at some point he's turned on the recording button, so I give up trying to write down what I'm singing.

"You let me fly free. There's a time limit, holding me. Living for those moments when I feel finally free."

I sing the chorus again, a tear on my cheek. I try to pretend that he's not there but it's not easy. He's not someone easily ignored.

"When will I finally be free of this destiny you've forced on me. When will you finally see that I'm not who you want me to be."

My voice cracks as I feel a sob rise in my throat. I wish my parents could hear this song except they'd not hear the meaning behind it. Instead they'd only see the money it can make them.

"Cause, I'm caged in, confined, restricted by words, wrapped in someone else's dream, someone else's dream."

I continue to play, ignoring how my heart is racing angrily in my chest, demanding that I allow myself to cry. *I can't cry.* Right now, I'm not Clover Levon. I play the piano so softly that the sound fades into almost no-existence and then I pull my fingers away, sitting back.

Rigby comes forward, pressing the button so that I can hear him.

"Let me in," he says softly, the anger from earlier seemingly gone.

Unsteadily, I get to my feet and unlock the door. He barrels in and pulls me into a bear hug. I'm surprised and my racing heart lurches with the shock. He pulls me back so that he can look at me.

"I'm sorry."

"You're sorry?" I ask because I'm a bit confused. I don't get how we've done a complete one eighty in a matter of minutes.

"I know the pressure your parents put on you. I should never have taken that conversation to heart."

I nod my head once, looking up at him beneath my lids as stealthily as possible.

"I'm really not going solo," I tell him and although it's not a lie - Creed is not going solo – I still feel like I'm lying to him.

His hands release my shoulders and for the first time since he entered the room, he looks away from me. His eyes wander to the piano.

"Your song is really good."

"Thanks."

I feel awkward receiving a compliment from him. He feels too close. The distance between us is not enough. But then I remind myself that to him at least, I'm not a girl.

Lately

Someone Else's Dream (#1)

Lately I found myself running

Been dreaming about you a lot

And up in my head I'm your boyfriend

But that's something you've already got

You're insecure

Because he's no good for you

You turn heads when you wiggle that ass

But he doesn't see exactly what he's got

He doesn't know just how lucky he is

Why don't you just walk out that door

Leave him standing there alone

Why don't you just walk out that door

I'll be there to take you home

Lately I tried playing it cool

But when I'm looking at you

Lust & Lyrics

I can't ever understand why you're still with him
When he doesn't know how beautiful you are

You're insecure
Because he's no good for you
You turn heads when you wiggle that ass
But he doesn't see exactly what he's got
He doesn't know just how lucky he is

Why don't you just walk out that door
Leave him standing there alone
Why don't you just walk out that door
I'll be there to take you home

One way or another you've got to walk out that door
Need you to see that I would treat you better
One way of another I need to stop running away
Need you to see that I would love you stronger
One way of another you've got to walk out that door
Need you to see that he's no good for you
But I can't compete with your boyfriend

Hanleigh Bradley

Need you to see

Need you to see

Need you to see

Lately I love you

RIGBY

I watch him walk away and it hits me that I'm wrong. There's no world in which Creed would leave us.

He loves Saving Creed even more than I do.

Ignoring the others, I follow after him. I hear the click of the door locking when he enters the studio. I watch as he tries to call someone before settling down to the piano.

I lean forward momentarily so that I can hit record. You never know, this could be our next number one.

The music he begins to play is the same tune he was humming last night in the car except it's sadder somehow. Then he starts singing and I'm floored.

Closing my eyes, it's hard to imagine that it's Creed singing. It sounds like him and it doesn't at the same time. It's not a key he often sings in, in fact, I would say the notes he's currently singing might have even been just out of his range last week.

The words are raw and full of emotion.

I open my eyes when he sings a particularly high note and our eyes catch. He's looking right at me and I feel like he's trying to tell me something, although I'm not at all sure what.

This song is far more serious than any of the songs he's written before. In the past we got all our serious songs from Clover, his sister.

I've heard a lot of rumours about her in the nine months that Saving Creed have been together. I don't believe half of what I've heard. But I don't doubt the twins are talented.

When Creed stops playing, I have to remind myself to do something. I can't just stand here and stare at the man, that's too weird. Asking him to let me in, I make my way towards him.

When he unlocks the door, I pull him into a hug surprising us both. I've hugged Creed before, but he feels different, softer.

I feel my forehead tightening with confusion as I pull him away from me so that I can look at him.

Has he lost weight? Is he sick?

His face looks skinnier than it was before... He feels more fragile, even his shoulders under my hands feel dainty.

Lust & Lyrics

Trying to clear my mind, I say, "I'm sorry."

It takes us a little while to get past our awkwardness but when we do, it's like we're best buds again. We settle in at the piano to work on the song together. Together, we assign parts and write the music for the other instruments but there's definitely something different about Creed. I just can't put my finger on what it is.

Time runs away with itself and before we know it, the others are dragging us out of the studio to go eat lunch.

"Oi, you two come on," Ziggy says as he pops his head through the door. "We're going for subway."

"Nice," I reply, ignoring the disappointment I feel in the pit of my stomach at having been disturbed.

My shoulder brushes against Creed's and my breath catches. It's an unexplainable reaction. Looking up at the others, I notice Jett giving me an odd look. But before I can analyse it, the look has gone to be replaced with a smile. He comes forward to pull Creed up.

"Come on," he says gently, resting his arm on the other guy's shoulder. He leans on him like he's about to die. "I'm starving!"

Creed laughs softly, in a way I've never heard Creed laugh before and again I feel that strange sense of disappointment at the idea that it isn't me that made him laugh. I've never been jealous of their friendship before and I'm not sure why I'm feeling this way now.

I walk slightly behind the others, trying to work my thoughts out. I'm relieved we're not still fighting but now instead of being full of anger, I'm seriously confused.

Crimson and Nona walk past us and Creed doesn't even glance at Nona. It's Ziggy who asks them if they'd like to join us for lunch. Nona falls into step next to Creed, but he just continues his conversation with Jett as if she's not there.

He's never said it, but I thought he liked her. The others seem oblivious to the fact that Creed's acting weird and I wonder if I'm imagining things.

Untitled

Someone Else's Dream (#2)

Do I need a reason to sing?

Do I need words to say?

Or can I just lose myself in a melody?

This love song doesn't need words

When you hear it you'll know what

I want to say

The notes combined in perfect harmony

Just like you and me

It's untitled

Indescribable

Unbelievable

It's untitled

Inexplicable

Completely magical

JETT

I'm struggling to keep a smile on my face as we sit here in Subway. Clover is next to Rigby and for some inexplicable reason it irritates me.

It's not like he knows she's a girl so why would it possibly bother me? As far as Rigby knows, Clover is Creed.

Earlier when we walked into the studio where Clover and Rigby had been, it had felt like we were intruding upon their private moment. There had been a definite atmosphere.

Nona is watching Clover closely, looking for an opportunity to engage her in conversation. She looks slightly put out. She's used to Creed showing her attention, perhaps not in the same way Ziggy does, but attention all the same. But now, Creed is as good as ignoring her.

I think the girl makes Clover nervous. She doesn't know how to act like her brother without causing a misunderstanding. She is scared to say too much, in case she says the wrong thing.

Watching them all, I wonder if any of them realise that Creed is not himself. As great as Clover is doing, she is not Creed. *Surely the boys can tell…*

Taking advantage of Creed's silence, Ziggy is trying to win Nona over. Nash is focused on his food and pretty much ignoring the rest of us. Rigby and Creed both seem distracted, glancing at each other every once and a while.

I feel a little bit responsible for Clover.

I should probably feel grateful that her and Rigby are no longer arguing but I'm less relieved than I am frustrated. My chest tightens at the idea of them getting on. Clover is smiling as if all the chaos of the last twenty-four hours hasn't happened. Rigby asks her a question about the song they were working on before we interrupted them, but she doesn't answer him because Creed's phone goes off in her pocket and after glancing at the screen, her face drops.

"Hi," she answers.

Everyone is watching her closely. It's probably because they've never seen Creed look so nervous, answering the phone. She literally looks like her world is about to fall apart.

"Can I go this afternoon?"

I lean forward, eager to hear about Creed. She glances my way and I see concern in her eyes. She's scared. That look is enough to tell me that

Creed still hasn't woken up. I'm not the only one watching her, Rigby is eyeing her closely and I find myself wondering if he can hear her conversation. From across the table, I'm basing everything on the look on her face. But Rigs is sitting right next to her.

"Thanks," she says softly. Hanging up the phone, she turns towards us all, opening her mouth to say something.

Before Clover can say whatever she has to say, Nash has cut across her.

"What happened to your new phone?"

"Huh?" Clover looks down at the phone in confusion.

"You changed your phone back to the blue one. What happened to the rose gold one?"

Shit. Everyone is looking at Clover, waiting for her explanation. She is staring at her phone as if hoping that it will give her an answer.

I prepare myself to answer for her but just as I go to reply, she answers calmly. She's strangely confident as she lies to us.

"I broke my cover in the crash, so I just used a spare one." The only sign that she might be less sure is the hand that goes through her hair. "I ordered a replacement online. It arrived today."

The guys seem to accept her explanation and I notice Crimson's shoulders sagging with relief.

"I need to go," Clover says. "I need to visit a friend."

"A friend?" Rigby asks. "How long will you be? We need to get back to the studio."

"Probably an hour," Clover says as she stands to her feet, preparing to leave.

Rigby's expression clouds over briefly but after a moment he forces a smile onto his face. Watching him, I try to determine what emotions I've just seen cross his expression. Disappointment? Anger? I'm not at all sure.

"Should I come with you?" I ask because I really want to see Creed. I won't believe he's okay until I see him for myself.

With a nod she gives her consent before she returns her attention to the others.

"We'll see you all in a bit."

I try to ignore the way Rigby smiles at her. It's not a smile that Rigby has ever given Creed before. It's too sweet, too soft.

Grabbing Clover's arm, I drag her out of there. I might be imagining it, but I don't want her getting too close to the others. I tell myself that it's because they will work out that she's lying to them, but I can't convince myself that that's the truth.

Truth is… I think I'm jealous.

"Should we go see your brother?" I ask once we're away from the others, dropping my hand from her wrist so I can take her hand.

If she's surprised, she doesn't let on.

I can't tell if I'm trying to comfort her or if I'm trying to claim her. Waiting for the car, I try to rein in my thoughts. Right now, Clover isn't Clover. I drop her hand as if it burnt me.

In reality, I'd hold onto her if I could. But right now, I can't. I need to treat her the way I treat Creed if I don't want the others to work out what's going on.

Blink Twice

Someone Else's Dream (#3)

I just want to know
Where you went when you left
Blinked twice and you were gone
Blinked twice and was left alone

I just want to know
What he gives you that I don't
Blinked twice and you were gone
Blinked twice and was left alone

You promised more than this
But words are easy to break
All I did was blink twice
Blinked twice
Blink once, you turn
Blink twice, you're gone

I just want to know

Hanleigh Bradley

What I did wrong

Blinked twice and you were gone

Blinked twice and was left alone

I just want to know

If there's a way to go back

Blinked twice and you were gone

Blinked twice and was left alone

Blinked twice

Blinked twice

CLOVER

The door handle is slick in my hands. I don't know what is waiting for me inside the hospital room. Breathing in and out, I try to pull myself together.

Jett pats me on the back, pushing me forward slightly.

My heart is drumming in my chest as I try to rationalise everything. He's okay, I tell myself. He's just asleep.

Jett's hand covers mine on the door handle, pulling it down. Without his help, I'd probably stand here for an hour or something stupid, waiting for the courage to open the blasted door.

Just inside the room, I see my brother. I have to remind myself that he's not dead. I've never seen my brother so still. He's pale too.

Jett is holding my hand and he gives it a reassuring squeeze as he leads me into the room. My mum is sat on a rickety looking chair next to the bed, clinging to my brother's hand much the same way

I am clinging to Jett. She climbs to her feet, reluctantly releasing Creed's hand. Her face is ashen, exhausted in a way I've never seen before.

Until this very moment, I've never seen my mum look anything less than perfect. Her hair that is usually flawless is currently flung into a messy bun and her face is completely devoid of makeup. I can see black circles under her eyes that don't belong there. Before I can inspect her further, she's pulling me into her arms.

"Thank you, Clover," she says directly into my ear.

"It's okay." I don't really know what else I'm supposed to say. I can hardly complain that she's asking too much when my brother is right in front of me, the way he is.

As she pulls away, she takes my face in between her hands.

"You really do look so much like him," she says, her voice filled with awe. "It's quite surreal."

Jett chuckles from somewhere behind me.

"Except she's prettier."

"That's true," my mum concedes.

Walking around my mum, I approach my brother. I reach out to touch him, but my hand falls short in the air in front of him. He's not dead, I remind myself again, forcing myself to take his hand in mine. It's not as cold as I expect. I glance at the screens around him. He's wired up to a heart monitor. His heartbeat sounds steady, although I have no idea what it should sound like really.

Jett and my mum say something about going to fetch us all a coffee but I'm not paying attention. A tear rolls down my cheek as I sit in the chair my mum previously occupied.

"What are you like?" I whisper, my voice breaking slightly. "Because of you, I've had to come home early and everything," I complain without conviction.

I begin to tell him all about everything he's missed over the last couple of days. It feels like I've been back longer than just the two days I have, so I'm surprised when I run out of things to tell him after rambling on for five minutes.

Taking a breath, I stop talking. He probably can't hear me anyway. I rub the back of his hand with my thumb.

"You've got to get better, Creed," I tell him after a moment's silence. "You owe me three months."

I laugh but it doesn't sound right. There's no humour in the sound at all.

Focusing on the sound of my brother's heartbeat, I slow my own racing heart. He's alive and that's all that matters. When my mum and Jett return, my eyes are closed. Having long ago ran out of things to say, I'm just sitting here holding my brother's hand as if my touch alone is enough to keep him with me. It's naïve but I'd do anything to keep my brother by my side.

Growing up, when my friends had talked about their siblings, they'd mostly complained. Me? Not so much. We never really argued as kids. Perhaps it was the twin thing, but we were always dead close, practically best friends. Even now when something goes wrong with me, he's the first to know about it.

If he was awake now, I'd tell him all about how much of a dick Rigby is, except if Creed was awake, I wouldn't have even met Rigby.

I can hear Jett and my mum talking but I have no idea what they're saying because all I can see is Creed and all I can hear is the sound of his heartbeat on the monitor. I listen to it closely, fearful that it might faulter.

When it's time to leave Creed's side, I know that I can't face the others. My face is blotchy from tears and I feel as if more could fall at any moment.

Turning to my mum, I ask, "can I spend the rest of the afternoon as myself?"

She looks confused, unsure what I'm asking.

"I want to spend some time in the studio," I say. She'll never deny me the opportunity to work on my music.

Pulling out a packet of tissues, she agrees with a soft nod of her head. She places a tissue in my hand.

"Jasper will make sure you have everything you need."

"I'll make an excuse with the lads," Jett tells us as he prepares to leave. "You'll let us know when he wakes up?" he asks my mum.

"Of course," she replies. "Thank you for looking after Clover."

"It's nothing." The smile that stretches across his face is enough to make my heart skip a beat.

NASH

As always nothing goes to plan. Waiting for Creed and Jett to return, Rigby's good mood begins to dissipate. Listening to him grumble about them being late, is a complete ball ache and when Jett returns alone, I feel a bone deep need to escape. Offering to fetch everyone a coffee, I'm out of there as quick as my feet will carry me.

Pulling out my headphones, I decide to listen to some music as I walk. I consider texting the girl I'm seeing but I can't really be bothered. I've never really been one for relationships and she's definitely the girlfriend sort of girl. In other words, she's someone else's sort of girl.

The coffee shop is only across the road, but I dawdle as much as possible, hoping that Rigby will have got his shit together by the time I get back. I take a few extra minutes in the coffee shop, enjoying the attention I get from the barista.

I glance up every few seconds from my phone as I wait for the lights to change on my way back. But when they change and I begin to cross the street, my eyes are glued to my phone and I almost completely miss her.

I almost drop the coffees when I first see her climb out of the car.

First all I see is a black high heeled shoe and a slender leg that leaves my dick twitching at the mere idea of what the rest of her looks like.

The woman who climbs out can't be any older than I am. She's in her early twenties.

Her hair is that rose gold colour that all the girls seem to like right now. She's wearing all black; black shorts, black low cut top, black jacket.

She's totally fuckable.

I watch as she confidently walks away from the car and right into the record label building. It's then that I notice Jasper. I want to ask him who she is but I'm not one for admitting an interest.

Following after her, I try not to focus too much on how amazing her arse looks in her shorts. She lets herself into one of the practice rooms and yet again I find myself wondering who she is. She's not signed with the label that I know of.

She might be new, I suppose.

Shaking my head, I tell myself to forget about her. The guys will be waiting and the coffees that I'm carrying will end up cold if I stay here for much longer.

I can't quite bring myself to walk away though. Instead, I follow after her. Staying in the shadows, I watch as she settles behind the keyboard. She begins playing and I'm surrounded by music. I can't take my eyes off her. She's beautiful. Her shades have been removed and I can finally see her eyes. They're a shocking green, completely enticing. As she plays, she hums to herself and I wonder if I'll be able to hear her sing.

Just as she opens her mouth, I hear Ziggy calling my name. Glancing down the corridor, I can see him watching me, a bemused expression on his face.

Looking back at the girl, I'm relieved she hasn't heard him. I nod to him, a silent acknowledgment. I want to hear her first, then I'll walk away.

"Don't ever stop."

I almost crumple against the wall at the sound of her voice. I can't describe what it is that I like about it exactly, except that I feel like she's singing exclusively for me.

"Don't ever leave. Don't faulter."

I tell myself that I must walk away, that I can't stay here watching her, but my feet don't move.

"The notes are weak. The rhythm uneasy. Please, don't faulter. Don't ever stop."

Although I could stand listening to her for as long as she would play, I force my feet off the ground and begin to walk away.

"I'll count the beats. Don't ever leave."

I stop. Her voice is gentle, sweet, so quiet, I almost miss it but in a completely ridiculous way it feels like she is telling me to stay. I have to remind myself that she doesn't even know that I am here.

"I'll keep your time. Don't faulter."

Entering the studio next door, I almost laugh out loud at the sight of my friends lounging about. There's something magical happening in the next room and they're completely oblivious. I consider telling them, but I'd like to keep the pretty nameless girl next door a secret for as long as I can. She's far too pretty to share.

"Still no Creed?" I ask.

"He got roped into helping his mum," Jett explains.

"What should we do then?" There's nothing I hate more than wasting time and it feels like all we've done today is waste flipping time. The only consolation is sitting in the room next door but I'm a bit scared that she might leave before I even get her name.

Beautiful Life

Someone Else's Dream (#4)

It's a beautiful life

With you by my side

It's a beautiful life

Every day

Holding your hand

There's nothing else I need

It's a beautiful life

Today, everyday

Your beautiful soul

Makes my life

More than it was before

It's a beautiful life

With you by my side

It's a beautiful life

Everyday

Lust & Lyrics

Even my worst days

Ain't bad anymore

It's a beautiful life

Today, everyday

You're beautiful heart

Makes my life

More than I could wish for

It's a beautiful life

Beautiful, beautiful life

ZIGGY

I'm not sure what's going on with everyone. We've given up for the day, having achieved nothing.

Rigby is back to being a dick, no real surprise there. Creed is AWOL again. Jett is distracted and Nash keeps trying to sneak into the recording studio next door. *Why? I don't know.*

Ignoring the others, I hide behind the drum kit. With my sticks, I tap out a gentle four four beat as I allow my mind to wander. Nona's face fills my thoughts as I try to come up with a plan.

She must know I like her. I've not exactly tried to hide it. But I don't stand a chance while ever she likes Creed. I hit the kit harder with my sticks as I feel frustration seep into my bones.

Until yesterday, I had thought Creed was into Nona too. I hadn't thought I stood a chance; it was just inevitable that they'd get together eventually. But then yesterday Creed had ignored Nona and my interest had flared up once more.

Lust & Lyrics

The emotions I'd been trying so hard to quash had come back fighting.

Sighing, I remind myself that even if Creed isn't interested in Nona, it doesn't change the fact that Nona likes Creed.

I'm not even on her radar. I'm not stupid. I know how she sees me. She looks at me and sees a cute little brother… someone who's hair she can ruffle and who's cheeks she can squeeze.

To Nona, I am about as far from being a man as Creed is to being a girl.

I don't notice when the others leave, I'm so preoccupied with my thoughts. It's only when it starts to go dark that I realise that I'm alone in the studio. The lads must have gone home without me, I realise irritably.

Stowing my sticks away in my backpack, I prepare to leave too. My hands pause over the bag's zip when the silence is broken by a voice that is both familiar yet new. I'm certain I've heard it before, but I can't place where.

Shoving the bag on my back, I exit the studio before preparing to enter the one next door. My hand is on the handle and I can hear that siren's voice coming from just inside when my phone rings.

The voice stops and I fear that I've disturbed her. Rushing to answer the phone, I don't even check the caller ID.

"Yeah?"

"Hurry up," Rigby says down the phone. "We're waiting in the lobby. Nash is hungry."

I hang up without replying and wait just a fraction longer than I should so as to see if she will start singing again. Instead I hear a shuffling and I panic. I don't want to be caught hovering like a weirdo outside her studio.

I dart down the hall, wishing that I could see her face at least once.

Creed is still missing when I reach the others and Rigby doesn't seem happy about it at all. As soon as he sees me, he takes off out the door, towards the car that's waiting for us. I join Nash and Jett as we follow after him.

Glancing back, I wonder if the girl from the studio is within view. I had been sure I'd heard her packing up. She's not there and I'm left feeling deflated. I'm so put out by missing my chance to see her face, I almost don't catch Nona and Crimson waving goodbye to me. The deflated feeling intensifies until I feel like my gut weighs a ton.

Nona will never like me the way I like her.

I've Been Waiting

Someone Else's Dream (#5)

I've been writing these songs

About why I can't be with you

I've been thinking all about

You and me and everything we're not

This is a one sided love

But I've been waiting

I've been waiting for you

I've been holding on to

The idea that you might

Come back one day

You've been clear from the start

About not wanting to be with me

But why can't you just lie to me

Just once tell me, you miss me

I don't want to want you

Hanleigh Bradley

But I don't know how to stop
Everyone else knows what I
Refuse to admit, refuse to see

Are you even listening to me?
Can't you just lie to me?
I've been waiting so patiently
Are you even listening to me?
Can't you see…?

I've been writing these songs
About why I can't be with you
But then you kiss me
And I'm pulled back into love
I can't be with you
But then you kiss me
I can't be with you

NONA

The second I see her I know exactly who she is. When people said they looked almost identical, they weren't exaggerating. She could be her brother if it wasn't for the colour of her hair and the slightness of her frame. She's definitely skinnier than Creed, curvier too.

She's a girl and as much as she looks just like Creed, there's no denying that she's all woman.

I consider approaching her. I've wanted to meet her for longer than I can remember. Creed talks about her a lot. He's always said they're really close and so I can't help but wonder if he's spoken to her about me.

Although based on the recent change in his attitude towards me, it probably doesn't matter either way. If he was interested last week, he doesn't seem to be now. It's disappointing but sort of to be expected, I suppose. Those boys get more attention than I get hot dinners. His eyes were bound to wander eventually.

It's not like he's made me any promises or even took me out on a date.

We've flirted, that's it.

If anything I got ahead of myself, thinking it was more than it actually was. I turn to walk away, trying my best to ignore the temptation to introduce myself, when she calls out my name.

"Nona!"

I'm floored. *How does she even know who I am?* Hope bubbles in my tummy and I begin to think that all might not be lost after all. I look her way and its definitely her who called me.

She's waving excitably with a big, friendly smile plastered on her face. I stand stock still as she strides the distance between us.

If Creed is a god, she's a goddess. Her long legs put mine to shame. I try to remind myself that she's wearing heals while I'm just in pumps, but it does nothing for my self-esteem.

Thank fuck I don't have to compete with her for Creed, I find myself thinking. Definitely better for the guy you like to have a super hot sister than a super hot ex.

When she's right in front of me I realise that I'm being rude.

"Hi," I say awkwardly.

"Nona, right?" She smiles at me as if seeing me has just made her day a hundred times better. "Fancy getting a drink?" She waits for my response and when it doesn't come she lets out a melodic laugh. "Sorry. I'm Clover, by the way."

Shaking my thoughts away, I grin at her.

"I guessed. You look…" I begin.

"Just like Creed?"

"Exactly like Creed! It's scary how…" My voice dwindles as I continue to stare at the face that is both familiar and new. I try to pick out all the things that make them different but it's not easy.

"My brother told me all about you," she's saying, and her words cause my breath to catch, "and so I really wanted to meet you for myself."

"Really?" I sound like a mouse, high pitched and squeaky.

"Yeah. I think he's working himself up to asking you out." She plays with her hair, glancing at me from behind her lashes, watching for my reaction. If I didn't know Creed better, I'd think he sent her to test the waters. "But he's a bit stressed at the moment with the new album so you'll probably get stuck waiting a little longer."

"Huh?" I'm completely lost. *What am I waiting for? Creed to ask me out?*

"I think he'll get around to asking you out after the launch of the new album. I heard today that they haven't even got one song ready." Her expression is covered in sisterly concern. "I came home to help them."

She pauses for a second before pulling on my arm so she can link hers with mine.

"Anyway, I'm totally rambling. Let's get that drink!" Then she's pulling me out the door by the arm and I'm following after her completely willingly.

She's super chatty as we walk the short distance to the nearest pub. I'm working up the courage to ask her about Creed. This might be the best chance I'll ever get to find out more about him.

"How long have you been back?" I ask a few moments later as we grab a table, drinks in hand.

"Just a few days."

"Because of Creed's accident?"

Her eyes dart to mine. She's not quick to reply. Suddenly the girl that hasn't stopped talking since the moment I met her is silent.

Just as I'm about to change the subject, she says, "yeah. My parents were quite scared."

The look on her face doesn't match the situation. Her brother is fine. He wasn't badly hurt at all and yet her expression could convince you that he'd died in that crash.

"Creed said you've been travelling," I try to ease the tension that the conversation has somehow created. "Where did you go?"

"Oh," her face brightens, "here and there." She giggles before listing off almost the whole of Europe and then some.

We sit there in that pub until its dark outside. I ask her about a million questions about Creed and she answers them without pause. She's eager to tell me and it makes me wonder just how much her brother has talked about me. Perhaps he does like me after all.

Saving My Heart

Someone Else's Dream (#6)

I kiss with my lips

I dance with my feet

I snuggle with my arms

She can have them all

But she can't have my heart

I'm saving it for you

I'm saving my heart

I'm saving it for you

I'm saving it for you

Those three words

I love you, I love you

I'm saving them for you

I'll give her pretty words

I'll show her a good time

I'll keep her happy

She can have it all

Lust & Lyrics

But she can't have my heart

I'm saving it for you

I'll show her the world

I'll buy her pretty shoes

She can wear me

Like an accessory

But she can't have my heart

I'm saving it for you

I haven't even met you yet

I don't know your name

The only thing I know is

She's not you, she's not you

So, I'm saving my heart

RIGBY

I spend the entire night waiting for Creed to come home. Not completely sure why his absence matters so much, I feel frustrated.

The others entertain themselves, joking around as we eat the pizza we have ordered. Jett keeps shoving Ziggy's hands away from the pizza box, reminding him to leave some for Creed. Usually I'd say that Creed can feed himself, but a protective urge stirs within me that is completely unfounded.

I pick up the box, walking away from the breakfast bar where we have all been perched for the last hour and place the leftover pizza in the fridge.

Without saying anything, I walk out of the kitchen.

I'm about to turn on the Xbox when I remember that Creed is out. That strange disappointed feeling that has been tugging at me since Creed left this afternoon, gives an almighty wrench at my chest. My shoulders slump as I trudge through the house to the piano room.

Sitting at the grand piano that the label bought us as a house warming present, I begin to let my fingers glide across the keys, hoping that they might create something without me having to think about it too much.

The sounds of the house around me, the lads larking about, all of it, is silenced by the tinkling sound of the piano. It's all I can hear. The melody doesn't reflect my mood at all. It's energetic and damn well perky.

I begin to sing although I'm not sure where the words come from. I almost choke on them once or twice as they cause me to chuckle.

"I kiss with my lips; I dance with my feet; I snuggle with my arms."

My foot is tapping to a beat that is pounding through my head.

"She can have them all, but she can't have my heart. I'm saving it for you."

It's only as the song comes towards its close that I realise that I'm not alone. Creed is stood leaning against the door frame. The look on his face is weird. It's a little bit too similar to the ones our fan's give us when we're on stage and it both makes me feel uneasy and pleased all at once.

He comes towards me and I'm tempted to tell him to stay away.

The air is thick between us, an unexplainable tension palpable almost to the touch. I clear my throat.

"Did you get your pizza?" I ask, trying to distract myself from whatever it is I'm feeling right now.

"Yeah. Thanks." His voice is softer than it should be. He plonks himself down next to me on the piano stool. "Play it again?"

I nod, sucking in as much oxygen as I can through my mouth because I know that if I breathe in through my nose, I'll be able to smell him. Except everything about him is wrong right now.

He smells different. He looks different. He sounds different.

And I feel different.

My fingers are slippery on the keys this time; I'm nervous. Scared even. Not that I'm sure why. I've done this with Creed a million times before, sitting at this very piano composing together but something is different now and I have no idea why.

Trying my best to appear unphased, I begin to sing. I'm more aware of Creed beside me than I am of the notes I'm playing and as a result, I make several little mistakes but where Creed would usually tease me in that way that brothers do, he simply offers me an encouraging smile. It's a smile he's never given me before but also a smile I want to see again.

It's everything that Creed isn't. It's soft, sweet and altogether intoxicating.

He sings the chorus with me as I feel my heart thudding in my chest.

"I'm saving my heart. I'm saving it for you. I'm saving it for you."

I try not to look at him as I sing.

"Those three words; I love you, I love you. I'm saving them for you."

I play without singing for the next few bars before I begin the next verse, staring straight at the wall in front of me.

"I'll give her pretty words. I'll show her a good time. I'll keep her happy."

Glancing his way, I catch his eye and for the briefest of moments I think they're green.

"She can have it all, but she can't have my heart. I'm saving it for you."

Focusing as best I can on the music, I ignore the way I feel drawn towards him. He's one of my best mates. *A guy. And I'm not into guys.*

Singing the next verse, I release all the pent up tension I feel into the lyrics.

"I'll show her the world. I'll buy her pretty shoes. She can wear me like an accessory but she can't have my heart. I'm saving it for you."

Then the song is ending, and I'm scared to look at him, scared that I might do something stupid, scared that I might see something in his eyes that I don't want to see.

His voice catches me off guard. "It's missing something."

That's all he says then he's leaning closer to me and I can't avoid breathing in the smell of his hair. The words are out my mouth before I can stop them.

"Have you changed your shampoo?"

His eyes go wide with surprise and then wider still as if he's suddenly realised just how close we're sitting. His lips are mere inches from mine. He glances down at them before biting down into his own in a fluid movement that has my cock twitching in my jeans. We both pull back as sharp as lightning and I'm clearing my throat as he focuses his attention on the piano once again.

"It needs a bridge," he says in a voice that is way too high.

He plays something before looking back at me questioningly, but I miss it because I'm still thinking about him biting his lip.

"Er... Play it again?"

Nodding his head, he plays it once more. This time I pay avid attention.

"Keep playing it," I say after a moment, resting a hand on his shoulder.

He jumps almost out of his seat from the touch as if I've just burnt him. He does as I ask though and plays the few bars of music on repeat for me to get a feel for it.

I allow myself to look at him again. He doesn't look the way I expect him to. His cheeks are flushed, and his pupils dilated, but what catches my attention the most is that his tattoo is missing. The edge of his tattoo that should just be peaking out over the neck of his t-shirt is not there.

Before I can rationalise what I've just seen, I'm singing. The words come quickly as I meet his eye.

"I haven't even met you yet. I don't even know your name. The only thing I know is she's not you. She's not you so I'm saving my heart."

It takes all the self control, I have not to pounce on him although I'm not sure if I want to kiss him or hit him. I don't know who the person sat next to me is but one thing I do know is that it is definitely not Creed.

CLOVER

Sitting so close to Rigby, it's almost impossible to remember that I am not myself. Right now, I'm supposed to be acting like Creed but everything about Rigby reminds me that I am very much a girl.

Even without touching him, my skin feels like it's on fire.

He's so close and yet completely out of reach. One thing is for sure, I need to get the hell away from him.

The words of the bridge, that he's just created while staring right at me, are intoxicating. And the look he's giving me right now makes me almost giddy, as if he's singing for me. As if I'm the one the words are about which is beyond stupid because he doesn't even know who I am.

He thinks I'm my brother.

Glancing at his lips, I feel drawn to them. I want to kiss him. My eyes travel up to his eyes. His brow is lowered as if he's concentrating on something, trying to work out a puzzle of some sort.

"I'm going to go to bed," I stutter out, gulping down the air between us so fast I almost choke.

He doesn't speak. He's just staring at me.

My heart's racing. I can't think straight.

If I'm not careful I'll do something I'll regret. I need to get the hell out of here.

Rushing to my feet, I almost knock us both flying along with the stool we're sat on. His arm wraps around my waist, catching me before I can fall and once again, I'm transfixed by the look in his eyes.

Apologising quickly, I try to right myself but end up pulled up against his chest.

It's a reminder of the hug we shared earlier, and it causes my body to alight with awareness. I push my hands against his chest and turning sharply I make a rush for the door.

It's only when I reach the living room and I hear the sound of the others talking that I realise that my breathing is erratic. I pause with my hand on the door handle, trying to rein in whatever control I can.

Rigby comes up behind me, taking me by surprise. He covers my hand with his and twists before pushing the door open.

"Not going in?" I hear his voice close to my ear.

I nod because words are bloody impossible and stumble into the room. I try to put as much distance as possible between myself and Rigby, choosing a seat at the far end of the room. I'm completely oblivious to what the others are saying, unable to focus on their conversation when I can still feel his eyes on me.

If I look at him, I'm positive that I'll find him looking right back at me, but I can't bring myself to check. Partly because I'm scared that I'm wrong but also because I'm scared that I'm right.

Even though we've got several metres between us, I feel the same way I did when we shared the piano stool. Something ripples in the air between us and I can't handle it any longer.

My voice spikes as I wish the guys all good night without so much as looking at them.

As I climb into Creed's bed, I silently pray that my brother will wake up soon. I don't know how much more of this I can take.

***

The next morning I'm woken by the sound of someone banging on my door.

"Get up!" I can hear Rigby shouting.

I roll over, rubbing my eyes. A glance at the alarm clock tells me it's still early.

"Fuck off," I grumble.

"Hurry up." I hear the handle turn, but the door doesn't budge. Thank hell I locked it last night. "Since when have you locked your room?"

"Erm," I panic, "I'll be down in a few minutes." Hoping that he won't press the topic, I wait for a response, but none comes.

Sighing with relief, I pull the covers off my body and look for some clothes in my brother's wardrobe.

Ten minutes later, I can at least say I'm clean and dressed. The only thing left to do before I can unlock the door is my hair. I've left the hardest job until last. Trying my best to catch all the hair in the cap that Crimson gave me, my head is upside down and I'm beginning to feel dizzy.

There's another bang at the door.

"You said ten. It's been at least fifteen."

I almost scream out in frustration. If only he knew what I am trying to do, then he'd shut the fuck up for sure. When I finally have all my own hair hidden beneath the cap and the wig in place, I give myself a quick once over in the mirror. I really do look just like Creed.

The knocking starts again and I'm making my way towards the door.

Opening it, I try to avoid looking at the gorgeous man on the other side but it's damn near impossible because he's taking up all the space directly outside my room. His presence is imposing but I try my best to conceal my reaction to him.

"Come on. We're all heading to the studio. I want to get at least one song nailed down today."

There's no room for discussion. He grabs my hand and as good as drags me down the stairs to where the others are already waiting.

Don't Wake Me Up

Someone Else's Dream (#7)

I know I'm dreaming
I'm dreaming about you
I know it's not real
But don't wake me up
I don't want to see

Reality, because
You're not mine in reality
You're not mine, no, no, no
Don't wake me up, up, up
Don't wake me up, up, up

I know it's all in my mind
It's a fantasy, pure delusion
My own wishful thinking
But don't wake me up
I don't want to see

Lust & Lyrics

I might as well be sleeping

Thoughts of you fill my head

I know it's not possible

But don't wake me up

I don't want to see

NASH

Creed plays us the song that he wrote yesterday, and I'm floored. It's far too serious to be something Creed has written.

"Are you sure you wrote this?" Ziggy asks, apparently I'm not the only one who finds it hard to believe.

Creed only smiles, leaning back in his seat. Smug bastard.

Rigby hands us each a sheet of music. Automatically I pick up the base and begin to play my part, acquainting myself with the sequence of notes. It seems simple enough.

"Should we give it a go?" Jett asks some time later, once we've all looked over the sheet music.

There's a murmuring of agreement and then we're playing the song. We don't get five bars in before Creed is stopping us to correct something. He's softer about it than usual though. Where normally he'd call us all lazy shits and tell us to sort our crap out, today he's fully constructive in his criticism.

He even borrows my bass guitar for a moment to show me how to play it, confusing the fuck out of me. *Since when has Creed been able to play bass?*

He's still a slave master though, not letting us stop until its damn near perfect.

Even when Nona and Crimson walk in with iced coffees, he simply raises his hand and asks them to wait a moment. I expect Crimson to get shitty with him – they've never got on – but instead she looks entertained. Her lips are turned up at the corners and her eyes seem to dance with humour.

When he finally puts down his guitar, Nona is the first to speak.

"Wow. I love the new song. Did you get it from Clover?"

Creed offers her a smile before shaking his head but it's Rigby that answers for him.

"Nah, Nona," he says as he wraps his arm around Creed's shoulder, "our boy Creed here wrote it himself."

Crimson looks even more entertained if that's at all possible and I'm left wondering what she knows that I don't. Ignoring the conversation, I watch her closely but she's giving nothing away. It's only when Nona says that she met Clover yesterday that my attention returns to the others.

"We went to the pub," Nona tells them. "She's really cool." She sounds like she's totally fangirling.

"Yeah, I guess so," Creed replies, rubbing the back of his neck with his hand.

It's not like Creed to be slow to praise his sister. We've heard a lot about her over the last nine months. Creed has always had a slightly protective edge to him when talking about her. She's as much his best friend as she is his sister. His hesitance makes me wonder if they've fallen out or something.

"You didn't tell us she was back," Ziggy is saying excitably. Having heard so much about her, we've always been eager to meet her.

Rigby is pulling a weird face as if he's suspicious of something, although I'm not sure what.

Realisation hits me. *The girl I saw yesterday with Jasper!*

"Did she come by the studio yesterday?" I ask, my words rushed.

It's Jett that answers.

"Yeah."

"Nona, what was she wearing?" I need to confirm it. "Is her hair pink?"

"Black shorts…" Nona looks thoughtful. "Her hair is rose gold, yeah."

It's her. The girl that I've had stuck on a loop in my mind for the last twenty-four hours is Clover. *Shit, she's Creed's sister.*

Before I can stop myself, I say, "She's really fit."

Instead of hitting me like I expect him to, Creed actually blushes. Jett doesn't hold back, swiping his hand across the back of my head before I can duck out.

"Back to work," Creed says more nervously than I've ever heard him before.

"You really do look alike," I say, turning my head as I consider his face. "Except she's like a million times better looking."

His eyebrow raises as he pulls his guitar over his head.

"Is she really that hot?" Ziggy asks.

"I mean… her legs are killer long."

"That's true," Nona pipes in. "I was seriously jealous of those yesterday."

Creed snorts.

"It's amazing what six inch heels will do."

"And her boobs." My voice is wistful as I recollect what she looked like.

"Enough." This time it's Rigby that cuts across the conversation. "We haven't got time for you to behave like a man whore."

"Hey!"

"I want to show this to Switch before we go home tonight," he says, his words final.

Caged

Someone Else's Dream (#8)

You leave the cage door open
Its an illusion, mocking me
Telling me that I am free
Telling me that I can escape

But, I'm caged in, confined
Restricted by words
Wrapped in someone else's dream
I'm caged in, confined
Restricted by words
Wrapped in someone else's dream

You let me fly free
There's a time limit, holding me
Living for those moments
When I feel finally free

But, I'm caged in, confined

Hanleigh Bradley

Restricted by words
Wrapped in someone else's dream

When will I finally be free
Of this destiny you've forced on me
When will you finally see
That I'm not who you want me to be

'cause, I'm caged in, confined
Restricted by words
Wrapped in someone else's dream
Someone else's dream

JETT

I spend the next few days walking on eggshells, convinced that Clover's secret will be revealed at any moment.

Most of our time is spent in the studio working on a couple of songs for the new album. Clover makes frequent visits to her father's office in an attempt to find out how Creed is doing but as of yet, he's still asleep.

There's no reason, as far as the doctors know, for him not waking up and so it feels like every day we're waiting for the news that he's finally awake. News that doesn't come.

Today we finally recorded Caged, the song that Clover wrote for us and it sounds bloody brilliant. Nash has insisted we celebrate. He wants to go out to a club.

"You can invite Clover," he says keenly.

"Er," Clover looks caught out, "I think she's busy."

"How do you know without checking?" he questions.

"Mum said something about going to the spa."

The lie sounds like it's been pulled out of the air and it's clear from their expressions that none of the guys believe her, but they don't press it.

"We could just get some beers and…" Rigby begins.

"But staying in is no fun," Nash complains.

"We can invite Nona and Crimson." Ziggy is practically bouncing on the balls of his feet with excitement.

"I guess we could have a house party," Nash concedes. "Are you sure Clover can't come?"

"Are you interested in Creed's sister?" I ask. "She's not the sort of girl you usually date."

"I don't date," Nash replies.

"Exactly."

As if on cue the others burst out laughing.

"I could date," he argues, a pout on his face.

"Unless you want Creed to slaughter you," Rigby smirks, "you should stay away from her."

"I can ask her to come," Clover says softly, and I almost bite her head off. I don't understand what she's doing at all. It's not like she can be two places at once. She comes up to stand beside Nash, kneeing him in the back of the knee, almost causing him to fall.

"But you can't hit on her."

"Can't make any promises." He gives Clover a cheeky grin.

If she was actually her brother, Nash could lose a limb or two but because she's not, the arse gets away with it.

"Should we leave right away?" Nash is saying but both Clover and Rigby are shaking their heads.

"Not bloody likely," Rigby says exchanging a conspiratorial look with Clover as she hands Nash his bass.

I'm not sure I like the look those two are sharing. It's a little too knowing, slightly too close and for some reason I'm a little bit jealous.

***

It isn't until much later that Clover allows us to stop. My fingers are seriously cramping up from playing the keyboard and Nash is grumbling about not having enough time to plan a party.

"Can't you just send a mass text?" Clover asks as she falls back on to the sofa with a sigh of relief. "Job done."

"Yeah but someone needs to go shopping."

"Just ask Switch," she says before yawning, "or I'll ask Jasper." She pulls out her brother's phone and sends a quick text to her mother's assistant.

Not two minutes later, Clover lets out the girliest scream I've ever heard, causing us all to scramble up from where we've settled on the floor.

Climbing up so she can stand on the sofa, she's pointing at something in the corner of the room. In her moment of panic, she's forgotten that Creed isn't scared of spiders and perhaps more importantly that Creed cannot scream like that.

"What's wrong?" Ziggy is asking, looking in the direction that she's pointing.

Nash is looking at her like she's bat shit crazy and I'm at a complete loss as to how we're supposed to rectify this situation.

Rigby simply grins before walking over to the spider and picking it up with his bare hands.

Show off.

Acting the part of her fucking white knight, he leaves the room to get rid of the spider.

"I didn't know you were scared of spiders, Creed," Ziggy says with a scratch of his head.

When Rigby returns the look of gratitude that Clover gives him is far too sweet.

CLOVER

What the hell have I just roped myself into? How the hell am I supposed to attend the party as both myself and Creed? I must be completely bonkers – *insanity probably runs in the family...*

I need a bloody plan or something. I'm pacing the distance from Creed's bedroom door to his window with angry long strides.

There's a knock at the door and I'm turning around on the spot. Jett enters, his expression serious.

"We can just tell them she said she couldn't come," he says and for a moment I'm lost as to who he's talking about. Then it hits me, he means me. The me that doesn't dress like a boy.

As impossible as I know it is, I'm still disappointed. There's a part of me that really wants to put on a pair of heels and a pretty dress. I would die to put on some make up. Pulling out Creed's phone, I make a stupid decision. I ignore the nagging feeling that I'll regret it, that I might actually get caught and send a text to Crimson asking for help.

Returning the phone to my pocket, I say, "help me sneak out?"

"What?"

"I need to leave without Creed leaving," I try to explain.

"But…" He doesn't like it. I can tell just from the look on his face. It's the look he gives me before he gives in to my stupid ideas. It's a look I'm familiar with. He sighs before relenting. "Fine."

"How?"

He smirks at me before saying, "You're the one that wants to escape why do I have to come up with the plan?"

"Because you're my friend," I say sweetly.

"Isn't it better to sneak out right in front of their eyes?"

"Huh?"

"Leave through the front door with a good excuse," Jett explains.

"But then when they don't see me come back…?"

"I'll lie and say I saw you come in."

I nod my head once before making my way over to my brother's wardrobe, pulling out a pair of running shorts, a t-shirt and hoody. My phone vibrates in my pocket, so I fling the clothes on the bed.

"Crimson is waiting outside," I tell Jett.

"I'll leave you to change," he says before leaving the room.

I must be daft. All because of a stupid party, I'm risking everything. If the guys find out about Creed… to be honest I don't know what would happen.

Would they be angry? Probably.

Would they blame me? Most likely.

Would they hate me? I'm not sure.

It's only been a few days, but I feel like I've become friends with them all. I don't want them to hate me without actually having the chance for them to get to know the real me, a chance to get to know Clover.

***

When I return to the house over an hour and a half later, I have a fully formulated plan. Crimson will help me change outfits periodically throughout the evening in Creed's room.

As nervous as I am, I'm super excited. I'm looking forward to meeting the guys as myself. It's also a huge relief to be wearing my own clothes instead of my brother's. I've never been much of a tomboy and dressing like a boy for the last few days has been far from comfortable.

I've felt invisible; lost… hidden away inside an exterior that is not my own.

Nervously I knock on the door to the house that I've been sleeping in since my return. It feels weird standing here as a guest that needs to be invited in.

Ziggy is the one to open the door. His smile is wide and sincere as he pulls me into a hug.

"You're Clover, right?"

"Yeah…" I say awkwardly as he releases me.

"I knew it the second I saw you're face," he's telling me. "You really are Creed's double."

He takes me by the hand, pulling me into the house.

"Guys! Clover's here!"

Several guests have already arrived. The guys all glance my way with interest while the girls glower in my direction.

Rigby, Jett and Nash are all in the kitchen stood around the breakfast bar when Ziggy rushes me in to meet them.

I'm almost scared to look at them in case they work it out. Ziggy makes the introductions.

"Clover, this is Rigby and Nash. You already know Jett… guys, where's Creed?"

"He's in the shower," Jett lies more naturally than I've ever seen him before and I'm grateful. I hate that I'm making him lie for me.

"Nice to meet you, Clover," Nash says, coming towards me. His eyes are twinkling with interest. He's forgotten the condition that I – Creed – gave him. He's forgotten that he's not allowed to hit on me.

Before he gets a chance though, Rigby is beside him, drawing my attention his way.

"We've heard a lot about you."

You're The Right Person

Someone Else's Dream (#9)

You're the right person

At the right moment

You're the girl I've been

Dreaming of until now

I'm now looking for a way

To tell you how I feel

Baby, I'm head over heels

In love with you

You're the right person

At the right moment

You're the reason

That I'm still smiling

I'm now looking for a way

To show you how I feel

Baby, I'm completely lost

In thoughts of you

Lust & Lyrics

Thoughts of you

It's you, it's you

I'd give it all up, if I could just

Keep you by my side

I need you, I need you

You're the beat that

Moves my heart

You're the song that's

Inside my soul

You're the one that

Fills my mind

Thoughts of you

It's you, it's you

I'd give it all up, if I could just

Keep you by my side

I need you, I need you

RIGBY

The second I see her face, I know. The person who sang Saved differently, the person who wrote Caged, the person who has been affecting me, it's not Creed, it's Clover.

My shoulders sag momentarily with relief before they puff out pretentiously as if I can pretend she hasn't seen how much of a dick I am. If she thinks first impressions count for something, she probably doesn't think very highly of me.

"Can I get you a drink?" Nash offers.

It's frustrating watching him flirt with her. I want to give him a good slap round the head, but I resist the urge. Instead I roll my eyes because this is just what Nash does. It means absolutely nothing.

I lead her into the living room.

The others are focused on her too, talking about how much she looks like Creed. But all I can see is how different she looks. She slight where he's bulky. Her eyes are not blue, they're green.

If I could have my own way, I'd drag her out of the room just so I can get her away from my friends. I offer her a seat on the sofa, watching her closely. The others follow behind us, only Nash leaving us to go and get Clover a drink. The rest of our guests are completely forgotten.

Jett is watching her protectively and Ziggy is sat at her feet as if she's a goddess that needs to be worshiped.

Nash brings her a beer before plonking himself down next to her on the sofa. I feel a rumble in my chest as I almost bark at him to get away from her. He's an absolute manwhore and as much as he might be my friend, I don't want him anywhere near her.

"So, what's it like having Creed for a brother?" Ziggy is asking her with the eagerness of a puppy.

"Pretty good. Can't complain," she says with a lilt that is definitely missing in Creed's voice. That lilt as well as everything else I can see about her has me wondering exactly how she's managed to fool us all into believing that she is her brother.

The questions continue until a couple of girls approach us, clearly put out that all of our attentions are focused on Clover. I take advantage of their appearance and take Clover's hand, pulling her through the house and into the piano room. Closing the door behind us, I turn to face her.

She's looking at me, biting her lip softly.

"Where's Creed?" I ask. I sound angrier than I mean to. I'm not mad, not at all.

Her eyes go wide, but she holds her tongue.

"What do you mean? I thought you said he was in the shower."

"I think we both know that Creed hasn't been in this house for several days."

She turns away from me, buying time but I pull her by the arm, causing her to turn and fall into my chest. I hold her there.

My voice is gruff when I ask, "Clover, where is your brother?"

"In the hospital."

Her eyes are cast down and her words floor me.

"Since the accident?"

She nods her head but says nothing.

"Is he okay?"

She shrugs her shoulders. It doesn't come across as uncaring but rather like she's trying to keep her shit together.

"I don't know."

Dropping to the floor, I pull her with me, so we can both sit beside each other with our backs to the door. I wrap an arm around her shoulder and pull her into my side.

"I'm sorry for being an arsehole," I tell her the only thing I can.

We sit there talking, completely ignoring the ruckus that is just beyond the door, the party raging throughout the house.

We talk until I feel her head droop and she falls asleep, then I carry her to Creed's bedroom, hoping the other's won't see. Placing her gently on the bed, I kiss her forehead before turning to leave.

"Where have you been mate?" Ziggy asks when I turn the corner into the living room.

"Just here and there."

"Where did Clover go?" he presses.

"Home," I lie.

He's disappointed. His shoulders droop and he returns his attention to whatever the fuck he was doing before I came into the room.

NASH

The angel is Creed's sister and what's more she's even more perfect close up. The party has died down and most of the guests have gone. I've even managed to evict the two girls who have been following me around for the last two hours.

The lads are all in the living room, playing on the Xbox. All except Creed. He's not been around all night.

Both Rigs and Jett have told me they saw him at the party but I definitely didn't. According to Rigby he's asleep in his room, completely shit faced. But that can't be real. That boy has a better tolerance than I do.

I want to talk to him about his damn sister and that boy is supposedly so wankered he's gone to bed early.

All the guys hounded Clover tonight, that is until she disappeared with fucking Rigs. There hadn't been a guy in the bloody house who wasn't interested in her. But I'm not daft, Creed wouldn't let me within a fucking inch of her. I'm not the sort of guy you want with your sister. I'm a father and brother's worse nightmare. Too much of a slag to be loyal, that's what they all think and for the most part, they're right.

But I've always liked to think that out there somewhere there's a woman that I'll want enough to change... *And pigs might fly too.*

Seeing Clover tonight though, that childish notion of a woman I could love – really love – came flooding back and I had felt myself wonder if she could be that girl.

And then Rigby had dragged her away and I'd reminded myself as I watched her walk away from me, that she's my mate's sister.

For guys like me, that makes her off limits. Fucking, dating, even loving her, could cause our band to break apart and my bandmates are the only real family I have. I can't fuck that up. Not even for the best piece of ass I've seen in a long time.

Leaving the others in the living room, I make my way up the stairs and stop only when I reach Creed's door. I knock once. I'm not really sure what I'm doing exactly. I know that talking to Creed about Clover is as good as wasting my breath. He'll tell me to stay away from her and he'll not be wrong. I can't keep a girlfriend for a month, let alone see it to the end; marriage, children, and all that shit.

Trying the door, I'm surprised when it opens. Creed's been acting a bit strange recently and this is the first time since his accident that I've found his door unlocked.

I walk into the room and take in the sight of the girl in the bed. At first, I think Creed has gotten lucky and I prepare to make a sharp exit. That is until, I recognise the hair… rose gold… It's Clover sleeping in Creed's bed.

Moving towards her, my eyes roam the room, looking for clues as to where her brother is. Both Jett and Rigs are convinced that Creed is the one asleep in here. Unless… My eyes land on a wig. I feel my forehead scrunch up in concentration as I consider what it could possibly mean.

Where the fuck is Creed?

I consider shaking the beautiful girl awake so that I can ask her where her brother is, but I can't bring myself to do it. Instead I approach the bed, sitting down gently on the edge so that I can touch her face. She's flawless.

I can't believe she's been acting the part of her brother. I can't decide if I should be livid or impressed.

Running my fingers along her cheek, I feel her perfect skin beneath my touch, causing my own skin to tingle with awareness. She's fairylike in her sleep; soft, innocent and yet potently dangerous.

Her eyes flutter open and she looks up at me in shock.

"Nash." Her voice is huskier than normal, heavy with sleep.

Leaning down, I kiss her. I know I shouldn't. I know her brother will kill me. I know the guys will string me up for this but when her lips touch mine, I can't bring myself to regret it.

CLOVER

Panic sweeps through me when I open my eyes to see Nash watching me sleep. He knows. It's impossible for me to keep this secret now. Not only do Jett and Rigby now know but Nash too.

The idea of explaining again makes me want to throw up.

My fear is overridden when he lowers his mouth to mine. His kiss is consuming and even though I like Rigby and care on some level for Jett, I give in to the sensations that his lips on me inspire. Lifting my hands to his neck, I pull myself up so that I'm clinging to him by the hair at the back of his neck.

The kiss we share is hard as neither one of us want to yield to the other. His hand is under my top and the feel of his touch on my skin causes me to arch my back as I let out a moan into his mouth.

My mind is shouting at me that I'm messing everything up but I ignore it completely.

Lust & Lyrics

In this moment, all I can think about is the way his other hand is on my arse, pulling my pants down so the globes of my bum sit above them. We're doing everything we shouldn't, and I can't bring myself to say no or stop.

The other boys are downstairs and yet that does nothing to stop me from revelling in the feel of his fingers entering me for the first time. Their names are on a loop in my ear – all the reasons why I shouldn't be doing this, but my mind is no longer calling the shots.

Before long he has me completely naked and he's removing his own clothes quicker than I can catch my breath. Then his hands are on me again – my boobs, my bum… his hands are everywhere. When he lines up his cock to enter me, his eyes are fixed on mine.

He slowly enters me, and I wrap my legs around his waist, pulling him closer, deeper into me. The sounds we make are far from quiet as the headboard bangs against the wall in time with our thrusts. I don't believe for one second that the boys downstairs don't know what's going on.

A twinge of guilt twists in my gut but it does nothing to stop the moan on the tip of my tongue from escaping.

This is everything I shouldn't be doing and like most forbidden things in the moment it definitely feels worth the trouble it's bound to cause.

ZIGGY

The morning after the party, everyone is behaving weird. Both Rigby and Nash are being nice towards Creed and for some unknown reason Jett keeps giving Nash a death glare. The only person behaving even close to their usual self is Creed.

He looks slightly awkward at the sudden extra attention but other than that he's usual old Creed.

Our journey to the studio is painful. No one speaks.

All eyes are on Creed and I can't help but wonder if I've missed something but I'm not sure what I could possibly have missed when the boy went to bed early last night. I put it down to the fact that all three guys are probably – almost definitely – interested in Clover.

I have to admit, when I saw her on our doorstep, I thought I might be falling in love. But I hadn't really had chance to get to know her because the others took over. Nash was his usual flirty self and Rigby as good as kidnapped her, cutting us all out of the game. With no opportunity to get to know her, I was left feeling pretty deflated.

Nash had been downright pissed when he couldn't find her or Rigby. Where he felt anger, I'd been disappointed. Disappointed that yet again the Siren that I'd heard singing in the studio, was out of my reach.

Her voice even when she was just speaking was magical. It captivated my imagination and drew my attention to her. The idea of seeing her today at the studio is the main reason why I'm allowing Rigby to drag me out the door and into the waiting car. Perhaps I'll even hear her sing again.

JETT

I don't think I'll ever get the sight of Nash fucking Clover out of my head. Right now, I fucking hate him and I don't feel much better towards her.

I've always liked her. A stupid crush on a friend's sister that I'd done my best to ignore. I'd always thought that she'd find a nice guy who I could concede to without any bitterness.

So long as he keeps her happy had been my mantra. But I had never imagined conceding to the likes of Nash.

A good guy. Someone kind. That I could see. But as much as Nash is one of my best mates, he's not the guy I want the girl I love to be with. Hell, realistically there is no guy I want her with except me.

Except we didn't stand a chance from the beginning. My best friend's sister was off limits and unlike Nash, I knew it.

As I was heading up to bed last night, I'd gone to check on her. She'd disappeared early and I'd been worried. I'd been surprised when I found her door unlocked and horrified when I saw what her and Nash were doing on her brother's bed.

The sight had twisted my gut and turned me on in equal measure. I didn't want to look. I wanted to run from that doorway and erase my memory of what I could see but I didn't. I couldn't. Because as much as I hated the sight of Clover with Nash, I couldn't take my eyes off them. My body had reacted, and I'd grown hard in my trousers.

I'd known Clover was beautiful, but I'd had no idea just how perfect she was until that moment, watching another man fuck her. Her hair was sprayed across the pillow, her legs wrapped around him as he pounded into her. I struggled not to let my hand wander. I needed release. I wanted to fuck her the way Nash was fucking her.

Instead, I pulled the door shut and made my way towards my own room ignoring the sounds of ecstasy that I was walking away from. Once in the privacy of my own room, I removed my clothes and began to pull roughly on my cock.

There was no time for being gentle. I needed release while the image of Clover close to orgasm was still in my mind. I'd desperately held onto that mental image until my hand was covered in my own come.

Now though, in the light of day, without the alcohol that had been rushing through my system the previous night, I can barely look at her. I'm embarrassed and angry at both myself, Nash and Clover.

Clover is pretending nothing happened with Nash and nothing in her behaviour suggests she saw me at her door last night. I'm relieved because I really don't want to have to explain that to her.

***

Rigby and Nash are all over her like a bad rash and I can't help but wonder if she's told them about Creed. They must know that she's not Creed, otherwise there's no way in hell they'd behave this way with Creed.

It's not even like they're trying to suck up to him, no they are all over him.

Nash is making sly passes at her arse while Rigby is trying to take her hand. After a morning of pure torture, I'm ready to lose my shit.

Pulling Clover into an empty studio, I try to keep my cool.

"What are you playing at, Clover?" I ask.

"What do you mean?" She plays innocent and as cute as she is, it pisses me off even more.

"You know exactly what I'm talking about. You told Rigby and Nash!"

"Er…" Finally, she has the good sense to look bashful. Biting her lip, she says, "they guessed."

"Guessed?"

"Rigby guessed the moment I arrived at the house, last night."

"And Nash?"

Her face turns scarlet and I know she doesn't want to tell me.

"He came to Creed's room last night."

"And you fucked him," I say even though I know I shouldn't.

She doesn't say anything.

"They're Creed's mates," I tell her, trying to put my own frustration aside. "Please, don't make things even more complicated. You're fucking Nash, flirting with Rigby and Ziggy would be following you around like a little puppy if he knew you were you."

"I know that. What happened last night wasn't intentional."

"Don't play with them," I say, silently thinking, *don't play with me.*

Your Heart Beats

Listening To Your Heart (#1)

I feel your heart

As if it beats in my chest

Your soul sings

Even when you can't speak

I hear you, I hear you

I hear the rhythm

Of your soul

I hear the melody

Of your dream

I'll keep it safe for you

I'll hold it close for you

Your heart beats, I hear it

Your heart beats, I feel it

Your heart beats, inside my chest

I feel your soul

As if it burns my skin

Lust & Lyrics

Your love calls me

Even when you can't see me

I hear you, I hear you

I feel your love

As if it rings in my ear

Your heart clings on

Even when I'm out of reach

I hear you, I hear you

Your heart beats, 1, 2, 3

Your heart beats, love

Your heart, your heart beats

Your heart beats, love

CLOVER

I try to spend the next few days focusing on the music for the new album, doing my best to ignore the guys I'm currently living with. It's not easy especially when they behave all flirty.

I see the way they look at each other though and I don't like the way I'm causing a rift between them. The only one oblivious to the drama is Ziggy, although he adds to it all the same by constantly asking about me.

When will Clover come to visit again? Will we see Clover today? Should we invite Clover?

Each question a reminder for the rest of us that our current situation is far from normal. It's been well over a week since the accident and my brother, Creed still hasn't woken up.

Jett is barely speaking to me and so my usual sounding board is missing. So instead I find myself seeking out Rigby in the music room. He's there behind the piano where I've grown attached to seeing him. He grins when he sees me but doesn't stop playing, simply scooting up the piano stool a little to make room for me.

He's playing a song I don't know, and I want to ask him if he's just written it. I want to ask if it's going to go on the album, but the words steal my attention.

"Do I need a reason to sing? Do I need words to say or can I just lose myself in a melody?" he sings, and his voice quiets my mind in an instant. "This love song doesn't need words. When you hear it, you'll know what I want to say."

As if by instinct, I know this song is for me. He's written it exclusively for me. The whole world might get to hear it, but it was written for me.

"The notes combined in perfect harmony, just like you and me."

My breath is stuck in my throat and it feels as if my heart has stopped beating.

"It's untitled, indescribable, unbelievable. It's untitled, inexplicable, completely magical."

I miss the moment when the song comes to an end and the music stops. It isn't until he kisses me that I realise his hands that had been playing the piano are now in my hair. His tongue is begging entry to my mouth and I can't refuse him.

Moving on the stool that we're both sharing, I straddle him. I can feel his dick beneath me, and I grind into it as I deepen our kiss. I know that I'm behaving like a completely wanton slut. I fucked his friend just a few days ago and yet here I am about to fuck him too. But I don't care. He grabs my hips and pushes his own up into me. He's hard and I know he wants me. It's strange because as much as I know he knows who I am, I still look like my brother right now.

"Clover," he groans out, still thrusting his hardness against me. I fear that he's going to stop us, that he'll tell me that we can't because I don't look like me right now, but he doesn't. Instead, he complains that I'm wearing too much clothes. Standing me to my feet, he begins to remove my jeans.

"I wish I could touch your hair," he says before removing my hoodie. When he has me naked all except my knickers and the bandage that has my boobs bound, he chuckles softly. "I think I'm going to unwrap you… it's like Christmas has come early."

I know I should try and pull away. As much as I like him, I shouldn't be doing this with another one of my brother's friends.

The air is electric around us, just as it always has been, and I can't resist it any longer. I want this. I want him.

He's different to Nash. He's gentler except you could never really call Rigby gentle. His fingers inside me are slightly callused from the thousands of hours he's spent playing his guitar and those same fingers are now playing me much the same way. His fingers move with an expertise across my clit, causing my entire body to spasm.

He's still sitting on the piano stool and I'm stood in the space between him and the piano. His mouth replaces his fingers and I almost scream out. He circles my clit once with his tongue before sucking on it. Then his tongue is plunging into my pussy as deep as it can go.

I cover my mouth with my hand and bite down in an attempt to hide my screams from the rest of the house. My other hand drops onto the keys of the piano, an almighty clashing of sound hitting my ear.

"Fuck," I cry out between whimpers. So much for talking.

JETT

I regret getting cross with Clover almost immediately and as time passes it gets harder and harder to apologise. Several days after our argument, I knock on her door.

She opens it wearily. Her wig is slightly lopsided as if she's just rushed to put it on.

"Wouldn't it be easier if you just told Ziggy?"

"Huh?"

"Then you could at least be yourself in the house." It seems obvious to me.

"I didn't…" She hadn't even considered it.

"I came to say sorry," I tell her. "I should never have spoken to you like that."

"It's okay." The words sound hollow and I think I've actually really hurt her. "I slept with Rigby."

Her words blow right through me. They sting more than I'd like as jealousy pulses inside me. I don't say anything, scared that I'll end up saying the wrong thing. I don't want to come across judgemental, but I can't work out what she's up to.

This isn't like her. She's not a girl who sleeps with just anyone.

"I like him," she admits with a whisper.

I count to five to steady myself before I speak.

"What about Nash?"

"I like him too," she says.

"If they knew…" I don't need to finish that sentence. She knows.

"They'd kill each other."

Sitting down on the bed, I ignore the way being so close to her makes me feel. I ignore the fact that I've wanted her far longer than either Nash or Rigby. I consider all the different things I can tell her, but nothing seems right. I don't want to just boss her about like some big brother. Instead, I do something I'll probably regret.

"I love you, Clover."

Her eyes widen with surprise. "What?"

"I love you."

She's silent and the expression on her face definitely can't be considered one of her most attractive looks. Her mouth is gaping wide as she fails to speak and her eyes are practically bulging from their sockets.

"You love me?" She finally gets the words out. "Since when?"

"Since always," I say it even though I know it's pointless. Her brother is my best friend. There's no world in which we can be together.

"Always?" The word catches in her throat and she almost sounds like she's choking on it.

She's climbing to her feet and pacing the room within seconds. I've just made her already complicated problem far more difficult. After a moment or two of watching her burn a hole into the carpet with her hurried steps, I come up behind her and wrap my arms around her.

"I love you, Clo." My selfish actions bring relief. To me. But definitely not her. I've told her how I feel, and I feel lighter as a result. The girl in my arms however, is weighed down with even more concerns than she had been five minutes ago. *I did that to her.*

Don't Faulter

Listening To Your Heart (#2)

Don't ever stop

Don't ever leave

Don't faulter

It's a sound I carry with me

Wherever I go

The sound of your life

As I hold it close

I try to protect it

It's more fragile than I knew

The notes are weak

The rhythm uneasy

Please, don't faulter

Don't ever stop

I'll count the beats

Don't ever leave

I'll keep your time

Hanleigh Bradley

Don't faulter

It's a sound that comforts me

You're always there

It's the sound of you

In my life, by my side

I try to hold it

Without breaking you

The notes are weak

The rhythm uneasy

Please, don't faulter

Don't ever stop

I'll count the beats

Don't ever leave

I'll keep your time

Don't faulter

Please, don't faulter

CLOVER

He loves me. He's not supposed to love me. If he'd told me that before I met Nash or Rigby my response would have been easy.

I've loved Jett since the first day I met him. That hasn't changed. The way I feel about him has never changed but everything else has.

Now those feelings aren't exclusively his. I care about Rigby and Nash as well. I feel like a complete whore just thinking about the mess I've made though.

With Jett I can talk about anything. He's the person who understands me best. But Rigby speaks to a part of me that I didn't think anyone knew was there. When we're sat behind a piano together the whole world just falls into place and I've never felt so safe. Then there's Nash. He's exciting and fun and with him I forget all about my family's expectations. He gives me a rush. He's heady like a drug. With him I feel like I can be anyone I want to be. I don't have to be the princess of rock or whatever daft thing my parents want me to be.

If I'm honest with myself, living with the four guys I've fallen for each of them. Even Ziggy. I might not have slept with him and he might not have told me he loves me but the way he looks at me and cares for me. He makes me feel cherished. With Ziggy I'm special.

But there's no world in which I can have all four and I think I'd have to be the most selfish human being alive to ask that of them. And what's more I can't bare to tell them what I've done.

As Jett's arms come around me, my shoulders tense. He shouldn't love me.

Angry, I turn on him. "How could you?"

His eyes show his bewilderment.

"Why the hell didn't you say something sooner?"

"Sooner?"

"If you had told me before…" I don't finish what I'm saying because I have no idea how I can tell him the truth – that I love him and always have. How can I tell him I love him only a few short breaths after telling him I've slept with not only one of his friends but two. What's worse that if I could I'd do it again…

I make my way towards the door, ignoring him when he calls me back. I practically run past Ziggy in the hallway and push past Nash and Rigby who are at the front door, tears are pouring down my face as I run down the street.

I don't stop running, not when I feel winded, nor when I stop crying. I only stop when I reach the hospital.

I hadn't even realised this was where I had been heading. Entering the building, I wipe my eyes. I make my way through the entry hall over to where the lift stands against a far wall. Pressing the button to call the lift, I wait. My foot is tapping impatiently as I watch the numbers decrease, the lift getting closer.

I feel relieved when I don't see my mum or dad in the lift. Making my way through the corridors of the hospital, I try to organise my thoughts.

My mind keeps flitting between the idea of getting on a plane and leaving and telling the boys everything except I definitely can't do that. As I open the door to my brother's room, I find myself wishing that my brother would just wake up already.

It's a selfish thought but I need my brother.

Not that I think I could possibly tell him what a hash of things I've made. No, instead if he's awake I'll be able to run away back to France at least for the remainder of the year.

CREED

Somewhere in the distance I can hear my sister crying. Even though I can hear her, I don't know where the sound is coming from.

No matter how much I want to, I can't get my eyes to open. She's speaking but the words sound muffled. She's apologising, I think. She seems to think she's fucked up somehow.

"Creed," her voice lacks its usual cheerfulness, "I need you to wake up."

I think I feel her hand in mine, but I can't be sure because my skin, much like my eyes, doesn't feel like it is my own. I try to squeeze her hand to comfort her, but I have no way of knowing if I'm successful.

"I was just trying to help but I've made everything worse. I love them."

I have no idea what she's talking about. Who does she love?

"I thought mum was bonkers asking me to pretend to be you…"

Hang on, rewind a bit, I try to tell her, but my mouth doesn't move.

She continues to talk but the words mumble together, and I'm left scraping together little titbits of information. All I know for sure is that my sister has been pretending to be me and she loves someone… although I can only guess as to who.

The idea that it might be one of the guys causes anger to flare within me. If Nash has messed with her, I'll bloody kill the git.

I need to wake the fuck up. Clover is still crying, and I can do jack shit about it, locked up inside this body.

CLOVER

When I leave the hospital, I'm significantly calmer. I rush back to the house so that I can pack a bag. Grabbing my passport, I prepare to leave.

I glance in the mirror. I can't go to the airport looking like Creed. I pull the wig off my head and the cap beneath it. I change my clothes as quickly as possible, hoping to be out of the house before any of the guys realise I'm even here.

The house is quiet but I'm not sure if it's because they're out, perhaps looking for me, or because they're all busy in their rooms doing their own thing.

Finally dressed, I put the rucksack over my shoulder and leave my brother's room. My eyes on the screen of my phone, I barrel headlong into someone.

"Clover?" Ziggy says as he takes a hold of me to stop me from falling. "Visiting Creed?"

I don't know how to respond. Instead, I just nod my head.

"Cool," he says, apparently oblivious to my awkwardness. "Do you want a drink?" He sounds eager as if he's keen to spend time with me.

"I can't. Sorry." I don't want him to know where I'm going. "I have an appointment."

His eyes land on the passport in my hand. I try to hide it discreetly, but I know he's seen it.

"Are you going away again?" He sounds disappointed but I refuse to acknowledge his emotions. My own feelings are already too much for me to understand. I don't think I can let myself worry about his too.

Or Jett's? a voice says in my mind. *Rigby? Nash?*

Pulling away from him, I try to distract him.

"I think Rigby has a new song he wants to show you guys."

His expression changes and I think he knows I'm lying but if he does, he doesn't let on. He just nods his head and gives me a hug. He holds me longer than would be expected from a normal, run of the mill goodbye hug between friends.

I don't pull away. I can't. I won't. The feel of his arms around me makes me feel both safe and loved all at once. When he lets go of me, I don't want to leave but I know I can't stay.

"I'll see you soon," I say quietly before leaving the house that had suddenly become my home.

***

The airport is as busy as always. I stand in front of the departures board as I try to decide where the fuck I'd like to go. Anywhere but here. There are too many options. As far away as possible.

After several moments of deliberation, I decide to head to Greece. I don't really care where I go. As long as it's not here.

I fling my bag on the ground as I offer my passport to the woman behind the customs desk.

"Do you have any luggage for the cabin?"

"No. Just carry on," I tell her.

She runs through all the questions they always ask, and I answer without any thought at all. My mind is split four ways and right now there's no time for me to think about the woman behind the desk.

Then she returns my passport to me, offering me a smile and I'm walking away. I check my gate number and then I'm queueing for security. Every few minutes I'm glancing towards the doors, hoping that one of them – no, all of them – will come through the doors, calling my name.

If any one of them walked through the doors right now, it wouldn't be enough to keep me here though. I've messed things up far too much.

JETT

The moment she is gone, I regret letting her go. But I can hardly force her to stay. Perhaps a bit of time to clear her head is exactly what she needs. I close Creed's door and cross the hall to my own room. Entering the room, I collapse on my bed.

The house is quiet. I have no clue where the others are.

I lie there on top of my bed, waiting for her to return. My ears are tuned, waiting for any noise at all. I struggle to keep my eyes open though, and they quickly start to droop and before I know it I'm asleep.

When I wake up, it's to the sound of my phone ringing. Hours have past and its beginning to get dark.

"Hello?" I answer my phone.

"Hi Jett." I'm surprised to hear Jasper on the other end of the line. "Is Clover with you?"

"No. Sorry. Why? What's wrong?"

"Creed's awake and we can't reach Clover."

He hangs up after asking me to call if I hear from her. I'm out of my room in a flash and banging on her door.

"Clover!" I call before opening it. She's not there.

"What's going on?" Rigby and Nash are stood at the bottom of the stairs.

"Where's Clover?"

"Dunno mate," Nash says.

"Why? What's going on?" Rigby asks.

"Creed is awake."

"What do you mean?" A voice comes from somewhere behind me. Turning on the spot, I see Ziggy. "What the hell is going on?"

I don't have time to explain this to him.

"Creed is in the hospital. Have you seen Clover?"

"She's gone to the airport."

"What?" I'm floored. "When?"

"She's gone?" Rigby looks cut up and Nash isn't much better as he throws his fist into the wall.

"What do we do?" I ask. I'm torn between going to the hospital to see my best mate and going to the airport to drag her back.

"We go get our girl back," Nash says without stopping to think. His words make me wonder if he realises that she loves us all.

Rigby is already on his way out the door and none of us question it as we follow after him. But I'm terrified that we're already too late.

All Mine

CREED

My eyes open and dart around the room, looking for Clover. She's not here.

Fucks sake.

Instead, my eyes land on my mum. She looks exhausted and usually I'd feel at least a little pity for her. But not now, not knowing what she forced Clover to do.

In what world would she make Clover take my place?

If Clover were here now, she'd just shake her head and blame it on the drugs. Pretty much all our parents' crazy antics get explained away by their supposedly reckless youth.

"Where's Clover?" I demand before my mum even realises that I'm awake.

Her eyes practically bug out of their sockets as she jumps out of her seat, moving closer. She's wrapping her arms around me, tears streaming down her face, but I don't give a shit.

"Where's my sister?" I ask again.

But mum isn't listening. She's overwhelmed by the fact that I'm awake or whatever. Or possibly just relieved that the family's money maker isn't in a coma.

It might sound seriously fucked up but that's just the way our family is. We're not the Levon kids, Clover and I, we're our parents' pensions.

"Mum get off me," I say irritably, gently pushing her away, "and tell me everything."

She must hear the stern tone in my voice because she backs up sharpish and pulls out her phone.

"I'll get Clover to come," she says.

I'm quiet as I listen to my mum's discussion with Jasper, her assistant. She takes her fucking time. She's in no rush to tell me what the fuck has been happening while I've been trapped here in the hospital.

When she finally hangs up, I look at her pointedly, waiting for her explanation. It doesn't come. At least not quickly.

"Well…?" I say when my patience is practically gone.

She looks almost apologetic which is funny because our parents don't ever apologise. No matter what crazy shit they pull, they act like they've never done anything wrong.

"You made Clover pretend to be me?" I ask.

She's clearly surprised that I know, and I can see the question 'how do you know?' practically written on her face, but she doesn't ask. Instead, she has the sense to look nervous.

"It was an emergency," she tells me.

"Tell me everything," I demand. I'm being shitty and disrespectful and if my dad were here, he'd skin me alive for speaking to my mum like this. But I can still hear Clover crying in my mind.

"I called Clover back early. We didn't think you'd be… I didn't think it would take this long. I thought it was just for one night."

I get it. I hate to admit it but I understand my parents' decision. I don't like it but I get it. It was simply a question of money. *Why waste all that ticket money when you can just put up the spare?*

"But it wasn't just one night," I say brusquely, hoping she'll get to the damn point and fast. "How long was it?"

"Er," she hesitates, "not long…"

"Mum," I chastise her.

"A week or so."

"You had her pretending to be me for weeks?" I have about a thousand questions but none of them are for mum. They're all for Clover and the guys.

My mum looks down at the floor sheepishly.

"I wasn't thinking straight, darling."

For a second, I almost pity her but it doesn't last. Especially when I ask, "where was she living? Did she stay with you?"

"No. She stayed with the band."

My anger flares at that.

"You put my sister into a house of hormonally driven arse heads?"

"Er… like I said, I didn't think it all through. It all just sort of happened."

"You forgot that your actions have bloody consequences like usual," I grumble, climbing from the bed.

"Where are you going? You shouldn't get out of bed until you've seen the doctor."

She tries to push me back down but I'm stronger than her and completely unwilling to comply.

"I'm going to find Clo."

"Jasper is looking for her."

"I don't give a shit."

"Creed please…"

"No. You've gone too far this time, mum. This is so far over the fucking line, I can't even see the line anymore," I roar angrily at her, my temper rising with each word.

Glancing her way, I see unshed tears lining her lower eyelids, but I can't bring myself to apologise. *It's her own damn fault.*

You've Gone Too Far

(Written by Creed)

Do you even see the line?

You crossed it so long ago.

You've gone too far.

You show no sign of slowing.

You're not stopping.

Stop it. Stop it.

Fuck this. Stop it. Stop it.

You've gone too fucking far,

This time. Stop it. Stop it.

I'm no longer listening.

Stop. Stop. Stop. Stop.

I said stop it.

Do you even know you're wrong?

You fucked us all right up.

It's all over.

But you still don't even see it.
You're not stopping.
Stop it. Stop it.

Fuck this. Stop it. Stop it.
You've gone too fucking far
This time. Stop it. Stop it.
I'm no longer listening.
Stop. Stop. Stop. Stop.
I said stop it.

It's all over now. There's no going back.
I said, it's all over now. All over now.
There's no going back this time.
STOP.

CLOVER

I don't want to go through security. I'm queueing to go through, but I can't bring myself to step out of the view of the airport's doors. I foolishly keep letting people pass me.

But I don't know what is holding me back. I should leave. It wouldn't matter if they all came barraging through those doors to stop me leaving. It's not like I can stay.

I can't tell them that I've fucked two of them and love all four of them... *That's just... delusional?*

My phone buzzes, giving me an excuse to step out of the queue. I tell myself that I'll answer the call – even though I really want to avoid it – and then I'll grab a coffee and hop back into the queue.

I've been ignoring my phone for hours, so I don't really know why the hell I'm picking it up now.

Exasperated, I say into the device, "what Jasper?"

"Clover? Where are you? I've been calling for ages?"

He sounds tired and excited all at once, but I don't have the energy to listen, not when my eyes are strained on the doors.

I desperately want someone, anyone to walk though them, and pull me back. I'm not one for all that romantic shit, but right now, I think I'm making a mistake.

But the alternative is almost unbearable. I really don't want to have to have that conversation where they all look at me with matching expressions of disappointment.

It's better if I just leave.

"I'm at the airport," I tell him. It's not like he can get here quick enough to stop me. *Not now.* Once I'm air side, none of them will be able to stop me.

"What? Don't leave. Creed is awake."

That causes me to pause. My eyes rove towards the queue that I just abandoned. It's moving slowly.

"I can't stay. I'm glad he's awake."

I'm about to hang up when he says, "Creed wants to see you. He'll meet you at the airport."

I plan to refuse. I have no intentions of waiting here, not for Rigby or any of the others. Not even my brother Creed.

But I don't get the chance because Jasper hangs up before I can respond.

Considering my options, I wander over to the café and order a cappuccino. Sitting just outside, close to the queue for security, I try to make a decision. I sip on my coffee and take a pen out of my bag. Grabbing a napkin, I begin to doodle lyrics on the scrap of tissue.

The words seem to pour onto the paper.

'This should be the end of our story. This should be goodbye.'

I put everything I feel into the words on the page. I'm so distracted writing the lyrics down that I'm completely oblivious to everything around me.

Not until I have the bones of a song written onto that tiny napkin do I lift my head. There standing directly in front of me, staring down at me, is Rigby.

The sight of him steals my breath. I stumble to my feet, pulling away from him, grateful for the table that is between us.

"Rigby," I begin, but I don't continue. I don't know what I intend to say to him.

Once again, I want to run. My eyes dart back to the queue that I shouldn't have left. If I hadn't, I'd safely be on the other side, unreachable.

"Clover, where the fuck do you think you're going?"

I can hardly tell him that I'm going anywhere that isn't here or that I'm literally running away from him and the others. Shrugging my shoulders, I try to play it off.

"Creed is awake," I tell him as if me leaving is perfectly reasonable. "I have no reason to stay."

"No reason?" he repeats, his eyes giving way to emotion that I really don't want to see. Hurt. Everything that I was hoping to avoid is there in his eyes. "I can think of four."

"Huh?"

I can think of four reasons to stay too but I can't imagine his four match mine. And I really can't forget that the four reasons I so desperately want to stay are the same four reasons demanding that I leave.

I can't pick and choose between the four of them, I want them all and that's just not possible.

This Should Be Goodbye

(Written by Clover)

This should be the end

Of our story

This should be goodbye

But I'm holding back

I'm not ready to turn away

This should be goodbye

But I'm holding back

I'm clinging to the way you make me feel

To the way you make me smile

The way you make it so easy to love you

I'm clinging onto that love

But this should be goodbye

This should be the end

Of our destiny

This should be goodbye

Lust & Lyrics

But I'm holding back

I'm not ready to leave you and me

This should be goodbye

But I'm holding back

I'm clinging onto a destiny

That isn't even mine

I'm clinging onto a love

That isn't even mine

I'm clinging onto a hope

That's doomed to fall

I've got to stop holding back.

It's time to say goodbye.

ZIGGY

I'm trying to understand what the hell is going on. Nothing that has happened in the last few minutes makes even the remotest bit of sense.

How the fuck is Creed in the hospital?

The others are so focused on the fact that Clover is leaving that none of them feel the fucking need to explain either, which is a fucking piss take.

"Step on it," Nash tells Jett. "Fuck the speed limit."

Weirdly, Jett doesn't argue with him. Normally that sentence would lead to a massive argument about road safety and back seat driving but not today. Today, Jett does as Nash says.

"Will someone tell me what the fuck is going on?" I say from where I'm sitting in the backseat with a stone faced Rigby.

"No time," Jett says.

"There's plenty," I argue. "We're over thirty minutes away from the airport."

I look between the three guys. Rigby is staring out the window, clearly ignoring me. Jett's eyes are focused on the road. It's Nash that replies to me.

"Creed has been in hospital since the day of the o2."

He literally drops that bomb and goes quiet and I'm left to try and piece the rest together on my own.

"Then…" *Who the hell has been living with us?* I don't need them to tell me, the answer comes quick enough on its own. *Clover.*

I don't say anything else for a few minutes as I try to make sense of it all.

"You all knew? And you didn't tell me?" It's hard not to feel hurt.

"It wasn't our story to tell," Jett says softly.

"She told you?" That hurts even more than the idea of my brothers not telling me.

"Not exactly. I knew the second we walked on stage," Jett replies, looking my way through the rear-view mirror.

Turning to the others, I wait for their answers.

"I found out," Nash says, not expanding on his answer at all.

"How?" I demand.

"I just… I just found out, mate."

"Rigby?"

He doesn't answer.

"Rigs?"

"What?" he answers eventually.

"How did you know?"

"She doesn't have his tattoo."

I feel jealousy pit in my stomach. *Just how close did they get that he saw that?* I mentally tell myself not to be so childish. It's not like it is the most discreet tattoo, taking up almost his entire shoulder.

"How long have you known?"

"I don't know Ziggy… a while."

We pull up into the airport carpark, abandoning the car, so that we can all run over to the terminal building. Several fans try to stop us, but we ignore them. There's no time to stop and play the role of celebrity.

I'm not completely sure why we're stopping her.

If she wants to leave, who are we to hold her back? I feel like I've not had anywhere enough time to get to know her. I only know that I want to, that I want to get to know her.

It's weird to think that she's been living with me and I didn't even know it. I've been stupidly oblivious to the amazing opportunity. Just the other day, I'd been cross that the others were commandeering all her time.

But actually, she has been here right under my nose all this time.

We split up when we enter the building, each of us going off in search of her. All rushing, hoping that we'll be the one to find her, rather than the others. It's a race to find her as much as it is a shared mission.

I head towards the check in desks. When I spot a girl with rose gold hair, my heart begins to pound in my chest. Reaching for her, my hand drops to her shoulder.

She turns but her eyes are brown and she's at least three years older than Clover.

Disappointed, I apologise before turning away, eyes roaming around the room, my feet moving hurriedly. I need to stop her, before someone else does.

I refuse to just sit back and accept that they've all had a chance, that she might like them, want them, choose them, when I haven't even tried yet.

I want a fucking fair fight.

RIGBY

I can't believe she left. I'm running aimlessly through the fucking airport terminal building trying to find her. I'm crashing into people, being a fucking bastard while at it, all in an attempt to reach her before she leaves me.

If she hasn't already that is. There's a real chance I'm already too late but I don't want to think about that.

After everything we've shared and to risk sounding like a fucking sap, I don't just mean the sex, *how could she just jump on a plane and desert me?*

Without even a fucking word.

No 'goodbye.'

No 'nice seeing you.'

Nothing. Not even a 'I'll see you in six months.' She's not even told me she's going, let alone if she'll come back.

I don't know what I'm going to do when I find her, if I find her. I might hug her, cling to her, beg her not to go. But I think it's more likely that I'll tear her a new one, shouting until my throat is raw.

I'm practically shaking with rage.

This is all some sort of twisted joke and I can't wrap my head around it. *How can she just leave?*

It shouldn't bother me as much as it does. We've not known each other long but the connection is real. *And she's fucking running from it!*

Glancing back towards the doors, I can see that Jett has been commandeered by fans. Nash is searching the security queue and Ziggy is over by the check in desks.

They haven't found her yet and I'm filled with dread.

I don't care who finds her so long as we do. *She can't leave!* There's a stream of curse words running on repeat in my head as I rush towards the café.

My girl loves her coffee.

'My girl' sounds almost sarcastic in my mind. She's bloody leaving me and I'm still thinking of her as my girl.

She's not mine. She's making that pretty damn clear.

I don't know how to describe what I feel when I spot her, head lowered over some paper, at one of the tables. She's probably writing some lyrics or something. Even in this situation, when my whole fucking world is turning upside down, she's writing fucking song lyrics.

Fuck my life! What is this shit?

I watch her for a second, trying to make sense of this crap. She doesn't look cut up. She's not crying her eyes out. She's not devasted. There is nothing about her that says that she doesn't want to leave, nothing that says that she wants me to come stop her.

And for a second I wonder if I should just let her go.

Except I really can't do that. There's no world in which I can just let her leave without at least having my say, without at least trying to stop her, without telling her I… telling her how I feel, even if I don't really know myself.

Slowing my steps, I approach her the way I would a wild animal, scared of spooking her. It isn't until I'm standing directly in front of her that she finally looks up.

She's startled, her eyes darting around for an escape route.

I don't understand. I can't comprehend where this went wrong. *Does she regret sleeping with me? Is it because the others clearly like her too?*

I don't care if they like her, so long as she's mine.

Neither of us say anything as her eyes finally settle on mine. Finally, I feel like I can breathe. She's in front of me and she's, at least for a moment, not going anywhere.

It's difficult to place the emotions on her face. She looks heartbroken, almost as if she's the one who has been dumped. As if she's resolved herself to end whatever there is between us.

"CLOVER!"

Instinctively, she looks away from me, towards whoever called out to her, but my eyes remain on her. My stomach drops when her face lights up into a wide, breath stealing and almost surreal smile.

I don't think I've ever seen her smile like that before and I feel jealousy deep in my gut at whoever inspired that glow.

But still I don't look.

I can't bring myself to find out who it is, not when she's leaving me.

"Clover, where the fuck are you going?"

That's a voice I recognise, and I'm flooded with relieve as I too turn towards it.

"Creed," I mumble more to myself than anyone else.

My Girl

(Written by Rigby)

You're leaving me

Jumping on a plane

Not even saying goodbye

Is this really how we end?

You're leaving me

But you're my girl, my girl, my girl

I still haven't played all my cards

I haven't told you I love you

You're still my girl, my girl, my girl

But you're my girl, my girl, my girl

I still have an ace up my sleeve

I haven't told you I love you

You're still my girl, my girl, my girl

Did I hurt you?

Lust & Lyrics

Am I the one to blame?

Where did this go so wrong?

Is this really how we end?

You're leaving me

It doesn't matter that you're my girl

Not when you're leaving me

Can't drag you back

Can't cling to you

Because you're my girl

And I still love you

CREED

"Is this really necessary?" my mum asks as she struggles to match my pace.

"If your sister wants to leave, we shouldn't try to stop her. She's still got three months…"

I don't bother to respond.

Technically, she's right. Clover has a deal with our dumb ass parents. She gets time to travel the world before doing what they want her to do.

They want her to be the 'Princess of Rock' or some other bogus shit. It's the family business, what they've been priming us for since we were barely walking. It's never occurred to our parents that we might not want what they way.

We should just let her leave but I can't, not when just hours ago she was crying in my hospital room.

I want a fucking explanation.

And then once I know what has been going on while I've been stuck in the bloody hospital, I'm going to deal with whatever arsehole fucking made my sister cry.

The terminal building is heaving with people; people off on their holidays, others saying goodbye to loved ones. Several fans try to accost me, grabbing at me, begging for autographs.

Jasper steps between us, blocking them and I roam my eyes over the crowds, searching for Clover's pink hair.

I don't expect to find her quickly so when I spot someone with rose gold hair, my eyes automatically continue past her, until I catch myself and look back.

There sitting in a café near the security queues is my twin sister.

She's not alone. Rigby is standing there almost blocking her from my view. They're not talking, just standing there, staring at each other.

Striding in their direction, I call out to her, "CLOVER!"

She practically jumps out of her skin in reaction. It's as if I've just broken into their silent little bubble, reminding her that they're not alone but rather surrounded by people in the middle of the airport's terminal building.

Clover doesn't say anything though.

Her eyes move from me to mum and then back to Rigby. She looks lost, almost scared, nothing like my crazy, strong sister.

Taking a seat at her table, I fold my arms.

Mum and Rigby are watching us, clearly both feeling awkward.

"Piss off," I tell them.

Mum bristles. I can't really say I blame her either. I shouldn't be swearing at her.

"Give us a second," I say.

Rigby looks like he's going to argue but with a sigh he steps back and then they're walking away, leaving us alone.

Clover doesn't say anything. She just looks down at a napkin that she's been writing on. I make a grab for it, reading the lyrics that she's written on it.

"It's good," I tell her after a moment.

Still she doesn't say anything.

"So, you and Rigby?" I ask, leaning back in my chair.

She shrugs her shoulders, lifting her eyes to meet mine for the first time.

"I've fucked up," she tells me. Her voice shakes.

"At least it's Rigby…" I tease, trying to comfort her. "I was scared it would be Nash. That boy is a complete manwhore."

Her face drops.

"Shit. It's Nash?" I'm going to fucking kill that boy.

She looks nervous as if she genuinely thinks I'm going to lose my shit with her for whatever she's done. But this is Clover we're talking about. There's no way she's done something that bad.

"Clo, are you going to tell me what's going on?"

"Do I have to?" she asks somewhat petulantly.

"You do if you want my help to fix it," I retort bluntly.

"I like them."

"Who?"

"Rigby… Nash… all four of them."

"What?" I don't really know how to reply. I don't know what she means.

"I had sex with Rigby," she tells me, "and Nash."

I'm quiet. It's not often my sister manages to leave me stumped. Clover isn't the sort of girl to just sleep with anyone. She doesn't really sleep around and so I can't work this out.

"And you like them both?" I ask after a pause.

"And Jett and Ziggy."

Her tone is low, her voice hushed, like she's embarrassed to admit her feelings.

"Look at you, Clo! Going all polly!" I say, offering her a big smile. I'm teasing her, trying to ease whatever pain she's trying to hide.

The last thing I want is for her to think I'm judging her so I lean across the table, taking her hand in my own and give it a squeeze.

JETT

When my eyes land on Clover, I'm flooded with relief. The panic that I'd first felt at the idea that she's leaving because of me, because of what I said, because I love her, finally beginning to ease.

I push through the crowds towards her only to be pulled back.

The others have gathered together a short distance from where Clover is sitting. Nash has his hand on my shoulder.

"Creed is talking to her," he tells me.

Mrs Levon is standing with Jasper, her assistant, making what looks to be awkward conversation with Ziggy and Rigby. She's the only one that looks completely oblivious to the tension that seems to permeate off the group.

"What's going on?" I ask.

Mrs Levon is the one to respond. "Apparently my children have no manners."

Stepping towards me and taking my arm, she continues, "Jett, you'll never believe what Creed just did."

She pauses for dramatic effect. It's pure Mrs Levon. She's always been like that, even when we were all little kids.

"He swore at his own mother!" she tells me, with a face that says she feels scandalised.

Ironically, if the stories are to be believed, she's done far worse to her parents. But now is not the time to remind her of that.

Instead, I simply pat her hand sympathetically and pray that Creed will hurry up. Glancing over towards them, I see that neither of them look to be in a rush.

"You don't think he's trying to convince her to sign with the label early, do you?"

I barely keep a straight face as I turn back towards Mrs Levon.

"Unfortunately, I don't think that's what he wants to talk to Clo about."

I don't tell her that I think he's fishing for information about who he needs to punch.

"That's a shame," she replies wistfully.

I plaster a smile on my face and wait quietly, letting the others lead the conversation. My mind wanders to my last conversation with Clover.

Her words are on repeat in my mind and they leave me feeling strangely responsible. 'Why the hell didn't you say something sooner?' I'd been so completely bewildered. I couldn't believe that she'd felt the same way. That she loved me too.

But then it had sunk in. If I'd have told her sooner, she wouldn't have… what? Slept with Nash? Rigby? She wouldn't have fallen for them? We could have been together?

This entire mess could have been averted if I'd only had the fucking balls to admit my feelings.

I straighten up from where I'm leaning against the wall, when I see Creed stand to his feet. When he moves around the table and embraces Clover, my heart begins to race as I panic again that she's going to leave.

He's saying goodbye, I think to myself.

I want to stop her leaving but I don't know how to. I made a right mess of telling her how I feel and now she's leaving and it's all my own damn fault.

When Creed takes her hand and they begin to walk towards her, I sigh in relief but I still feel uneasy. I wait nervously as they close the distance between us.

Creed is the first to speak.

"Jasper, can you get Clover's bag back? She won't be flying today."

His words are ominous, suggesting that she may well leave tomorrow.

"Does that mean that you'll sign with the label, Clover?" Mrs Levon steps forward.

But it's Creed that replies, "no, mum. Not today."

"Tomorrow?"

"We'll see. Clover has something she needs to take care of. Once she's done with that, she will decide what she wants to do."

His tone is firm, leaving even his mother no room to negotiate. She merely nods her head in acceptance. Then we're all making our way towards the entrance.

No one speaks. Although there's clearly a lot that each of us wants to say. Creed is literally giving off vibes that say, 'open your mouth and I'll glue it shut.'

It isn't until we have Clover's bags back and we've said an awkward goodbye to Mrs Levon and Jasper that anyone dares to speak.

"There's too many of us," Ziggy says, looking between my car and the six people we need to fit in it.

"Jett, give me your keys," Creed says.

I hesitate.

"You've just gotten out of the hospital."

"Give. Me. Your. Keys."

I feel like telling him it's my bloody car, but I've never seen my best friend so pissed and I really don't want us all to have a fight in the middle of the airport carpark. Reaching into my back pocket, I fling my keys at him.

He catches them easily before turning to Clover.

"You take the front seat." Then he's turning towards us. "You four get in the back."

No one bothers to argue, even Rigby looks like he knows it's a fight he can't really win. Or perhaps he just doesn't want to look bad in front of the girl he likes or her brother.

NASH

I feel like a little kid that is about to get told off by his parents. As soon as we enter the apartment, Creed points towards the sofa and tells us all to sit down.

He's not normally this much of a bossy git. It's usually Rigs that does that sort of shit. If the situation wasn't so awful, I'd probably roll my eyes at the role reversal.

No one questions it though. We all just do as we're bloody told.

I'm surprised how nervous I feel. It's just Creed. He's a friend. And yet, he's not. Not now. He's Clover's brother and that trumps our friendship.

In fact, that little fact might be enough to destroy our friendship.

My foot is tapping on the carpet, probably making me look impatient. I'm not. Actually, I'd like to avoid the impending conversation for as long as possible.

But Creed's exactly like a dog with a bone so there's no way we'll be able to duck out.

Clover looks bloody terrified and I don't feel much better. I can see it coming. I'm going to land a black eye. The others don't exactly look happy but I'm not sure why they look quite so bothered. It's not like they've fucked her too… *She's mine.*

They might like her but I'm definitely the one that will get the brunt of Creed's anger.

Creed is apparently not in a rush. He sits himself down and leans forward, not saying anything, looking at each of us in turn. Clover is bright red, her face clashing with her pink hair.

"I don't want to interfere," Creed says eventually.

But you're going to, almost pops out of my mouth.

"It's not really any of my business," he says. He clearly feels crazy awkward, but he perseveres. "Look, I don't want Clover to leave just yet."

That's not quite what I was expecting him to say. I was expecting punches.

"Neither do I," Ziggy pipes in, only to be shot down with a glare.

"But you all seem to have made a right bloody mess of things," Creed continues, "and so…"

"So… you want to have a meeting about it," Jett retorts, looking more entertained than he should.

He'll be lucky if he doesn't get a slap to the back of his head.

Creed glowers at him, not bothering to reply.

"I get that you all like Clo," Creed says, "but…"

"But we can't all have her," Rigby finishes for him.

"That's not it," Creed replies, shaking his head. "I mean she's not a fucking piece of meat or a meal you can all bloody well share."

Unlike the other fools, I have the sense to keep my mouth shut and wait for whatever the fuck Creed is trying to say.

"It's completely up to Clover if she wants to date any of you," he tells us.

Well… No duh! I think to myself.

"From what I understand, she likes you all, so I think she should date you all, at least for a while."

"Huh?" I finally break my silence. I can't actually believe my ears. He can't be bloody serious. I was expecting blood and bruises, not permission.

"You heard what I said Nash," Creed grits out. "If any of you want to date Clover, then you have to accept the fact that she wants to date all four of you."

"Even me?" Ziggy asks, his face lighting up.

Creed almost cracks a smile but somehow manages to keep his face straight even when myself, Rigby and Jett all start snickering.

"So, what do you all say?"

Ziggy jumps to his feet eagerly.

"Count me in!"

Biting my tongue, I try not to laugh as I nod my head.

"I'm game."

The others agree just as quickly, no one wanting to be left out.

"That's settled then," Creed says. "Just so everyone is on an even playing field, you should all know that Clover has slept with Rigs and Nash."

He says it so easily, although the look in his eyes tells me he wants to stab me.

"Fuck. I need a bloody beer," he says, standing up and stretching. "Clover, I'd offer to get you a drink, but I think these four should have it handled."

Let's Play

(Written By Nash)

Relationships ain't serious

Love I don't do that shit

Hearts and kisses

I won't write that shit

Chocolate and flowers

You won't get that shit

I just want to play

I'm not in for the long haul

That's why they say I'm a man ho

I'm not in for the long haul

That's why they say I'm a man ho

There's no doubt I'll break your heart

Your friends will hate my guts

Your brother will break my nose

Your dad will want to hunt me down

Lust & Lyrics

Do you still want to play?

Marriage ain't for me

Vows I will break that shit

Sweet I love yous

You won't hear that shit

Kids, lets avoid

That shit.

I just want to play

CLOVER

I'm going to kill Creed. After dropping that massive bombshell, he up and walks out of the room, leaving me to deal with the aftermath alone.

He'd tell me I should be grateful. He said what I couldn't bring myself to. But instead of feeling grateful, I feel fucking mortified.

I should probably say something, but I have absolutely no idea what I'm supposed to say to follow that. The others are quiet too, probably waiting for me to speak first.

"I…" I try but I don't know how to finish the sentence.

"Let's just see what happens, Clo," Jett says softly. "No pressure."

I don't say anything back, not really knowing what to say. Instead, I just smile at him.

Ziggy stands to his feet.

"Right, who wants a drink?" Although the question is directed at everyone, he looks at me.

Nodding my head, I tell him that I'd kill for a beer.

Not going to lie. I'd happily get completely wasted right now. Anything to avoid this weird awkwardness. I don't know where to look or what to do. And the worst part of it all is that they are ALL looking at me.

Creed and Ziggy re-enter the room several minutes later, chatting happily between themselves, each carrying several beers.

"Rigs, wanna play?" Creed asks, nodding his head towards the Xbox.

"Sure," Rigby replies and like that we all settle in as if it's just any other night.

"Should we order in?" Nash asks, pulling out his phone.

There is a murmur of agreement before Nash turns to me.

"What would you like, Clover?"

"Indian?"

"Sure thing," he says, with a killer smile that must destroy his fans. It's seriously dazzling.

The awkwardness begins to dissipate, especially when someone brings up Saving Creed's new album.

"We really need to get these songs tied down," Rigby is saying, not even taking his eyes off the screen. He looks so focused, his forehead creased slightly, and his lips pressed in a hard line.

"Yeah man, but we've got Clo now," Creed replies, clearly unconcerned.

"And here was I thinking you were being a good brother," I quip, raising my eyebrow.

"Well… that too," he says before turning to Rigby and adding, "but the band might as well benefit from having her around, right?"

"Hey! I can hear you. You know?"

The guys are all laughing, clearly finding our interactions entertaining. It's always been like this with me and Creed. One teases the other and then it flips.

Tomorrow I will get him back…

"I think I might call Nona," I say innocently, raising my eyebrow in challenge.

Creed reacts. I see it. It definitely happens. But then the evidence is gone, his expression returning to a teasing smirk.

"You do that, Clo," he replies, "and make sure to tell her I want a date."

"You want me to ask her out for you?" I'm flabbergasted.

"I just did you a solid. You owe me. I just asked out four guys for you, the least you could do is ask out Nona for me."

He sounds serious. But he's not. There's no way.

"Okay. No problem." I pull out my phone. Unlocking it, I take my time to find her contact information, giving him plenty of time to back down. But he doesn't.

"You guys need to stop joshing," Nash pipes in. "Creed, I think she'll actually do it."

"He's forgotten I have his phone," I tell Nash in a mock whisper. "Forget asking her out…"

Creed looks less impressed now. He looks like he's going to lunge for me any moment. Knowing it's coming, I consider who to hide behind. Rigby is still focused on their game and Jett is happily reading a book which leaves Nash and Ziggy.

I grab them both by the wrist, forcing them to their feet and push them in front of me, creating a human wall between myself and Creed, just in time for him to attack.

He tries his best to reach between them for his phone which I'm brandishing about like it's a fucking prize.

"Dear Nona," I begin, pretending to type it as I speak, struggling to get out the words between bouts of laughter.

Rigby looks up when he notices that his opponent isn't playing anymore and comes to stand behind me. I'm struggling to breathe as I feel his chest against my back. His hand stretches out and takes the phone from me. I'm so surprised I don't even stop him.

I turn to face him. He's looking at me, his eyes playful. He raises the phone above his head, out of my reach.

"Whose side are you on?" I ask, my eyes narrowed, reaching up to try and take it.

"Yours, obviously," he replies, his other hand going to my waist, pulling me towards him.

The others notice when I let out a squeak and the wall breaks, all of us landing on the floor.

"Who the fuck has my phone?" Creed asks as he struggles to right himself.

ZIGGY

For the next week we spend practically every second of every day in the studio. When we're not eating and sleeping, we're practising for the new album. I don't get so much as a moment alone with Clover. It's not for want of trying either. She's just too bloody busy.

Her, Creed and Rigby pretty much live in the studio, working together on writing several new songs.

Rigby is back to his usual bossy, shitty self. The only one who doesn't get the brunt of it is Clover. To her, he's nothing but smiles. She's pretty good at easing his temper though. Every time he gets close to blowing up at one of us, Clover jumps in and intervenes, distracting him surprisingly easily.

With Clover here, it's a lot calmer. Whoever said she was a genius was not exaggerating. For the last album, Rigs and Creed were like a pair of crazy hounds chomping at the bit, ready to kill us.

Every day Clover seems to have a new song for us.

Hanleigh Bradley

I'm slick at playing the drums, but I can't write lyrics for shit. I don't know how she does it. It seems so natural, easy almost.

She frequently gets lost in her thoughts when we're talking to her and then she's reaching for paper and a pen so she can jot something down and next thing we know she's got a whole song composed.

What I like the most is that she seems to love challenging us. Every song is more challenging than the last, the rhythm a little quicker, an extra beat that I have to make room for or some complex pattern that seems impossible to play, until I've actually played it.

Clover never doubts that I can either. She gives me the music and sits there smiling at me as I grumble that I'll never be able to play whatever piece she's just given me.

It's becoming a bit of a game. She's now sitting on my stool, her legs stretched out, twirling back and forth while I complain that she's asking too much.

She doesn't say anything straight away, letting me rant for a few moments, before she looks up at me, her face bright with excitement and a tinge of pink to her cheeks.

You wouldn't know to look at her that she's had next to no sleep in the last week. She's fucking gorgeous.

Shrugging her shoulders, she grins.

"I didn't think it was that hard. I can clap it out so it can't be that hard, right?" she asks, her eyebrow raised.

She's right, of course but I don't want to tell her that. I enjoy these little exchanges, the few moments where I get to actually talk to her for a few moments before she leaves me alone again to practice.

"Do you want to try playing it?" I ask, folding my arms in mock anger.

"Where are your sticks?" she replies, completely straight faced.

"Can you even play?" I ask, bewildered. I've heard rumours that she can play guitar and piano, but no one ever mentioned anything about the drums.

"I can play most things," she says with a shrug.

I'm floored. I don't know what to say. She's a fucking genius, I swear.

"Except I can't play the drums," she tells me after a moment, giving me a blinding smile.

Laughing, I return her smile with a gentle shake of my head.

"So, you'll do it?" she asks softly, leaning forward.

"You're the boss," I reply. It's not as if I ever planned not to.

Then without another word, she's getting to her feet and I'm wishing that I'd argued the toss for just a moment longer. Just one more moment to enjoy her company.

She walks towards the door before turning back, her hand on the doorframe.

"See you at lunch."

She doesn't wait for me to respond. She's gone as soon as she says it and I'm left alone.

Shaking my head, I tear my eyes away from the door. We're on a deadline. I shouldn't be thinking about Clover at all. Pulling up my sleeves, I stretch before starting to tap out the rhythm of the new song.

It takes me a while to get the hang of it but when I do, I quickly loose track of time, losing myself in the rhythm.

She's A Movie Star

(Written By Creed)

She's not like the rest, she's something else
She knows she's the best, she's got the looks
She's not like the rest, she's an A star

She's everything I'm looking for
She's a movie star, a fuckin' movie star
She the queen of hearts, queen of hearts
She's everything I'm looking for

She's not like the rest, she's on the red carpet
She knows she's the best, she's got it all
She's not like the rest, she's an A star

One look, you're a goner
One look, she steals your soul

NONA

It's been a week since I found out about Creed's crash and I've barely seen him. He's been holed up in the studio with Rigby and Clover. He's texted me a few times but it's awkward and whatever progress I thought we'd made, seems to have stalled.

My mood is pretty sour. It's not just because I've not seen much of Creed either.

Crimson and I aren't talking. When I found out that she knew about Creed's accident I kind of lost my temper with her. Sure, I get it that it was her job and that she was sworn to secrecy by the Levons but I would have thought she'd tell me…

We're supposed to be best friends.

I know I should just apologise to her. Even if I think she should have told me, I shouldn't have screamed at her. But call me stubborn, I don't want to apologise.

When I return to the label after popping across the street for a coffee, I see Creed talking to

Crimson and instantly, I feel jealous. I know I'm being daft. They hate each other but it still feels strange seeing them together.

They'll be talking business. There's nothing else between them.

In a fit of stupidity, jealousy or outright spite, I don't know which, I walk right past them, completely ignoring the smile that Creed sends my way when he sees me.

I don't know why it bothers me seeing them together. I remember when I first joined the company there were rumours about them. People used to say the reason they were always at odds was because they used to screw.

But I'd asked Crimson and she'd outright denied it and call me stupid, but I usually try to trust my friends.

It's only when I'm alone in the wardrobe room that I take a deep breath, allowing my shoulders to sag, releasing all the tension I'm carrying. I begin to flip through clothes, arranging the clothes for Saving Creed's TV appearance tomorrow.

I jump out of my skin when I hear Creed's voice in my ear, "are you avoiding me?" His voice is a sexy husk, soft, almost gentle, it's so quiet.

"No," I squeak, turning abruptly to find him directly behind me.

He's so close. Too close.

I swallow suddenly nervous.

"So, it's Crimson you're avoiding then?" he asks, leaning in closer.

I go to step back but there's nowhere for me to go.

"We're not really talking," I admit.

"I thought you guys were tight."

"We are. We're just…"

"Fighting?"

"Yeah." I don't want to tell him that I'm being a petty bitch, so I don't tell him anything, instead changing the subject. "How's the album coming?"

"Great," he tells me. I don't know how he can talk so calmly with so little space between us. I can hardly think straight, let alone make coherent sentences.

"That's good." My voice comes out breathy.

"I've missed you, Nona," he whispers directly into my ear, before pulling away slightly so that he can give me one of those blinding smiles that make all the girls weak.

I don't really know how to respond.

"I…"

He doesn't let me finish though. His lips are on mine in a flash. I don't hesitate for a second, kissing him back. I lean towards him, allowing his tongue entry into my mouth.

I don't know how long we stay there in that tiny room. I only know that when he pulls away, I'm practically wrapped around him like a Kuala.

"Wanna get something to eat?" he asks, looking down at me.

Slightly breathless and definitely speechless, I nod my head.

Creed holds my hand as we make our way through the building. It's only when we reach the lobby that he drops it with a sigh. Crimson, Clover and the rest of Saving Creed are all standing there chatting.

Ziggy is the first to spot us and is waving us down.

"So much for time alone," Creed mumbles under his breath.

I open my mouth to tell him I don't mind, but it would be a total lie. I totally mind. I was enjoying myself a moment ago, on cloud nine or whatever, but now with everyone else here it all feels a little bit unreal.

Turning to face me, he says, "tonight. Make time tonight."

He smirks and I'm picturing all the things that one word suggests.

What Do You Think About Us?

(Written By Rigby)

What do ya think about us?

Do we even have a chance?

Is this destiny or an illusion?

The way I feel right now

Feels so real, so real

But what do you think?

What do ya think about us?

Nobody knows how I feel about ya

Baby, you're addictive

Baby, you're like a drug

Nobody knows how I feel about ya

Baby, when you dance

Baby, when you sing

Na Na Na I lose my mind

Na Na Na I lose my mind

Hanleigh Bradley

What do ya think about us?

Do we look good together?

Are you playing for keeps?

The way I feel right now

Feels so real, so real

But what do you think?

What do you think about us?

RIGBY

I'm bloody starving. I've eaten nothing but MacDonald's and Subway all week and as much as I dig a good sandwich or burger, I've definitely had my fill.

We're still standing in the lobby trying to decide what to eat. No one can agree for more than two seconds.

Everyone is looking at Clover as if she's the deciding vote.

"Er…" She's unwilling to take sides. It's written all over her face. She just wants some damn food. "I could kill for a steak."

Thank fuck for my girl, that's all I can say. Real bloody food. I'm not going to lie. I got a little scared for a moment that she'd start asking for a salad – rabbit food – but Clover Levon isn't like other girls.

"Steak it is," I say, clapping my hands together in finality.

"Is that okay?"

She looks uncertain but everyone is nodding their consent. Not that it matters. I'd have dragged her out of here and abandoned the lot of them, just to get some real fucking red meat.

It's been a shit's storm of a week but I'm in no rush for it to end. If I could I'd stay holed up in the studio with Clover every day. But I can't. As soon as we finish writing the album, we'll spend a few weeks hashing out the recording and then we'll be back in front of the cameras full time and back on the fucking bus, touring.

Then I'll have no time to spend with Clover at all.

I guess I should be grateful that she's not somewhere in Europe, doing god knows what. Taking Clover's hand, I lead the others out the building. I completely ignore the grumbles that come from the others at me holding her hand. I don't give a shit about playing fair. The way I see it, unless she pulls away, unless she refuses, I'm going to keep doing whatever the fuck I like.

You snooze, you lose. It's not my fault I'm quicker to move than the rest of them. The three of them, Jett, Nash and Ziggy, follow after us with matching dark faces, clearly pissed.

Pulling Clover closer, I wrap my arm around her shoulder when we step outside into the rain.

"Since when has it been raining?" Creed asks.

He's forgotten that we've barely left the studio all week. Nine times out of ten, someone has even brought food to us. It's not like there isn't everything we need inside the label building. Everything from showers to clothes and food.

"All fuckin' week mate," Nash replies with a grin.

Lucky bastard. While we've been slaving away writing the album, he's been skiving off, supposedly practising his bass. That's not quite true. While we've been writing the new songs, he, Jett and Ziggy have been keeping up appearances, going on TV and doing interviews and all that bogus shit. *Can't really say I envy them.*

"We won't all fit in the van," Jett says. "Clover, do you want to come in my car?"

His smirk is so fucking annoying. It says he thinks he's got one over on us all. He hasn't.

"Why don't the five of us go in your car?" I suggest, matching his expression, pointing at Ziggy and Nash.

"It will be cramped," he argues back.

"We don't mind, do we Clover?"

Clover doesn't get a chance to respond before Creed gives me a wallop around the back of the head and I get a kick to the shin from Nash.

Pouting, I cuddle into Clover's side, while she rubs my head soothingly. If I could see my own face right now, I just know I'd look like I'm gloating. *Unlucky sods.*

Jett offers Clover the front seat, but I quickly remind him that Nash has seriously long legs and that Clover will be perfectly comfortable between me and Ziggy in the back.

I know I'm seriously pissing them all off and Clover is giving me a look that tells me I should watch it, but I can't resist.

Creed just shakes his head as he climbs into the van with Crimson and Nona. Jett is mumbling to himself about how much of a git I am, but I don't give a crap. I settle into the backseat and help Clover put on her belt before taking her hand once more.

The journey to the restaurant is pretty fun. Nash and Jett are clearly livid. Ziggy, on the other hand, is practically over the fucking moon. He's almost giddy.

I watch as he struggles to keep his hands on his knees, his hand itching to take Clover's other hand. It's funny and kind of sweet.

But because I'm a dick, I drop the hand I'm holding, the one closest to me and stretch, wrapping my arm around her. Then with my other hand I take the hand that Ziggy wants to hold.

Clover is completely oblivious and just curls her head into my shoulder, closing her eyes for a moment. If anyone were to ask, I'd tell them I'm just being thoughtful, considering how little sleep she's had but truth is, I'm a selfish son of a bitch and I don't want to share.

CREED

I fumble with the temperature controls.

Seriously, I swear this van is stuffy. At least if the others had joined us in the van, I wouldn't be stuck in bloody London traffic alone with Nona and Crimson.

This is a disaster waiting to happen and not just because Nona and Crimson aren't talking. No. This is going to be disastrous because I'm sitting in a fucking car with the girl I want to fuck and the girl I once fucked on a drunken night out.

I should have grabbed Ziggy and forced him to join us. But I couldn't do that, not when his little face lit up like a fuckin' light bulb at the mere idea of sitting next to Clo.

It's not like me and Crimson dated or anything. We just fucked. I was drunk. She was drunk. It was the night of our very first gig. I was high as a kite on bloody endorphins and adrenalin.

I'd have probably fucked anything, not that she wasn't hot. She was. She was fucking smoking.

She was good too. Crimson can do things that most guys just dream about their girlfriends doing.

But the next morning it was hella awkward and neither of us handled it particularly well. The woman who was a fucking firecracker in bed, had become all shy and I… well… I don't really know what I was thinking.

I think I felt guilty.

Neither of us were sober and I have a rule, actually the law has a rule… You shouldn't fuck someone who's had too much to drink. That's clearly a fucking consent issue.

Problem is I was wasted too, so common sense, curtesy and morality all flew out the fucking window.

If Crimson and Nona were not in the middle of a stand off, it wouldn't be so bad. They'd talk happily between themselves, practically ignoring me, including me whenever they felt like it and I'd just drive.

But with them not talking, I'm left in the bloody middle, somewhere I definitely don't want to be. Except, it could be pretty hot… For a second, I picture just how hot that could be before blowing out a long breath and tightening my grip on the steering wheel.

I'm not quite as progressive as Clover. *Perhaps it's all that time she's spent in Europe*, I muse to myself.

I'm not sure even my sister knows what she's getting herself into with the guys.

As tempting as it is, I try not to think about Crimson and Nona naked in my bed.

"So…" I begin, hoping to try and start a conversation. Anything to break the awkward silence and distract myself from the tightening in my jeans. "You guys aren't talking?"

As soon as the words drop out of my mouth, I regret them. Now instead of giving each other evils, both women are staring daggers at me. *Damn!*

Neither of them reply before looking out of their respective windows and I'm left feeling like a moron. It doesn't help that we're stuck in traffic. I turn the radio on, hoping to at least ease the tension with some tunes.

"I don't really know what I've done to piss you off," Crimson says eventually over the sound of the music. Her voice is exasperated, and I feel like I want to be anywhere but here. All hell is about to let loose.

We're not moving at all. We're literally head to fucking tail and going nowhere fast. I'm humming under my breath, my eyes focused on the car in front, wishing that I was supernaturally enhanced with the power of invisibility.

I bite down on my tongue, trying my best to keep my mouth shut. The last thing I want to do is say something else and make the whole thing even worse.

"It's not like I had a choice," she continues.

"If it was the other way around, I'd have told you," Nona replies, her voice quiet.

"Yeah. You're right. You would have. You wouldn't have thought twice about the chance of getting fired because you can afford to lose this fucking job. I can't."

Blinking, I try to process what they are saying. *Are they actually fighting about work? Surely not?*

"He was in the hospital," Nona says, turning abruptly in the passenger's seat to turn to face Crimson, "and I knew nothing."

Only then do I realise that I'm the elephant in the car. I'm what is coming between them, and suddenly I feel like a complete arse.

A Perfect Night

(Written By Creed)

The stars are out tonight
Everything feels bright
You and I, we're here
Tonight. Just give me
Tonight.

I don't care what we do
I don't need anything else
Only you, only you
I don't care where we go
I don't want anything else
Only you, only you

This all feels so right
I'm holding you tight
You and I, we're here
Tonight. Just give me

Lust & Lyrics

Tonight.

I don't care what we do
I don't need anything else
Only you, only you
I don't care where we go
I don't want anything else
Only you, only you

All I need is one perfect night
Just one night, one night with you
Just give me one night with you

I don't care what we do
I don't need anything else
Only you, only you
I don't care where we go
I don't want anything else
Only you, only you
Only you, only you

Hanleigh Bradley

Just give me one night with you

CRIMSON

"He was in the hospital and I knew nothing."

"What do you want?" I retort. "I couldn't tell you."

My foot is tapping impatiently, frustration seeping into my bones. My knuckles tighten as I try to hold in my temper.

"You should have told me!"

"I couldn't. How many bloody times do I have to tell you, I couldn't?"

"He was in a coma!" she practically screams at me. She's shaking with rage, angrier than I've ever seen her.

Creed looks shocked. Everyone knows that Nona is a softy. But this argument has been brewing for a week.

"I couldn't tell you," I say again through gritted teeth.

"Guys, maybe…" Creed tries to intervene.

"So, it's my fault?" Nona is furious. "I'm being fucking unreasonable? The guy I like was in a coma in the fucking hospital and it's completely unreasonable for me to expect that my best bloody friend would actually tell me."

Nona never swears. She's too sweet, gentle for that. She never shouts.

I know I fucked up, but I also know that I would do the exact same thing again. I didn't have a fucking choice.

"Just want to point out that I'm okay," Creed says, trying to defuse the tension in the van.

"I'm sorry."

I don't know what else I'm supposed to say, especially with Creed here. I'm not a big fan of showing weakness. I don't really mind with Nona. She's my best mate. But everyone else, not so much.

My eyes dart between Nona and Creed, torn between fixing things with my bestie and keeping my pride in front of someone…

Someone I like.

I shouldn't like him. The first time Nona told me she liked him, I told myself to stop. Chicks before dicks and all that. But it's a lot easier telling yourself not to like someone than it is to actually stop liking them.

I had thought it would be easy. I mean, it was only one night. One really hot, amazing night, but still only one night. But that one night had proven impossible to forget.

Letting out a loud sigh, I close my eyes, throwing away my pride.

"I'm sorry. I wasn't thinking about you, Nona."

It's not a dig. I don't mean to try and make her sound selfish but it's the truth. She was not my top priority, or anywhere close.

"Mrs Levon said I'd lose my job if I told anyone. I can't lose this job, Nona."

Even I can hear the panic in my voice.

Nona's eyes soften for a moment. She knows how important this job is to me.

"My dad…" My voice catches. "I can't lose this job, Nona. Who else will pay for…?" My voice dies. Unable to continue, tears rimming my eyes, I turn back towards the window.

I don't know what else I can say to make her understand. I'm not like her. If she lost her job, she could just get a new one. It's just her. She could even ask her parents for help. She would be fine.

But I'm not like her. It's not just me. If I lost my job, there'd be no one to pay my father's care costs.

"I'm sorry," Nona says mildly, reaching back to take my hand. "I know." She gives it a gentle squeeze.

Rubbing my eyes, I turn to smile at her. My eyes brush past Creed, trying to ignore that he's even here. I notice him glancing my way in the mirror and I hold my breath, trying to control my expressions.

"How is the album coming?" I ask Creed, trying to move the conversation onto safer territory.

Creed's face lights up as his eyes meet mine in the mirror again.

"It's amazing. Absolutely fucking amazing!"

Creed talks for a solid five minutes about all the new songs that he just can't wait for us to hear and I sit there, breathing in the sound of his voice, wishing that things between us had gone slightly better. All the while, holding Nona's hand.

I'm a pretty shitty friend.

"We're here," Creed tells us, bringing my attention back, as he pulls into the restaurant's carpark. This is going to be one long bloody day.

JETT

A waitress leads us to a large, round table towards the back of the restaurant. Rigby pulls out Clover's seat and then moves to sit next to her, but I move quicker, stealing the seat.

"I don't really think you need to sit in my lap, Rigs," I say snidely.

This whole situation is a bit ridiculous. It's not like any of us actually have enough bloody time to date Clover and yet we're fighting over her like a piece of meat. Well… Not quite.

I ignore Rigby's mumbled response as I lean in towards Clover beginning a conversation about the latest song she's working on. My attention focused on Clover, it's easy to lose track of time.

I barely even remember to tell the waitress what I want to eat.

"You're going to stay, right?" I ask, even now I'm terrified that she might jump on the next plane out of here. *It would be just her MO.*

"For now." Her response gives me no security.

I take her hand, trying to keep her here with me but I know it's pointless. She'll go wherever she damn well pleases. That's how Clover is, and I don't want to change her.

"Are you coming with us for the TV interview this afternoon?" I ask.

"Can't," she replies. "I'll be holed up in the studio, writing your next number one."

Chuckling, I lean closer.

"You're pretty sure of yourself," I say beneath my breath, so close I could almost kiss her.

I want to kiss her.

Her eyes move to my lips, before returning to meet my gaze. Shrugging, she just smiles.

With only one hand, we both struggle to eat, but neither of us pulls our hand away, our fingers staying entwined under the table. The others aren't happy. If looks could kill, I'd be a dead man three times over.

Sitting here with Clover's hand in mine, I find myself wondering if it's even possible for us to make this work. I don't know what the end game is.

Does she want to be with all of us?

Is she working towards picking one of us?

Are we supposed to be trying to fight for her?

Glancing at the others, I try to imagine what our future might look like. Nash would tell me it doesn't matter, that I should just enjoy the here and now with Clover. Rigby would tell me that Clover's future is all his.

If she seriously does decide that she wants us all, I don't actually know what I'll do. I don't know if I can live my life sharing her.

In fact, I'm almost positive I probably can't.

That scares me because I'm almost positive that if I say that aloud, we'll be over before we've even started.

"Are you okay?" she asks, her face etched with concern.

I nod my head because I don't know what else I'm supposed to do. I can hardly tell her that I'm jealous as hell that she's slept with Rigby and Nash. Or that I don't want to have to share her. Not if we're just dating and definitely not if this gets more serious.

"I'm going to go outside," I tell her. "I need some air."

"Should I come too?" she offers sweetly.

I don't know how to respond. Of course, I want her to come with me but equally I think it might be her I'm running from.

I can't say no to her though, so I find myself nodding and excusing us from the table. Rigby and Nash's faces are marred with annoyance while Ziggy just looks disappointed.

When we're finally outside and alone, at last I feel like I can breathe again. I pull Clover against my chest, hugging her tightly.

"Are you okay?" she asks again.

"Yeah, all better now," I tell her with a smile.

I don't hesitate for a second, before pushing Clover against the wall of the pub building that we've just exited, my mouth on hers.

Relishing in the moment that I've been imagining for years, decades even, I lose all rationale. It's hurried and forceful and completely desperate.

I stumble against her, unable to keep myself upright. Then she's pushing against me, moving so I'm now the one with my back to the wall, trapped.

I was a fool if I thought I could live even another day without this, without her.

My hands are wandering under her top. I shouldn't. We're outside, in a public place, but I want to…

I want to touch her.

But I know that won't be enough either. One kiss… One touch… I know without doubt that it will escalate until we're both in a fucking jail cell for having sex in public.

I pull away, not because I want to, not because I have doubts about our future, but because if I don't we'll both be in trouble.

Taking her hand, I lead her back inside. She grumbles a complaint against my back, trying to pull me back, but I don't give in. I need to fuck her now and we're not doing it outside for all the bloody world to see.

Hardly caring if anyone spots us, I lead her into the ladies' loos. Shagging in the toilets is kind of grim but right now I couldn't give a shit.

Pushing her into a stall, I close and lock the door behind me.

I always thought I'd take my time to enjoy having sex with Clover for the first time. I'd been imagining it for long enough. But right now, I have zero patience as I practically throw myself at her.

Can I Let You Go?

(Written By Jett)

You'll probably never be all mine

But I can't pull back now

You're all I want, You're a dream

Can I let you go? Can I walk away?

This might not be destiny

But I don't want to be alone anymore

Dreaming, wishing you here with me

I don't know, I don't know, I don't know

If I can let you go.

Kissing you is practically a crime

But I can't pull back now

You're all I want, You're a dream

Can I let you go? Can I walk away?

You're a runner, a free spirit by design

Lust & Lyrics

But I can't pull back now

With you, I'm the cat that got the cream

Can I let you go? Can I walk away?

You'll never be all mine

We don't have that sort of destiny

You'll never be all mine

But I don't know if I can just accept a share

You'll never be all mine

But that's everything I want

All mine, All mine, All mine

Can I let you go?

CLOVER

This is probably the least sexy place I've ever had sex. It's totally disgusting but I'm not saying no. Instead, my hands go to the button of Jett's black jeans.

We won't have long before someone comes looking for us.

His kiss is urgent as he pushes me against the stall wall. He doesn't even break the kiss to undo and push down my shorts. When they're around my ankles, he lifts me up so that my legs wrap around his hips, leaving the shorts on the floor.

If I was in my right mind, I'd be super worried about what sort of crappy germs are going to be on my shorts when I put them back on, but I'm definitely not sane right now.

He doesn't bother removing any of his own clothes, just pushing his jeans and boxers down slightly to release his cock. And then he's entering me.

I'm not ready. I hiss out in surprise and almost bite down on his tongue, causing him to chuckle into my mouth.

Jett thrusts into me, pushing me back into the wall behind me noisily. I don't care if anyone hears me, but Jett apparently does. He covers my mouth with his hand as his mouth goes to attack my neck, sucking and nipping my skin in a way that is guaranteed to mark.

We don't last long. I come undone, my body shivering, him pulsing within me. His forehead is sleek with sweat as he drops it to my shoulder.

I bite down on his palm playfully, trying to tell him that I need to catch my breath. Then with another chuckle, he's releasing his grip and lowering me so that I can stand on my own feet.

Quickly I pull my shorts on and we try and make ourselves look a little bit more presentable, just as I hear a knock at the door.

"Clover? Are you in there?" I hear Nona through the door.

I panic. It's one thing to have sex in these dingy toilets, it's another thing for everyone else to know about it.

"You go first," Jett whispers before dropping a quick peck to my lips. "I'll follow after you in a minute."

Suddenly shy, I nod my head, before unlocking the stall door.

I can't meet Nona's eye when I step out. I'm tempted to outright ask her if she knows what I was doing in the loos. But I can't do that to the poor girl. She'd probably have a fright.

The others are still at the table. No one looks particularly happy. Creed and Crimson just look awkward, like they have no idea what they should talk about, while Rigby looks almost murderous. Nash has his arms folded and is tapping his foot impatiently on the floor.

But it's the look on Ziggy's face that causes me to pause. His eyes meet mine and he looks hurt. His eyes are glistening as he blinks at me like I've just destroyed a precious gift he's just offered me.

And perhaps that's exactly what I've done.

It's impossible not to feel guilty when I'm stringing them all along.

No one says anything and the silence is deafening. I just sit there waiting for Jett to come back, silently praying that he will hurry the fuck up.

"Where the fuck is he?" Rigby roars after five minutes and I jump in my seat at the sudden outburst.

"I'm going to wait outside," Nash says without looking at me.

I stare at a spot directly in front of me on the table, trying my best to keep myself from crying. Maybe this was a mistake. Perhaps I should have just left.

My brother gives me a sad smile and I want to ask him to get me out of here. I want his help to escape but I don't think I can do that. I'd be leaving Jett to deal with the ramifications alone.

With my back to the door to the bathrooms, I completely miss the moment he makes a reappearance, but I feel his hand on my shoulder and I hear his voice in my ear, "let's go."

He takes my hand as I get to my feet and I'm nervous as hell. I'm pretty sure everything is about to blow up.

NASH

No one says anything on the way back to the label. It's hella awkward. Rigby isn't even in the bloody car. He decided to go back in the van with Creed and the girls, leaving only Jett, Ziggy and me to ride with Clover.

You'd think that would make things easier since Rigs is in a shitty mood, but not so much.

Mostly because he's not the only one feeling super pissed off right now. I'm not exactly happy myself and Ziggy looks like his entire world has just fallen apart – no exaggeration.

The poor lad is probably feeling a little bit left out.

He's the only one who hasn't gotten any yet, I think bitterly.

Logically, I know I don't really have the right to feel possessive. We all walked into this knowing exactly what was happening. We knew that she was going to date the four of us. And it's not like I haven't already fucked her.

Jett is just evening out the playing field…

And yet I still feel betrayed. Like I thought she'd go on a few dates and then pick me. I don't know what I thought would happen, but I definitely didn't think Clover would fuck Jett in the pub loos while I was eating a fucking steak. It's almost funny.

When we arrive, I don't bother saying anything before heading off to get ready for my TV interview. I try not to notice that Clover looks hurt but it's almost impossible and I almost end up turning back just so I can hug her.

I really don't like being angry with her. I'm not even convinced it's her I'm angry with. I think I'm more annoyed with myself and my blasted pride. And Jett… *I'm definitely pissed with Jett.*

How could I not be? He just fucked my girl.

Except she's not mine. Not just mine, at least. For the time being, I'm supposed to be willing to bloody share her. *How did I get myself into this mess?*

I don't know why I'm even asking myself that. I know the answer without thinking… I was just too damn scared she'd leave.

Clover makes her way towards the studio, leaving Jett and Ziggy to follow after me to hair and makeup. I really don't want to spend the afternoon with Jett with a fucking fake smile plastered on my bloody face, but I don't think I have much choice.

He looks like he wants to say something. It's probably not an apology so I don't want to hear it.

"Guys," I hear his voice from behind me, but I don't slow my steps or turn back to look at him. If I do, I think I might punch him and that will definitely not go down well at the interview. "I…"

"What do you want to say?" I ask brusquely. "It's not like you're sorry you fucked her. And it's not like we have some fucking claim to her."

My voice comes out angry as I turn on the spot, stepping towards him, entering his personal space.

"So, what the fuck is it that you think you need to say?"

He doesn't say anything. He doesn't know what to say, any more than I do.

The truth is none of us know what the fuck is going on. Not really. We're all lost, falling in love with a girl that somehow can't choose between us.

My pride doesn't like it. I'm not used to having to chase girls. The girls usually fall all over me. But Clover is different. For her, I have to compete with my best mates and that pisses me right off.

Sighing, I remind myself that the reason I like Clover so much is that she's so completely different to the rest.

I told myself I could handle her dating us all but that was because I'd arrogantly assumed, she'd pick me in the end. Now though, I'm not so sure. There is a very real chance that she will pick one of the others.

Or that she'll just leave.

Or that she might just expect us to stay in this fucking limbo for fucking forever. I don't need tradition, I don't need to put a ring on her finger or anything stupid like that, but I want to at least be able to say that she's MINE and not someone else's.

RIGBY

Clover is already sitting behind the piano when I arrive. Her fingers are moving seamlessly, crafting a melody so gentle and intricate that I don't know if anyone else would be able to play it the way she is.

The sight of her like this, doing what she does best, is almost enough to make my anger just wash away. But I cling on to it, desperate not to lose it.

I don't want us to get distracted and just pretend that everything is fine. I want us to move forward from this shit.

There's a tear in her eye when she starts singing and I find myself wondering if it's my fault she's crying. Or if something happened in the car on the way back. If one of the guys upset her, I'll have them, I find myself thinking to myself, a sudden urge to protect her rising up.

"I never knew what love was until I met you," she sings, her voice hollow, "and now I don't know what I'm meant to do."

I keep my distance, watching her, listening to her. I don't want to disturb her. Call me selfish but I want the song almost as much as I want Clover. I want this album written already so I can actually spend time with her.

"Everything I'm putting you through," she sings, seemingly oblivious to the fact I'm even here, "everything I'm making you do."

"You're giving me it all, why do I feel so blue?" The song speeds up, her fingers moving quicker. "You're giving me it all, why do I feel so blue?"

She's singing her heart out, tears flooding down her cheeks. She's stunning even with a red, blotchy face. I want to close the distance between us and pull her into my arms but she won't appreciate that when she's composing.

She needs the emotions that are driving this song forward.

"I never knew, I never knew, I never knew, how much it would cost you, cost you."

As I listen to her words all my anger fades away. It's hard to be angry when she's hurting so much more than I am. It takes all my patience to wait until she's finished before I take a step towards her and pull her up from where she's sat so I can hold her.

"I'm sorry," she whimpers.

I don't know what she's apologising for exactly.

Fucking Jett? Probably not. It's not like she doesn't have the right to screw whoever she damn well pleases.

Crying? That's more likely. Clover isn't a big crier. She's used to putting all her feelings into her music.

"Shh," I whisper, my hand running through her hair soothingly.

"I'm asking too much," she continues. "I'm sorry."

"Stop saying sorry, Clover," I say. "You've done nothing wrong."

"But…"

Pulling away slightly so I can look at her properly, I run the pad of my thumbs beneath her eyes, wiping away her tears.

"Let's go home," I tell her. I can't imagine we're going to get much done with her like this.

"The album…"

"Can wait."

She looks like she's going to argue with me, so I shake my head.

"You need to rest," I tell her. "All this shit is wearing thin on your nerves, Clo."

It's no joke either. She's not had a proper night's sleep in I don't know how long. Neither have I. Today wouldn't have happened if we weren't all so bloody tired.

It's hard not to be a jealous idiot when you're fucking exhausted.

"Let me at least write this song down first," she negotiates.

I can hardly refuse her. It's a damn good song. Nodding my head, I tell her that I'll wait for her. Then she's searching for some manuscript paper and a pen.

Taking a seat on the sofa in the corner, I lean forward watching her. I'm not daft, it will be at least another hour before we actually leave. Her creative juices are flowing and there's no way in hell, she'll leave a song half finished.

She bites down on her lower lip as she tries to recall what she's just played. She's looks bloody adorable and yet sexy as sin.

I Never Knew

(Written by Clover)

I never knew what love was until I met you
And now I don't know what I'm meant to do
Everything I'm putting you through
Everything I'm making you do

You're giving me it all, why do I feel so blue
You're giving me it all, why do I feel so blue
I never knew, I never knew, I never knew
How much it would cost you, cost you
You might lose it all then what will you do?
What will you do? What will you do?

I never knew what love was until I met you
And now I don't know what I'm meant to do
Could you give me a bloody clue?
Can a love like this even be true?

Lust & Lyrics

I never knew what love was until I met you
And now I don't know what I'm meant to do
It would be easier if it was just us two
But what's a girl to do?

I'm asking too much, far too much
You're going to end up hating me
I never knew I'd end up losing you

ZIGGY

The house is quiet when we arrive back. It's a bit surprising, seeing as how Creed said Rigby and Clover would be here. I'd been expecting to walk in and find them chatting away in the living room or something. What I hadn't expected was silence.

"I wonder where they are," Nash voices what I'm thinking.

Creed just shrugs his shoulders, telling us he's going to have a lie down and heads towards the stairs.

"Don't you want dinner?" Jett calls after him.

"Wake me up when it's here," Creed replies.

"But what do you want?"

Creed just waves off the question and begins to climb the stairs.

"Pizza?" Nash asks.

"Sure," I agree.

I'm not really bothered so long as I don't have to cook. Which is pretty much the way it always is. None of us particularly like cooking. In fact, we've had way more home cooked meals since Clover came to stay. She can cook, unlike the rest of us.

"I'm going to go look for Clover and Rigby."

"They're probably in the piano room," Jett tells me as he settles down onto the couch, pulling up the delivery app on his phone.

"Okay. Thanks," I reply awkwardly.

It bothers me that they all seem to know Clover better than I do. It probably sounds silly, but I want to be the one to know where she goes, I want to know her hideouts…

My jealousy eases when I let myself into the piano room only to find it empty.

Jett might not know her as well as he thinks he does, I think to myself. It's childish and probably a little bit pathetic.

Especially since it wasn't that long ago I thought I was in love with Nona. But then I'd heard Clover sing and my whole world felt as if it was realigned.

I quickly make my way through the house looking for them. When I reach Rig's door, I suddenly feel nervous.

What if they're in the middle of something? Maybe I should just leave them alone…

Rapping my fist on the door, I try to ignore my apprehension. They're probably not even in there, I tell myself.

"Come in," I hear Rigby say from inside.

Opening the door, I almost close my eyes, scared what I might see but Rigby is sat behind his desk working on his laptop and I let out a relieved sigh.

I open my mouth to speak but Rigby points towards the bed, raising his finger to his mouth, shushing me.

"Whisper. She's asleep."

Jealousy roars in my stomach for a brief second and I don't say anything as I stare at the sleeping girl. She's fully dressed as if she just threw herself into the bed and fell asleep.

"She's really been doing too much," Rigby tells me quietly.

I approach the bed, sitting on the edge. She's so peaceful like this, pink hair splayed on the pillow behind her.

"I was worried," I tell Rigby without taking my eyes off her, "after that shitstorm at lunch."

"Yeah, she was pretty upset. That's why I brought her home."

Reaching for her face, I brush a lock of her hair out of her eyes.

"How are we supposed to not get jealous?"

"You've got me there. I have no idea," Rigby replies. "Even now, having you sit there, I want to punch you."

I chuckle lightly at that idea. I'd happily take the punch if it means I can stay close to Clover.

"Do you think she'll pick soon?" I ask, although I'm secretly hoping she doesn't. I'm at a serious disadvantage as the only one who's not slept with her

"Who says she'll definitely pick," Rigby asks. "I don't get that vibe."

"What do you mean?"

"She likes all of us."

"Yeah but she can't have all of us, can she?"

"Can't she?" Rigby asks, shrugging his shoulders. "If we're all game, why should she give up something or someone she wants?"

"Huh?"

"I'm just saying."

"Just saying what?"

"Plenty of people do it, you know… Have multiple partners. If we can make it work, she doesn't have to lose anything."

"But we can't actually do that…"

"Can't we?"

"Can you seriously put your jealousy aside?"

Rigby shrugs his shoulders again.

"For her, I'm willing to try."

I'm Never Ever Going To Let You Go

(Written by Ziggy)

Even if every day is like today

Even if you betray me, destroy me

It doesn't matter because you

Belong to me, belong with me

I'm never ever going to let you go

There's just no way, There's just no way

I need you near, I want you here

There's just no way to let you go

Even if you scream and rage every day

Even if you cheat on me, hurt me

It doesn't matter because you

Belong to me, belong with me

I'm never ever going to let you go

Hanleigh Bradley

I'm never ever

Never ever, Never ever

Never going to let you go

I'm never ever going to let you go

There's just no way, there's just no way

I need you near, I want you here

There's just no way to let you go

Tell me what you need

Tell me your demands

Tell me what you need

Coz I'm never ever,

Never ever, Never ever

Never going to let you go

Less Than Conventional

RIGBY

I'm willing to try, I remind myself as a sleeping Clover wraps herself around Ziggy.

I struggle to control my expression, rein in my jealousy, but its near impossible. Every part of me wants to cross the room and pull my girl away from him.

Except I have no more claim to her than he does. She's no more my girl, than she is his.

She mumbles something in her sleep but I'm too far away to hear.

Standing to my feet, I approach the bed. Not because I want to pull them apart but because I want to hear her clearer.

I hadn't been aware that Clover talked in her sleep and the sudden realisation makes me see her slightly differently. The incredibly sexy woman before me is surprisingly cute.

Sitting on the edge of the bed, in a hushed whisper I ask Ziggy if he heard what she said.

But he doesn't answer.

He's too busy straining to hear her again, his ear almost pressed to her lips.

It's almost ridiculous, the two of us sitting here, eagerly waiting to hear Clover sleep talk. My pride hopes that she's dreaming of me and not one of the others, especially when I finally hear her words clearly.

"I think I love you."

Ziggy pulls back, his eyes wide with surprise, taking in a huge breath of air. He glances towards me.

"Do you think she means…"

Normally if your girlfriend says that she loves someone in her sleep you can comfortably trust that she means you. With Clover there's only a twenty-five percent chance that she means me.

I don't say anything. There's no point.

Instead, I move up the bed so that I'm leaning against the headboard next to Clover. Ziggy's arm is wrapped around her and I try to tell myself that it doesn't bother me, even though I know it does.

Closing my eyes, I rest my head back.

It's been a bloody awful day and it's not over yet. We have a lot to discuss. We need to work out how we can make this work.

It doesn't seem possible but I don't think Clover is going to choose. It's not like she ever told us she would though, so I can hardly get angry.

Clover moves next to me and looking down at her, I see her nuzzling in closer to Ziggy, rubbing her nose along his neck like an adorable kitten.

I'm tempted to leave the room.

My self control is dwindling. I want to pull her away, throw Ziggy out of my room… anything, to get them away from each other.

When her lips inch towards his, I'm barely breathing.

Bloody hell! I can't watch this.

Her eyes still closed, she reaches up, her hands moving to Ziggy's hair, pulling him closer.

I find myself wondering if she even knows where she fucking is. She's in my bloody room. She should be kissing me.

Sucking in a breath, I'm staring at them horrified.

I said I was willing to try, not that I was willing to watch them fuck. I'm not even convinced she's fully awake. Surely if she was, she wouldn't be doing this here…

She turns towards me, her eyes hooded with lust and she offers me a smile before pulling me towards her.

Kissing me, she takes me completely by surprise. Her lips are as soft as ever but she tastes slightly different.

I can taste him on her and I don't like it. Jealousy soars inside me but it's not enough to make me pull away, instead I pull her closer.

She's straddling Ziggy while kissing me.

It's surreal and insane and it definitely doesn't make sense, but I tell myself not to think about it. Nothing matters except her lips against mine.

Let's Try

Written By Rigby

Let's give it a try

Let's give it a go

Let's do it again

Until we get it right

I'll give you the world

Just give me your heart

I'll make it okay

So don't leave again

Let's try to make this work

Let's try to love again

Let's try to not forget

What we are to each other

Lust & Lyrics

Let's give it a try

Let's give it a go

Let's do it again

Until we get it right

I'll give you my heart

If you give me a smile

I'll make it okay

So don't leave again

I want to try so don't leave me again

I want to try so don't leave me again

Don't leave me again, I want to try

I want to try so don't leave me again

ZIGGY

Watching her kiss Rigby, I can't decide if I want to punch the git or just enjoy the moment. Clover's hand is inching up my jeaned thigh and it's hard to focus on anything else – even my jealousy – when she is this close.

"Fuck it," I say under my breath as I shrug my shoulders.

Then I lean forward, coming behind her so I can kiss a trail along her neck.

It doesn't matter that they got her first so long as I get my share.

My hands play with the hem of Clover's top, slowly exposing the flesh beneath it. Breathless, Clover pulls back from Rigby, breaking their kiss. She leans her head against my shoulder, her back to my chest as she catches her breath.

I continue my onslaught, kissing along her collarbone. Glancing at Rigby, I can't actually believe we're doing this. It's so completely beyond normal. He doesn't look phased in the slightest as he stares at Clover hungrily, eager for more.

I'm impatient too.

Lifting her top, I pull it over her head in one motion. My eyes linger on her breasts before moving up to her face so I can meet her eye, her head turned towards me.

She looks perfect like this. Perfectly decadent. Cheeks tinted pink, her chest heaving in time with her unsteady breaths.

Reaching for her, I pull her around so I can kiss her again. My kiss is dominant, demanding and consuming as I try to remove all trace of Rigby from her mouth, a primitive voice in the back of my mind laying claim to her over and over again.

Rigby lets me, surprisingly. He doesn't seem to be in a rush to take her back, even though I know he wants to. Instead, he's lifting his t-shirt over his head and undoing his jeans. I try to ignore him, pretend he's not here. That it's just me and Clover – alone.

My fingers curl around the clasp of her bra, releasing it. The straps fall to her elbows and I pull back to see her. I need to see her.

Sitting there, her bra still covering her, just, her eyes bright with lust, I've never seen anything more enticing.

She allows the bra to fall completely away, pushing it off the bed and I correct myself. If I thought she looked tempting a moment ago, it has nothing on the sight of her now.

I practically pounce on her, scared that if I don't, Rigby will. There's no time to waste when there's a queue of guys all wanting their fill of her.

Pushing her back so she's lying on the bed, I hover over her considering my options. I want to enjoy this, make it last.

I take one of her pebbled nipples in my mouth and suck on it before nipping at it gently, my hand moving to her other breast, kneading it like dough.

She moans and I almost want to brag to Rigby that I'm the one making her feel this good. But I'm not a complete shit, and perhaps more to the point, I don't want to waste a second on Rigby when it could be spent ravishing Clover.

I begin to move down her body, trailing kisses along her skin, hopefully marking her. I want the others to see where I've been, see what I've done, see that she's mine.

I hear a sigh behind me, Rigby's patience thinning.

"Ziggy, needs to learn to share," Rigby says petulantly, as he moves up the bed so he can kiss Clover again.

He's naked and I need to catch up. There's no way I'm letting him have her first.

I remove my clothes hastily. We won't have long before the others will barge in and tell us the pizza has arrived and we have a lot to do before then.

Once I've removed my own clothes, I begin to remove what's left of Clover's, and then I burry my face between her thighs. I start slow, licking almost tentatively, teasing her as she squirms against me.

Then I push my tongue inside her and bring my fingers to her clit, rubbing circles in time with the thrusts of my tongue. She begins to buck her hips, craving more, until her hips are completely off the bed, as I hold her in place against my face.

Glancing up at her, I gasp in surprise at the sight of her swollen lips wrapped around Rigby's cock. *Fucking bastard.*

CLOVER

This moment is everything I shouldn't want. It's hedonistic and damn selfish but I can't bring myself to care. I can't restrain myself, can't say no… I won't hold back.

I want them both. I can't deny it.

Would I be happy if I chose just one of them? It's hard to believe that with both of them touching me.

Impossible even.

I can barely think straight. I'm so distracted by how good it feels.

Will I regret this?

Maybe.

But I don't care. Not even a little bit, not when it feels so damn good.

Ziggy pulls away, my hips bucking, demanding that he continue. I glare at him as best I can with my mouth full of Rigby's dick.

Ziggy turns momentarily towards Rigby, asking where he keeps his condoms and it suddenly hits me that we're actually doing this.

Rigby grunts out an answer, pointing towards his bedside table.

I watch as Ziggy rolls a condom onto his dick, eagerly anticipating what is coming next.

Rigby pokes my cheek with his finger and I lift my gaze to meet his. His expression is teasing, silently berating me for getting distracted from the task at hand, but beneath that there's something else, a possessiveness, a need to keep me all to himself.

Once again, I find myself wondering if I'm too selfish. If I'm hurting them by not choosing.

But it doesn't stop me craving this moment. It's pure torment, wanting what I shouldn't have.

Except shouldn't doesn't automatically mean that I can't. I can have this. This perfect moment, with both Rigby and Ziggy here, proves it.

Selfish or not, this is what I want.

Rigby's hand moves to the back of my head, grasping my hair.

My eyes lock on his as I suck his cock deeper into my mouth. I love the way he looks at me like I'm his whole world. That look makes me want to please him, satisfy his every whim.

But it also makes me feel guilty.

I'm enough for him. I'm everything he wants and needs. But I'm not sure I can say the same.

No matter how much I love him – and fuck me, I definitely love him – I'm not sure it's enough. I still want the others. I feel like I need them, just as much as I need him.

There's no competition in my mind. They're all equal. And there's no way I can possibly choose. Not now.

Rigby comes in my mouth, taking me by surprise and forcing me back into the moment and out of my own head.

He pulls out of my mouth and I rub the back of my hand across my mouth, not once looking away from him.

Rigby glances towards Ziggy, his expression momentarily clouded.

"I'm not sure I want to be here for this," he mutters to himself.

I don't know what I want him to do. Do I want him to leave? Stay?

People live their lives like this, loving multiple people… I have no idea how they do it.

My concerns for Rigby are practically forgotten when Ziggy's dick pushes into me. Automatically,

I reach out for Rigby, digging my fingernails into his thigh.

Rigby leans forward, kissing a path from my ear to my collarbone, before whispering into my ear that I look hot.

Then he's kissing me. It's a fight for distraction. He's doing everything he can to ignore the fact that Ziggy is fucking me.

I moan into his mouth, clinging to his leg even tighter. I push up to meet Ziggy's thrusts. His pace is brutal, he's hurried as if we haven't got enough time. As if we'll be disturbed at any moment.

He may well be right but I don't care. Right now, nothing matters except how good this feels.

The others could barge in and I probably wouldn't even notice.

I wrap myself around them both, clinging to them, pulling them both closer. My fist wraps around Rigby's cock, stroking it up and down, although it's hard to focus when it feels so good.

Their hands are on me and I can't tell where one ends and the other begins. It's pure heaven. One tweaking at a nipple, the other grasping my hip, so tightly I'll most likely bruise.

I can feel my orgasm building, every touch prickling my skin as if it burns. I think Ziggy is close too. His movements are less controlled. My favourite drummer is struggling to keep his rhythm and that idea brings a smile to my face. I make him lose it.

I'll Give You What You Need

Written by Nash

I can't promise much

I'm not that guy

You know the one

He'll meet your folks

Put a ring on your finger

Bow the fucking knee

But that's not me

I can't promise much

I'm not that guy

But I promise you this

I'll give you what you need

What you really need

Hanleigh Bradley

I'm the guy your parents

Pray you'll never meet

But they don't know

What you need

Not the way I do

I'll make you cry out

Screaming my name

As your body caves

To my demands

I can't promise much

But I'll promise you this

I'll give you this

I'll give you what you need

What you really need

I've got what you need

I've got what you need

JETT

We're sitting around the breakfast bar eating pizza. It should be a pretty normal, everyday sort of occurrence but it's not. Nowhere close.

It's slightly awkward.

Clover is flushed and it's easy to imagine what she's been doing.

Ziggy and Rigby are avoiding each other's eye. Their embarrassed sideway glances are hilarious. It leaves me wondering what the hell I've missed but I'm not sure I want to know.

Nash doesn't share my self-preservation instinct apparently. He asks them outright what is going on, bringing a blush to Ziggy's cheeks.

I do my best not to laugh, biting down on the inside of my cheek.

"Er," Rigby struggles for the right words as Clover chokes on her pizza.

I pat Clover's back as she splutters.

No one says anything as Rigby gives up trying to explain.

"Anyway," I say, trying to ease the tension.

Creed is making no attempt to help his sister out of her awkward situation. If anything, he looks highly entertained. I almost expect him to start teasing her. I wouldn't put it past the bugger.

We eat in silence for a few moments, none of us knowing what to say, until Rigby clears his throat.

"I think we need to settle some stuff," he says firmly.

He's clearly feeling uncomfortable. He's tapping his fingers on the bar top impatiently.

"We need to work out a way to," he begins before pausing, unsure how to proceed.

He has everyone's attention, except Creed's.

Creed climbs to his feet, yawning with a stretch.

"I'm calling it a night. I'll leave you guys to all your relationship drama."

No one bothers to reply. I don't even look at him as I nod my head in acknowledgment.

"Night," Ziggy eventually says, his voice surprisingly high pitched.

"I love Clover," Rigby says sincerely and I feel suddenly scared.

My heart races as I feel myself growing fearful that he'll tell us to back off, that Clover is his, that he's won.

"I'm not going to pretend to know how any of you feel."

He pauses again, a frown on his face as he considers his words carefully. He doesn't want to piss any of us off it seems.

"I don't think you're going to choose, are you Clover?" he asks bluntly.

Her eyes widen and it's pretty obvious she's terrified. She doesn't want to have to answer that question. She knows there's no right answer and she's going to upset us either way.

"It's okay," Rigby says surprisingly softly. "It's okay. You don't have to."

Nash bristles, his shoulders straightening. He doesn't like where this is going and I can't pretend I do either.

Except I don't like the alternative.

Either I lose her, we all do, bar one lucky sod, or we share her, something that seems incomprehensible.

I want to tell her it's wrong, that someone will get hurt, but I think she's already hurting either considering making the choice and so perhaps I should just give in and let her have what she wants.

Let her have us all.

I don't want to share. I want to shout that I've loved her longer but I shouldn't be petulant. It would achieve nothing and would definitely hurt her, the one person I want to protect.

Steadying myself, I ask Rigby, "what do you have in mind?"

"Hang on," Nash cuts in, his tone harsh, angry even. "You can't be agreeing to this, Jett."

I shrug my shoulders. I don't know what to tell him.. Logically, he's right. I don't want this but I want her.

"You're joking?"

He's on his feet, pushing his barstool back. He's about to lose it, his temper rising.

"Man, what choice do we have?" I ask calmly. "Are you going to give her up?"

Clover lets out a hiss of breath, my words hurting her though I don't mean them to.

"No but that doesn't mean I'm willing to keep this bullshit going forever. Clover will work out who she wants and then we'll all accept her decision."

His words are sensible and usually I'd agree with him. With any other girl, I'd be on his side of this argument. But I know Clover.

She's not going to pick. She'd rather lose us all than have to choose between us.

NASH

I'm struggling to hold my temper in. I'm furious, shaking with fury. Have they all completely lost it?

I always thought I was the most sexually open. It's not like I've not had a threesome before. When it comes to sex, the way I see it, anything goes.

But this isn't about sex. Not really.

It's more than just sex.

I love her. I actually love her. I want more than just sex with her and if I want more, I have no intentions of sharing that more. It's mine. She's mine.

Mine to love. Mine to fuck.

Mine.

"Are you fucking insane?"

My voice is rising. I need to control myself, rein in my anger because the last thing I want to do is hurt Clover.

I see her flinch though. I've already hurt her.

"What else can we do?" Rigby asks.

"Rigs, tell me this," I demand, my arms folded in front of my chest, "how are you going to take this shit home to meet your mum?"

I regret the words as soon as they leave my mouth. I'm not calling Clover shit. That's not what I mean but its definitely what it sounds like.

Clover gets to her feet, her eyes wet with unshed tears.

I might regret the words I've just said, but that regret doesn't make it any less true. How do you take your girlfriend home to meet your mum when she brings four other guys along? Talk about awkward.

It's a logistical nightmare for one thing.

But more than that, there's no way anyone else will support us. Her parents won't.

Forget that though. I don't even want to try.

I want her and I want her to want me. Only me. Is that too much to fucking ask?

I wasn't bothered when I thought she'd pick eventually, when this was just a fun diversion before we settle into something more. That I could handle.

But if this is it, I'm not down for that.

I won't do it. I can't.

I'm waiting for Clover to say something, but she doesn't. She's not even looking at me. I can't tell if it's because she feels hurt or if she's angry with me.

Either way, I don't like it.

She turns away from me and it hits me. She'll leave me if I don't concede. I'll lose her.

"Clover," I say, working hard to sound calmer.

I wait until she turns back. She's still not looking at me and Jett is wrapping a protective arm around her shoulder. That arm annoys me, causing jealousy to course through me.

"What do you want from me?" I ask her. "I love you but…"

I don't know how to finish the sentence. I don't want to give her an ultimatum. I don't want to force her hand.

She's staring at the bar top and I can't tell if she's trying to formulate her answer or if she's just going to remain silent.

"I don't know," she whispers so quietly I almost fail to hear her. "I don't know. I'm sorry."

Rigby rushes to her side, pulling her into his arms.

"You have nothing to be sorry for," he tells her.

He's right. She's done nothing wrong. She's promised me nothing but I want everything.

I'm the one asking for more than she's willing to give. It's ironic. Usually I'm the one saying no, the one being chased.

I don't know what to say to her.

With a sigh, I sit back down, rubbing my eyes.

"Tell us what you want and we'll make it work," I tell her.

I might not like it but I can't end it here and if that means sharing her, then I'll learn to play fair.

"Er," she hesitates.

She doesn't know what to say. She's just as overwhelmed as I am. This is abnormal for her too.

Rigby smirks. He doesn't expect Clover to answer me.

"How about we set some ground rules?" Jett suggests.

"Rules?" I laugh bitterly.

The last thing I want is to create a list of rules. I'm a spontaneous guy and have never been particularly good at keeping within the rules.

"Rules are made to be broken, right?" I add with a shrug.

I Can Be That For You

Written by Nash

My mamma always told me

To be a good man

But that's not me

But I can be that for you

I've been a bad bad man

But for you I can be a good man

Yeah for you

I can be that for you

My papa always told me

To be a bad man

But that's not the

Me you want

Lust & Lyrics

It never has been

So for you I can be a good man

Yeah for you

I can be that for you

My mamma always told me

To be a good man

But that's not me

It never has been

I'm a player, I'm a cheat

But for you I can be a good man

Yeah for you

I can be that for you

CREED

I feel bad leaving Clover to deal with the guys on her own, my brotherly instinct to protect her kicking in.

Except seriously, it's her problem and I can't be bothered to play the fucking referee in that drama.

As I walk away, I hear their voices begin to rise.

Nash is clearly pissed, his voice cutting.

I can't really say I blame him. I know how I'd feel if I was in his place. I'd be furious.

My phone buzzes in my pocket. I don't check it. I want to enjoy the anticipation a little longer. It might be Nona.

Climbing the stairs, I take two at a time, eager to get to my room so I can answer the text.

When I make it to my room, I fling myself down on the bed, resting my head on my left forearm. Then and only then, do I check my phone.

The name that lights up the screen should disappoint me – it's not Nona – but I can't ignore the excitement I feel, my heart pounding in my chest.

There's no reason for Crimson to message me.

She hates me. Literally hates me.

She's Nona's best friend and she's a one night stand I've never forgotten.

It was just one night, one fucking amazing night.

Staring down at my phone, I swipe my thumb across the screen, opening the text. My palms feel sticky; I'm nervous.

Can we talk?

Three words. That's it. I have no idea what we could possibly have to talk about. I hesitate. I should avoid letting myself get too close to her.

She's dangerous.

She always has been.

If we'd handled that one night stand better, if we'd gotten together, Nona and I would be a none entity. Nona would just be my girlfriend's best friend.

But somewhere along the way, everything got twisted.

I love Nona. I do. And I don't want to fuck that up.

But Crimson is pure temptation. She's Nona's polar opposite.

Instead of replying to her text, I hit the call button. I wait impatiently for her to answer.

"Hello?" Her voice is surprisingly timid.

"Hi."

I don't know what else to say so I just wait for her to say something instead. She's the one who wanted to talk.

But she's not quick to say anything.

"Er…"

"What's up, Crimson?" I ask gently.

It's a voice I can't remember ever using with her. It holds the sort of tenderness that girls like Nona inspire. The cute, innocent girls that need protecting.

But Crimson isn't like that.

I don't feel like she needs my protection or like she even needs me at all. With her, I've always been all business. Even sex. We weren't gentle with each other.

It was rough, passionate and perhaps a little bit kinky, just the way I like it.

"I just wanted to…" She's whispering. "I thought we should…"

She pauses before continuing, her voice steadier.

"I thought we should air things out, if you and Nona are serious."

Her words surprise me. We've never discussed what happened between us. It's been a sort of unwritten rule to avoid the topic all together.

"We can do that if you like," I say even though there's no way in hell I'll tell her the truth.

I can't do that.

I can't tell her that I still think about that night or that I regret how it ended or worse that I like her.

None of those things can be said, not if I love her best friend.

"I just wanted to say I never thought you took advantage or anything. We were both drunk. It was a mistake."

She's rushing the words out as if she's scared that she won't get them out.

I'm grateful that we're talking on the phone. I'd hate for her to see how her words affect me. They hurt and I'm pretty sure it's written across my face.

"We will probably see a lot more of each other if you're with Nona. She's my best friend… I really want her to be happy."

Nodding my head, I breathe in. She's right. Everything she is saying is true except…

"It wasn't a mistake."

"Huh?"

Home

Written by Jett

I'm heading home

To where you're waiting

Waiting for me

It's cold outside

Coz I'm so

fucking far away

Far away from

Where you are

I'm heading home

I'm heading home

A day without you

Hanleigh Bradley

Is a day too long
My feet have a heavy beat
Rushing to get to
Where you are

I'm a little tongue tied
Too many things I want
To say to you
But my voice won't carry
To where you are

I'm heading home
To where you're waiting
Waiting for me

Are you waiting?

CRIMSON

"Huh?"

I can barely process what he's saying. His words just don't make sense. How could that night possibly be anything except a mistake?

We were drunk… stupid… and he's…

With Nona now.

So nothing else matters.

That's the only thing that counts.

"It wasn't a mistake," he says it again.

I wish he wouldn't.

He should have said it the morning after or taken it to the fucking grave.

This is not what this conversation is supposed to be about. We were supposed to clear the air so I could finally put my feelings aside and move the fuck on.

He wasn't supposed to make this more complicated.

"I liked you," he says.

His voice is too soft, this conversation too intimate.

I need to be strong.

I can't ask him any of the questions currently running through my head. If I do, I'll be a shitty friend.

I can't do it. I shouldn't do it. The words 'I love you' are on the tip of my tongue. I bite down on the inside of my cheek.

I can't say it.

"Crimson?"

I can't speak. I don't know what I'm supposed to say. All the worlds I want to use need to go unsaid.

"Please stop," I say eventually.

I'm practically begging him. I can't let myself listen to him.

He's silent for a moment. I can hear his breathing. Slow and steady, it's comforting.

"What do you want me to say instead?" he asks.

"That it was a mistake. That it doesn't matter anymore. That you've forgotten…"

"You want me to lie?"

"If necessary."

"I don't want to."

His tone is downright petulant.

"You're with Nona now," I say. "This conversation is pointless."

"You started it."

He's exasperating. What the fuck does he want from me?

"I shouldn't have called you."

"I'm glad you did."

His reply makes me hesitate, my finger hovering, ready to hang up.

"Crimson, I'm sorry if I hurt you."

I want to tell him that he hasn't but I can't. I don't want to lie. It's silly really. I called him, knowing everything I was planning on saying was a lie but now I can't bring myself to lie to him.

But I certainly can't tell him the truth.

"I'm sorry too."

"You have nothing to be sorry about."

I hate how gentle his voice sounds and the way it makes me feel. But more than anything I hate how much I like him.

I shouldn't like him.

"I shouldn't have avoided you," I whisper.

"I can understand why you did," he responds. "It was pretty awkward"

"I was scared."

"Scared? What of?"

"You."

"Me?"

"That you regretted it."

"What?"

He sounds flabbergasted like he really can't believe my words.

"We were drunk. You'd probably have fucked anyone…"

My words are harsh but he doesn't disagree with them.

"Possibly. But I was glad it was you and not anyone else."

"Really?"

I don't like how needy I sound.

"I didn't regret it, Crimson."

The way he husks my name down the line feels too intimate.

"What about now? Do you regret it now? Now that you're with Nona?"

"No." He doesn't hesitate. "No. I don't."

I want to ask him why but I'm not sure I want to hear his answer. And I'm pretty sure his answer will be dangerous.

"The only thing I ever regretted was not doing it again."

I breathe in sharply, unable to comprehend what he is saying.

"Huh?"

Apparently English is failing me. I don't know what to say but even if I did I'm not convinced I'd actually be able to say it anyway.

I feel too nervous; my head spinning, my heart racing. I can't say anything. Partly because of how nervous he makes me but also because Nona is my best fucking friend.

"I wish we'd handled it better back then," he says. "Then we would have had a chance to see what could come of it."

"But Nona…"

"I'm not saying I wouldn't want to be with Nona, I just wish we'd give ourselves a chance."

"A chance?"

"To see where it could have gone."

Where it could have gone? That's something I can't even let myself consider. If I do, I'll only get hurt. I'll only want what I shouldn't want. Covet what isn't mine.

NASH

Over the next few days we spend most of our time in the studio, finally nailing down the recording of the album. There's little time to think about the bizarre situation we've all gotten ourselves into, and for once I'm too tired to feel jealous of the others.

If anything we're all surprisingly at ease as if the argument we had a few nights back cleared the air somehow or maybe we're just too busy to think about anything except work.

The tension that had been evident between us all had seemingly just disappeared. But that doesn't sound likely, does it?

Nothing has actually changed.

Nothing has been resolved.

She hasn't chosen.

And apparently she has no intention to either.

I can't say I'm happy about it. The others are either acting like they don't care or they've actually lost their bloody minds.

I'm not actually sure which is more likely.

Right now though, I'm too tired to care.

We've been recording all fucking day and the production guys have finally told us we can call it a day.

I don't even know what time it is. The only evidence I have that its late is just how much my stomach is rumbling.

The guys are all talking about food as they clear away their instruments but my eyes are on Clover. I can see her through the window, talking to her dad – probably something about the song we've just recorded.

Our eyes meet and she smiles. It's practically blinding.

I don't know how I can possibly let her go. She's kind of like a drug, one I really can't quit. And I'm not sure I want to either.

I've never felt like this before. I usually dump the girls I fuck long before I even have a chance to feel anything, let alone this.

Usually I don't even have the time to feel sorry for leaving so quickly, let alone love them.

She holds my gaze no more than a few seconds before turning back to her father.

I as good as jump out of my skin when Ziggy comes up beside me, wrapping an arm around my neck.

"Come on man! I'm half starved."

I smirk down at him momentarily before my eyes wander back to Clover.

"What should we eat?" I ask, barely paying him any attention at all, not really waiting for his answer.

"Burgers?"

"Sure. If you like." I'd agree to anything right now, so long as I can keep Clover by my side.

I allow Ziggy to pull me out of the studio, Jett and Rigby following just behind us.

Clover's dad smiles widely at us all. I can practically see the pound signs in his eyes. He knows we've just recorded a number one.

"You worked hard," he says. "Take the rest of the day off and come back fresh tomorrow so we can nail down the last song."

The last song...

I can't believe we're so close to finishing the album. I should be ecstatic but it's bittersweet. As exhausting as it has been recording the album, at least Clover has been here with us.

We can't take her on tour with us.

She'll join us for some of it but it won't be the same. We won't be living in the same house. We won't have the privacy we do now.

Instead everyone will be watching our every move. Usually I live for this shit. I love it. Performing every night, the buzz of being on the road… But I don't want to be separated from Clover.

At home, I can kiss her whenever I want but on tour there will be too many people watching. And the last thing we need is for anyone to find out about our less than conventional relationship.

It's fucking frustrating but there's not much any of us can do about it.

Just thinking about it, makes me reach out for Clover's hand. Creed is walking his father out of the room, discussing the song we'll be recording tomorrow. It's just us, Clover, me and the other guys left in the room.

Her fingers twine with mine and I pull her closer. The words 'I don't want to go on tour,' are on the tip of my tongue but I can't bring myself to say them.

"You'll come with us on tour? Right, Clover?" Ziggy asks.

He's such a kid. He hasn't even thought about how busy we're going to be or that everyone will be watching.

"For some of it," she says, smiling at him.

"We still haven't resolved everything," Jett says matter-of-factly, straightening his glasses.

Clover nods her head, her expression resolute, her jaw tight.

"We can't put it off any longer," she says, still nodding.

Stay By Your Side

Written by Jett

Is it too much to ask

That you and I

Could just stay this way

Live this way

Each day

Can I just stay

Each day by your side

Is it too much to ask

Will you let me stay

Can I cling to you

Love you, depend on you

Hold you, sing to you

Lust & Lyrics

Can I stay by your side

Right in this moment

Or is it just a dream

A fool's errand

A little wishful thinking

Is it too much to ask

That you and I

Could just stay this way

Live this way

Each day

Can I just stay

Each day by your side

Is it too much to ask

I swear it's where I belong

Everything will be okay so long

As I can

Stay by your side

Hanleigh Bradley

Is it too much to ask

That you and I

Could just stay this way

Love this way

Each day

Can I just stay

Forever by your side

Is it too much to ask

CLOVER

They're all wearing matching sour expressions.

"But Clover its three months," Ziggy is complaining from where he is sitting opposite me at the breakfast bar.

Rigby refused to let us go out for food, insisting that certain conversations should be had at home away from prying eyes.

Of course, he's right but with this lot, food always comes first and so the others insisted on picking up some pizzas on the way back.

I don't know how they look so good, toned and perfectly sculpted when they eat so much crap. Seriously, it just isn't fair!

Ziggy is waiting for my response but my mind is in the gutter, filled with thoughts of muscles and flesh and…

"I can't spend my whole life following after you four," I say jokingly.

"What will you do instead?"

The tone of his voice suggests he can't imagine what I could possibly want to do on my own.

I want to tell him that I have my own life but his adorable pout makes it impossible. I just can't chastise him.

"Maybe record some stuff…"

Truth is, I haven't really thought about it.

"That won't take three months."

"No but I already said I'd visit."

I grin at him, he's so fucking cute when he pouts.

Rigby is quiet, leaning his elbows on the table but both Jett and Nash are nodding. At least they seem to realise why I can't go with them.

The rumours would be a nightmare, especially given our uneasy truce. All it would take was one photograph of me and one of them, one article and we'd be at war… well, not literally.

But the last thing we need is another bout of jealousy.

"It's a wise decision," Jett says. "We don't want anyone to start asking questions."

"Why not?" Ziggy asks. "I'll happily tell everyone that Clover is my girlfriend."

With a sigh, Rigby sits up.

"What are you going to tell them about me and Clover too? Or Nash and Jett? How will you explain that?"

Ziggy's shoulders slump.

"I don't care what they think," he says after a moment.

"But it's not just about you," Nash cuts in.

"Besides," I reach across the breakfast bar, taking Ziggy's hand in my own, "I have my own dreams. While you're living yours, I want to find mine."

Rigby shakes his head before turning his stool around so he's facing away from the others, his back resting on the edge of the bar top.

He reaches over and takes my other hand.

"This is why we all need to talk," he says resolutely. "We can't leave things as they are."

"But what choice do we have?" Nash retorts. "You're not going to give her up and neither am I."

"That's not what I mean."

"Then what do you mean?" Nash sounds exasperated.

"I mean we should decide on some rules or something, we should set out how exactly we can make this work."

There is a murmur of agreement from the others. As always, Rigby takes charge and the others eventually follow.

"First, I think we need to decide what we're going to do if anyone finds out."

My heart races at the mere thought of someone finding out. My palms are sweaty and no doubt both Rigby and Ziggy will be able to tell how anxious I suddenly feel.

Rigby gives my hand a gentle squeeze before continuing, "I think we should just remind people that Clover is Creed's sister."

"Yeah," Nash agrees, "I can play the whole 'Creed would castrate me before letting me near his sister' card."

That gets a chuckle from the others. Still grinning, Jett adds, "I can say we practically grew up together. She's like a sister to me."

"Okay but what if we actually get caught?" Ziggy asks, suddenly nervous.

Rigby turns to face me, his expression stoic, giving nothing away. He takes my hand from Ziggy, holding both of them now in his lap.

"If we're serious about this, if it's really what you want, we won't be able to keep it a secret forever. Eventually, someone will find out."

"I know," I whisper before saying louder, "if that happens, we just tell the truth."

"But what is the truth?" Nash asks.

"That love doesn't always come to you the way you might expect or even hope for it to. That I love you all and you love me."

I pause, trying to put what I feel into words.

"It might not be normal and people might not like it but this is what our love looks like."

"So they can go fuck themselves if they don't like it," Nash adds.

RIGBY

"Bedtime," I say firmly when Clover yawns for the tenth time.

She scrunches up her face like a child refused cake.

"Where are you sleeping tonight, Clover?" Ziggy asks.

That boy seriously lacks tact.

Clover shrugs. She hasn't decided it would seem.

"Do we need some sort of schedule?" Jett asks, his inner geek making an appearance.

There's an explosion of laughter as we all look at him in complete bewilderment.

"I'm serious," he says, his pride wounded.

"Oh, we know you are." Nash is quick with the comeback.

"Maybe we need a bigger bed…" Ziggy starts.

"I'm not sharing a bed with you, Ziggy." Nash's face has turned white, his expression stony.

"Okay…" I say, shaking my head. "We can readdress this in the morning. I'm dead beat."

"But we still don't know where Clover is sleeping."

"Clover is a big girl. She knows her options. I think she can decide on her own."

I offer her a quick wink before leaving the room completely ignoring the guys' reactions.

Fools.

Not ten minutes later, there's a gentle knock at my door. I make my way across the room in just my boxers, trying my best to remove any sign of gloating from my expression.

When I open the door, Clover smiles sweetly at me.

"They're still arguing," she tells me by way of explanation.

"No need to explain. You can pick me any time," I reply, pulling the door wider so she can make her way inside.

Thank fuck my friends are morons…

Well, stupid enough to not realise that Clover doesn't want to deal with that shit. She wants to sleep. And if I'm lucky, fuck.

"I should thank them," I tell her wolfishly as I close the door, "for practically driving you to my bed."

Turning to face her, I ask, "are you here to just sleep or..?"

I'm surprised to find her turned towards me, her fingers working their way down the buttons of her shirt.

She says nothing.

I hold my breath as I watch her undress. Her eyes hold mine as she steps out of her jeans before approaching me in just a thong and her bra.

"What do you think?"

"I think not." Her intentions are pretty clear.

She nods her head once and then she's kissing me, her lips meeting mine. They're soft and pliant and yet surprisingly demanding.

My dick is already hard, worked up from her little strip tease. Fingers on the clasp of her bra, I want her naked now. I'm impatient.

Kissing her back, I begin to walk towards her, causing her to back up towards the bed. Right where I want her.

Except I'm not quick enough.

It's impossible to ignore the thundering of three sets of feet on the stairs or their complaints that I played them.

And then our perfect moment of solitude is disturbed as all three barge into my room.

"Rigs, you're a dick." Nash is the first to break the tension.

"You snooze, you lose," I reply without turning to look at them.

My eyes are trained on Clover, gaging her reaction. She's clearly embarrassed but not as much as you might expect.

Twisting my neck, I smirk back the others.

"Either, join us or get out."

When I notice Clover shivering, I brush my hands up and down her arms trying to warm her while the others just stand there stock still, clearly lost for what to do.

"Five," I begin to count down.

Still nothing.

Returning my attention to Clover, I resume what we were doing before we were interrupted, kissing her deeply.

When the back of her calves hit the edge of the bed, I pull back momentarily.

"Four."

I don't wait for a response this time before I push Clover back so she's sprawled across my bed.

Dropping to my knees, I pull her by the legs towards me so her arse is hanging off the edge of the mattress. Then I begin to shimmy her thong down her thighs before removing it completely.

"Three," I call back, unsure if they're still even there.

I don't give a shit either way.

Spreading her thighs, I bury my face in her pretty little snatch.

I'm Watching

Written by Rigby

He's kissing you

I'm standing here

But I can't move

I'm watching you

You and him

Like a horror show

I can't look away

It's a horror show

It's a car wreck

On slow-mo

I can't walk away

I can't stand to look

Hanleigh Bradley

But I'm watching you

You and him

Him and you

It's a horror show

It's a car wreck

On slow-mo

But I can't look away

He's touching you

I'm sitting here

I can't look away

I'm watching him

Him and you

Like a car wreck on slow-mo

I can't look away

JETT

I need to move. I can't just stand here watching like some creepy perv. My hands are sweating, my heart pounding in my chest, my breathing heavy.

In a perfect world, I'd never witness Clover being tongue fucked by someone else. But this isn't a perfect world.

Both Ziggy and Nash look just as conflicted as I feel, unable to leave but unsure what else to do.

And Rigby is fucking counting down, making my anxiety rise.

It's now or never. I need to make a decision.

Ziggy is the first to step forward. He walks around the bed, removing his clothes as he goes. Then he's leaning down and kissing Clover.

My dick throbs with anticipation. It wants in on whatever crazy gangbang shit is about to go down even if I don't. If my dick had its way I'd have flung myself right into the fray without a moment's hesitation.

Nash smacks me across the back, causing me to stumble forward.

His eyebrows rising mischievously, he says, "if you can't beat them…"

"Join them," I mutter as I watch him approach the bed too.

Rubbing my hand down my face, I catch it on my glasses. I remove them, leaving the room slightly blurry.

I turn around to close the door behind me.

The last thing any of us need is for Creed to accidentally walk in on us. If this situation isn't awkward enough already.

I put my glasses down on Rigby's desk, taking a deep stabilising breath before approaching the bed.

Clover is moaning, her fingers digging into the sheets, her back arching.

I ignore everything else. I don't want to think about Rigby's tongue licking her out or the way Nash is kissing a trail of hickeys down her throat. And I certainly don't want to think about the way Ziggy is stroking his cock while leaning over her.

None of that matters.

With my eyesight blurry, it's easy to pretend I can't see any of it.

Climbing onto the bed, I reach for Clover's tit, squeezing it gently between my fingers.

Clover's eyes open, her gaze meeting mine. She smiles and it's fucking blinding.

I'm doing all sorts of things I wouldn't ever normally do. All for this one girl.

And that smile is a reminder she's worth it.

Leaning forward, I lick a circle around her pebbled nipple, barely touching her. It's just enough to drive her crazy. My hand moves to the other breast, pinching and squeezing it as my mouth assaults that perfect little nipple.

She whimpers and I tell myself that I'm the one responsible for that sound.

She's shaking, close to orgasm, ready to come, desperate even.

"Please," she begs. Who I'm not sure.

"Not yet," Rigby replies.

"Let her come, Rigs, you dick," Ziggy argues, but Nash pushes him, silently telling him to shut up.

It's hard to imagine they're not here when they open their fucking mouths. I focus my attention back on Clover's tits, trying my best to ignore everything else, everyone else.

My cock is uncomfortable in my jeans. I readjust myself before biting down on her nipple. This time when Clover screams out, I'm pretty confident I can take credit for it.

Whimpering, she begins to trash, desperately humping against Rigby's face.

I suck on her tit as I move my hands to the button of my trousers. My cock is painfully hard.

Sitting up to remove my clothes, I watch as Clover orgasms loudly. She's practically delirious, unaware of anything around her except for how good she feels right now.

No one waits for her to recollect herself. She's still coming when Rigby sheathes his condom clad dick inside her. Then without even a second's hesitation he begins pounding into her in an unrelenting rhythm.

Nash fills Clover's mouth with his cock and Ziggy has taken my place fondling her breasts.

I'm surprised when Clover's hand wraps around my dick, stroking it gently. She starts slow, almost torturously slow, but quickly picks up the pace, tightening her grip.

My cock is weeping, throbbing needily.

I try to control my reaction, hissing out a harsh breath. I don't want to come. I want to save it all for the moment when I'll finally be inside her.

But I can't stop myself. My cock pulses, come squirting out onto the bedsheets.

I crumble forward, leaning close to kiss Clover's cheek. I hesitate for a fraction of a second at being so close to Nash's fucking dick.

Quickly, I realise that none of that matters.

All that matters is Clover.

ZIGGY

Come morning none of us have gotten much sleep. I'm yawning as I take a quick shower, getting ready to return to the studio.

Today we'll finally record the last song for the album. If everything goes to plan, tonight we'll be celebrating.

My forehead rests against the glass as my mind returns to the night before. I could get used to living like this. Working together, we played Clover's body like it was some mystical musical instrument.

My fist twists around my dick, tugging it harshly as the water cascades down like rain against my back.

There's no time. The others will be waiting but I can't go down like this, with a rock hard cock.

There's a knock at the door. Opening my eyes sharply, I find myself face to face with Clover.

Her eyes wander down to my cock before she returns her gaze to mine, smiling widely.

"I was sent to tell you to hurry the fuck up," she tells me, quickly removing her clothes. "Want some help?"

I'd never refuse her.

Nodding my head, I continue to rub my dick.

Once naked, she walks into the shower before dropping to her knees before me.

"Fuck!" I grit out when her warm mouth engulfs my cock.

My fingers twist around her hair. The water is causing it to tangle but she still looks bloody beautiful looking up at me, her cheeks hollowed as she sucks on my cock.

Her head bobs up and down as I lean back against the cold tiles of the shower wall.

"I'm going to…" I try to warn her but I don't get the words out.

My dick jerks as it shoots jets of come into her waiting throat. Once it stops, she allows it to drop from her mouth with a plop as she swallows the last drop.

"What about you?" I ask.

She shakes her head.

"There's no time."

I don't like that answer. Fuck everything else. The guys can wait. The album can wait. Everything else can fucking wait.

"We'll be quick."

Pulling her to her feet, I guide her so her chest is squashed against the glass of the shower cubicle.

It's easy to imagine how fucking hot she looks right now through the glass but there's not time to check.

Instead, I lift one of her legs, giving myself better access and then I push two fingers into her.

Even though I've just come, it doesn't take much for me to grow hard again as I thrust my fingers in and out of Clover's wet heat.

Removing my fingers, I align my cock before slowly pushing into her. Once fully sheaved, I begin pounding against her, my hands grasping tightly onto her hips.

She pushes back against me, her arse pushing higher as she slides down the glass slightly. Her raised leg wraps loosely around my thigh and I reach around her to run my fingers along her clit.

She yelps desperately as our movements grow frantic.

I'm going to come again but not before she does. I wait for her, trying my best to ignore just how wonderfully tight she.

She crumples against the glass as her orgasm hits her. I hold her up before reaching for a flannels so I can clean her up.

After a moment, she takes my shampoo from the shelf beneath the shower. Clover lavers it into her hair before washing it out as I run the flannel along the skin of her thighs.

Dropping the flannel to the ground, I stand up to wrap my hand around her neck, kissing her deeply.

When I pull back, I smile at her.

"You smell like me," I tease, pointedly looking at her hair, twirling a strand between my fingers.

She simply smirks at me before walking out of the shower, grabbing a towel from the rail by the door. She dries herself off quickly as I approach her, reaching behind her to take my own towel from the rail.

I drop a kiss to her cheek before pulling back. I wrap the towel around my waist and leave the ensuite bathroom.

In my bedroom, I make quick work of finding clothes to wear and am just buttoning my jeans when Clover finally leaves the bathroom, now fully dressed, her hair twisted into a plate.

"Ready?" I ask, holding my hand out for her to take.

It's A Good Day

Written by Clover

Holding hands with you
It don't matter that it's raining
Not when you're smiling
It's enough to have me singing
A merry little tune

It's a good day
Coz you're smiling
It's a good day
I'm not lying
It's a good day
You're a' loving

Lust & Lyrics

The sky is blue

Every day that I'm with you

The sky is blue

Every day that I'm with you

NONA

When I arrive at the label, I'm surprised to find Creed waiting for me. He's leaning against the wall outside the makeup room where I often work.

He holds out a coffee for me.

"Morning," he says lazily.

"Thank you," I say as I accept the drink.

Taking a sip, I let us into the small room that is more like a storage cupboard than a room where several people work. It's cluttered with makeup and clothes everywhere. I hurriedly move things around so Creed can sit down.

"Have you heard if you're coming on tour yet?"

"Not yet. Crimson thinks they'll tell us today."

Nodding his head, he leans back, completely at ease. It's as if he's oblivious to just how nervous he makes me. I watch as he drinks his own coffee.

"NONA!" Crimson comes barging into the room only to stop short when she notices Creed. "Oh. Creed, you're here."

"Morning," he smiles at her before getting to his feet, stretching his long limbs. "Guess I should get going."

He barely even glances my way before turning to leave, almost as if he's avoiding eye contact. But that doesn't make sense so I push the thought aside.

I give myself a gentle mental shake before turning my attention to Crimson.

"What's up?"

"We're on the list!"

"We're going?" I ask, suddenly excited.

"Mrs Levon just told me.

"Brilliant."

I want to go and tell Creed immediately, my feet itching to chase him down. Except I know he's busy and that I shouldn't disturb him while he's recording the album.

"She gave me a crazy long list of shit to buy today."

Crimson's face gives way to a frown. If there's one thing Clover doesn't like, it's shopping.

"Should we go together?" I ask.

Unlike Crimson, I love shopping.

"Yay… or you could just go on your own."

"Come on! It will be fun," I tell her, taking her by the arm and pulling her from the room.

Crimson drags her feet. She doesn't want to go but she'll do it because she has no choice. She'll do it but she won't enjoy it and what's more she won't let me either, if her mood is anything to go by.

"I'll drive," she says with a sigh.

"I can't believe I have to go buy boxers and condoms for your boyfriend and his mates," she grumbles.

"Are you serious?" I ask with a giggle.

"Look." She flings the list at me. "You won't believe what Mrs Levon put on that list. Makes me wonder just how crazy her and Mr Levon were when they were touring."

Most of the list seems reasonable enough. Far more realistic than the riders I'd received off some artists in the past, but occasionally something would catch my eye.

With a blush, I ask, "who are the butt plugs for?"

"God only knows! That woman is whack. Completely lost her fucking rocker."

"Should we ask the guys if there's anything they want us to get?"

Truth is I just want to see Creed. I could just as easily text them all, but I want to see his face even if its only for a moment.

"Sure. Whatever they ask for won't be as embarrassing as this shit."

Joking easily about Creed's parents we make our way to the studio where Saving Creed are working. We arrive just in time. The guys are still talking and have yet to enter the box.

Clover smiles widely at us as we enter.

"Hiya!"

Jumping to her feet, she wraps us both in her arms, hugging us tightly.

"Mum said you two are going on the tour. I bet you're excited!"

"Yeah," I respond. "Can't wait."

"We'll have to hang out," she tells us. "I'm going for the first five shows."

"Is that all? I would have thought you'd be…"

"Clover will be working on her own album."

I almost jump out of my own skin at the sound of Mr Levon's voice. It's so cold and authorative. I turn to find him standing in the doorway, his arms folded across his chest.

"Right ladies, we've got to get cracking. Is there something you need?"

"We're going shopping for the tour and just wanted to check if there was anything the guys need," Crimson explains.

He nods his head before making his way into the room. The guys gather round to add things to the list.

After several minutes, Creed's eyes widen as he reads over the list. There's got to be at least five things on that list that could cause his surprise.

"Who asked for butt plugs?" he asks with a smirk.

"Your mum," Crimson tells him bluntly, trying to keep her volume low so Mr Levon won't hear.

The boys all laugh, thinking that Crimson is joking.

"No. Seriously?" Creed waits for the truth. He doesn't believe us.

"Yeah… your mum…"

His eyes rove over Crimson's expression as if trying to decide if she's lying to him, then he glances at me, searching me for some sort of tell.

"Fuck!" He whistles out. "I did not need to know that."

With a shiver, he thrusts the list at me and enters the box.

We leave the room, clutching at our sides unable to control our laughter.

CRIMSON

I'm kicking myself. Well, not literally. My mood is downright shitty and is showing every sign of worsening.

Nona hasn't stopped talking about Creed. It shouldn't bother me but it does.

I try to ignore her, umming and ahhing whenever she expects a response. I need to get a fucking grip!

This morning when I walked in on them talking I was crazy green with jealousy. They were only talking for god sake! And even if they weren't, what right would I have to care?

When we arrive back at the label, it's already getting dark outside. Our arms are heavily ladled with bags.

Saving Creed are making their way out of the studio. It's close to six o'clock in the evening and yet it seems too early for them to be finished.

But it's impossible to deny that there is celebratory atmosphere around the guys. They're loud and energetic.

Clover is the first to spot us and immediately takes some of the bags from Nona.

"Wow. You guys have been shopping all this time?" she asks.

The guys fight to carry the bags for her but she redirects them towards us.

"Where's Creed?" Nona asks as she hands over the last of her bags to Ziggy.

Nash and Jett take most of the bags I'm carrying but I tell them I can still carry the last few.

Then a voice coming from directly behind me startles me.

"I'm here," Creed says, taking the last of my bags as he steadies me with a hand to the base of my spine.

I can't breathe.

It's a none touch. Meaningless. He's just helping to keep me balanced after I nearly fell on my arse but it doesn't feel like that.

Everyone turns to face him but I'm stood between them completely immobile.

I stumble back, out of the way, brushing his hand away. I want to run away and hide.

Talking to him was supposed to help, we were supposed to put everything behind us, that night behind us.

But he went and confused me even more.

They're all talking but I can't focus on what they're saying. My heart is still racing, my breath catching. And he's still too close.

"You'll come, right? Crimson?"

Clover is talking directly to me.

"Eh. Sorry. What?"

"We're all going out to celebrate. You'll come with us, right?"

"Eh. No. I don't think I can."

There's a murmur of disappointment.

But seriously what do they want me to do? Just go and be a fucking massive wheel?

"Come on, Crimson," Nona starts up. "It will be fun."

Yeah for you, I almost say. The last thing I want is to have to watch as she hangs all over Creed.

"Please?" Nona grabs hold of me, her eyes begging for me to come with them.

Rolling my eyes, I nod my head.

I'm a fucking sucker for punishment.

"I'll try," I tell her non-committedly.

"YAY!"

She pulls me into a tight hug with an enthusiasm I can't share. I really don't want to go.

My eyes meet Creed's over her head, and he smiles at me hesitantly. I want to hate him. I want to blame him for all this. But I can't.

It's no more his fault than mine.

Except he was stupid enough to say all the things we weren't supposed to say.

"Mr Levon has rented us a bar for the night," Ziggy tells me, "and he's paying for everything."

He says it like these kids need to save their money, like he loves a good bargain. It makes me chuckle for a second.

Occasionally, his Northern side shows. Most of the guys grew up in the South but not Ziggy. He's a Geordie through and through even if his accent has faded some.

"We'll meet you in the limo," Creed says, his eyes flitting between Nona and me. He holds up the bags by way of explanation.

"Limo?"

I'm practically dragged out of the lobby by Clover and Nona.

"Yeah." Clover explains, "Apparently, my dad went all out. So fucking cheesy."

I giggle hollowly, not really sharing the other girls excitement.

When we reach the limo that's waiting outside for us, the driver opens the door for us to climb in. Nona is the first to enter and Clover turns abruptly to look at me.

I swear she sees more than I'd like her to.

Her eyes are critical as she accesses me. I don't feel judged but I get the distinct impression she's worried about me.

I'm surprised when she pulls me into a hug.

"It's okay," she whispers before pulling back and climbing into the car.

On My Mind

Written by Creed

You're always on my mind

I've got you stuck on

repeat and rewind

You're always on my mind

Was this all your design

On my mind

On my mind

I can't stop though I know I must

I can't stop though they say I ought

You're always on my mind

Hanleigh Bradley

I've got you stuck on
Repeat and rewind
You're always on my mind
Was this all your design

On my mind
You're always on my mind
You're always on my mind
Always on my mind

CREED

Tonight has not exactly been my definition of fun. My parents and several of the label's higher ups are sitting in one of the booths, talking business.

That's not really a problem.

Except they keep trying to drag me and Clover into their conversation.

The guys are all on their best behaviour, scared out off their wits that my parents might find out about their unconventional relationship with Clover.

To be honest I haven't got the foggiest clue how my parents would react. Everything I know about their past suggests they'd be pretty cool about it but realistically, I know they're still parents.

Do as I say, not as I do.

I almost want to expose the secret just to see their reaction, except I'm not a dick.

My fingers curl around my pint as I sit between Ziggy and Nona. Everyone else is talking excitably about our tour but I just can't get into the conversation.

Lifting the beer to my mouth, I gulp down, my eyes wandering to where I've been telling myself not to look. Crimson is sat directly opposite me, talking happily to my sister.

I'm furious with myself for still liking her.

Our eyes meet and she tilts her neck slightly, probably trying to work out why the fuck I'm staring at her.

Fuck my life! What the hell am I playing at?

Nona reaches for me, drawing my attention away from her best friend. I try my best to hide the frown that is written across my face.

Grimacing at her, I wait for her to speak.

"I'm going to the bar. Do you want anything?" she asks sweetly.

My beer is almost finished so I nod my head.

"Yes please."

Then she's gone and I'm left to stew. My eyes return to Crimson. Her expression is animated as she talks to the others.

I want to go home.

No. That's a lie. I don't want to go home. I want to take Crimson home.

But I definitely can't do that.

Rubbing a hand across my face, I get to my feet and make my way outside.

I need some bloody air.

Once outside I'm able to breathe. I take a seat on a bench and drop my head into my hands.

I like Crimson. I've always liked Crimson.

But I like Nona too.

My eyes closed, I try to forget it all. I can't have them both; I'm not Clover.

I should just go home and get some sleep. Perhaps after a good rest, I'll be able to clear my head.

The door squeaks open, taking me by surprise and my eyes open abruptly.

"Sorry," Crimson says, her voice surprisingly soft. "I didn't know you were out here. I'll go."

"No. It's okay. I'm going anyway," I reply, climbing to my feet.

We stand there for a moment, neither of us saying anything. I should leave but I don't.

"Non…" she begins.

Raising a finger to her lip, I stop her. The last thing I want to hear is Nona's name. That one word will make me feel guilty for what I'm about to do.

Stepping forward, I move my finger from her lips to cup her cheek. She shivers slightly, presumably from the cold. My hand is freezing.

"You're warm," I whisper.

She doesn't say anything. She doesn't move either.

"Creed," she whispers when I don't say anything.

I like the way my name sounds on her lips. I'd like to hear it again and again, preferably while she's coming.

"Yes, Crimson?" I reply, a hint of a smile on my face.

It's the first time I've felt anything close to happiness all evening.

"We shouldn't. She's looking for you."

I shake my head. She's not telling me anything I don't already know.

"I don't care," I say.

I should care.

"I care."

"I know you do," I reply, pulling my hand away and stepping back with a sigh.

"I think you should go inside," she says, no longer looking at me.

Nodding my head, I concede that she's right. I walk around her, purposefully keeping as big a gap between us as possible.

It's only when my hand is on the door handle that I hesitate.

Hesitate… That's all I've ever done with Crimson.

Turning on my heels, I stride the small space between us. Looking down into her face, I notice a solitary tear running down her cheek.

Leaning down, I kiss it away before moving my lips down to hers, kissing her gently. She doesn't react immediately, I've clearly taken her by surprise.

My hands wrap into her hair and I take a step towards her. She opens her mouth, responding to the kiss, grabbing hold of the hem of my shirt, pulling me closer.

CLOVER

"Have you seen Creed?" Nona asks me.

Shaking my head, I search the room for my brother but he's nowhere to be seen. But he's not the only one missing…

"I'll go look for him," I tell her. "You sit here and chat to the guys."

She looks like she's going to refuse but I silently ask the guys for help and they quickly engage her in conversation.

Wandering around almost aimlessly, I search for Creed and Crimson but they're nowhere to be found. Pulling out my phone, I dial Creed's number and step out into the garden.

A shrill ringing sound hits my ear and I turn to see my brother and Crimson making out.

I can't exactly judge him. I have four boyfriends.

Quickly closing the door, I cough loudly causing them to pull apart.

Crimson looks horrified as she hides behind Creed but my brother just looks pissed.

"What do you want Clo?" he asks brusquely.

I can't exactly tell him that he shouldn't be doing this. I'm hardly in a position to judge him, except at least the guys know what's going on.

But they didn't always, a little voice reminds me.

It was Creed that helped me explain everything to them.

"I…" I don't really know what I want to say to them both. "Just be careful. Nona is looking for you."

His expression drops as if he's only just remembered that Nona even exists.

"Shit," Crimson mutters. "I…"

She looks like she wants to explain herself. She's scared what I think.

"No judgement here," I say without any emotion. It's not that I condone what they're doing but I can understand it.

I know what it's like to love more than one person.

"I'm going back inside," I say. "If you like I can tell Nona you went home."

"No," Crimson begins, taking a step back towards the door but Creed pulls her back.

"Please Clo," he says.

Nodding my head, I turn to leave.

"No. Wait. I'm coming with you."

"Crimson," Creed starts.

"What?" she retorts angrily.

"We need to talk," he says quietly.

"Talking is what caused this problem," she rebuffs.

"But…"

Crimson pulls away from him and walks past me, re-entering the bar.

I hover even though I'm not sure I should. My brother looks cut up. It's not at all like him to get emotional.

"Fucks sake!" he growls as he kicks the wall before sitting down on it.

He's quiet for a moment but then he says, "I've made a right mess of things, Clover."

I can't exactly tell him he's wrong.

"I don't know what to do."

Coming to sit next to him on the cold wall I recall what he told me when I found myself in a similar situation. He'd teased me for my polyamory but I don't think I can do the same.

"I don't know how you do it, Clover."

"Do what?"

"Love those four idiots."

I don't have an answer for him. Loving them is as natural as breathing. I can't imagine my life without a single one of them.

"I slept with Crimson ages ago…"

I nod my head. I'd kind of guessed. They had that vibe. That one you have when there's more between you than you'd like to admit.

"We were drunk… and we never talked about it properly afterwards. I thought she regretted it."

Leaning forward, stretching his legs out, he continues, "I really liked her though."

"But you started liking Nona?"

"Yeah… I guess, I thought Crimson wasn't interested so I tried to distract myself and at some point, I started liking Nona."

"That's why it took you so long to ask Nona out?"

I'd always thought it was odd that I'd known about Nona for months, he'd been talking about her non-stop, but he never asked her out.

He nods his head. "But then Crimson thought she'd clear the air between us and we talked... I said things..."

I don't say anything. There's nothing I really can say. I don't know what the right answer is, any more than he does.

"I really don't know who to choose..."

He pauses.

"I should just break up with Nona and keep away from them both."

Logically, he's probably right. I could try and convince him to choose them both but that would be telling him to be just as selfish as I am. I'm not sure I can do that.

"What if I don't want to give them up?"

He looks at me with the same expression he used to give me when he wanted me to cover for him, keep him out of trouble with mum and dad. It's a face I've never been able to ignore.

"Then don't," I say, taking his hand in my own. "Just be up front about it with both of them."

Shaking his head, he lets out a harsh bark of laughter.

"Yeah. I can't do that."

"Why not?" I ask.

"I'm not you, Clover. You got lucky with those four idiots. There aren't a lot of people on this planet willing to share."

This Ain't Love

Written by Creed

I'm not saying this is love

I refuse to accept this is us

All we are, just a pair of fools

Moved by serotonin

I'm not saying this is love

I don't believe in that drug induced word

I don't believe in that drug induced word

Instead, I'm a'believing this is heaven

I'm a'believing this is something better

Not just a hormone induced ecstasy

I'm not saying this is love

Lust & Lyrics

I refuse to accept this is us

All we are, just a pair of fools

Moved by serotonin

I'm not saying this is love

This ain't love

It's not possible

That you're as foolish

As I am, A serotonin

Addict, lost in a

Hormone induced ecstasy

RIGBY

The morning after we finished the album, the house is especially quiet. Surprisingly, not because we're all hung over but because we're all packing for the tour.

We'll be leaving in a matter of days and Mrs Levon has filled our schedules with interviews and television appearances, leaving us with no spare time to do anything, let alone pack.

Clover is sitting on my bed reading a book as I move around the room flinging things into my case.

She glances up from her book, taking in the disarray that is my packing.

Raising an eyebrow at me, she smirks. She stole that expression from Nash but in my opinion, she wears it a thousand times better than he does.

It's bizarre how we're all rubbing off on her in our ways.

"Need a hand?" she asks, her voice dripping with sarcasm.

"You're alright. You just stay right where you are."

"You're really shit at packing," she remarks, climbing up onto her shins and peering into my case with a look of mock horror.

"Thanks," I reply, rolling my eyes before leaning down to kiss her.

"Just saying."

She shrugs before moving back to lean against the headboard. I like seeing her there on my bed. The only thing that could make the sight better is if she was naked.

Nash and Ziggy disturb our moment as they come barging into the room without knocking.

"CLOVER!" Ziggy is practically shouting.

He's so fucking loud and energetic. I really don't see what Clover sees in him... Except she clearly does because her face is lit up as if she's fucking delighted to see him.

"What?" she replies mirroring his excitement in her expression.

"Come watch a movie with us?"

He's like a fucking puppy waiting to be petted.

Rolling my eyes, I speed up my packing. I don't doubt that Clover will go with them and I'm okay with that but I don't want to be away from her.

Closing my case with a thump, I cross my arms over my chest, feeling proud I could even shut the damn thing.

"Finished?" she asks.

Nodding my head, I don't tell her that I'll need to repack it tonight so everything doesn't get crazy creased.

"What movie are you thinking?" She turns back to the others.

"Whatever you want."

Nash is quiet, more than willing to let Ziggy do all the talking.

"Okay. Cool," She says, climbing to her feet.

She leaves her book on my bedside table, bringing a smile to my face. She's planning to come back.

Ziggy grabs Clover's hand and all but drags her from the room, Nash and I following after them. Once we enter the living room, Ziggy hurries to pull Clover down onto the sofa, laying claim to the space next to her.

Nash grins gloatingly at me before squeezing into the space on her other side. He reaches forward to take the TV remote off the coffee table before offering it to Clover.

The one thing about having so much blasted competition is that we're probably all more attentive boyfriends for it, always competing to the sweetest, the kindest, the sexiest, the best in bed…

There's no room for complacency when your girl has options.

Striding across the room, I settle myself on the floor in front of her. Instinctively she moves her legs apart to give me space between them. Wrapping one arm around her shin, I aimlessly begin to draw patterns over her jeans.

"Where are Creed and Jett?" I ask.

"Went for food," Nash tells me.

"Cool. What food?" I ask, silently hoping he won't say pizza. I swear all we eat is pizza. I'm fucking lucky I still have abs.

"Chinese, mate," Nash says before suggesting a movie to Clover.

"I wanted pizza," Ziggy grumbles.

"I don't," Nash retorts.

"Yeah, you said that already."

"We always have pizza," I point out.

Ziggy doesn't say anything. He sighs heavily as if we're all a bunch of unfair shits.

Clover scrolls through the movie options, regularly asking each of us for our opinion. Considering our slightly unusual predicament I find myself chuckling.

"What's so funny?" Clover asks, giving me a gentle nudge with her foot.

"Just thinking that we bring a whole new meaning to Netflix and Chill."

I twist round so I can see their reaction. Nash and Ziggy both smirk but Clover turns bright red at the implication. I love that blush.

"Ziggy, go get a blanket," Nash demands, his tone only half joking.

"We're not doing anything under a blanket if my brother is watching this movie with us," she tells us firmly.

With a snigger. Nash retorts with the weirdest puppy dog expression I've ever seen, "I only wanted to hold your hand."

"Bullshit," Clover replies.

"It's alright, Nash. You can hold my hand," I say struggling to keep a straight face.

Wiping fake tears from his face, Nash takes my hand.

"Thanks, mate. I don't know where I'd be without you."

Neither one of us can hold in our laughter any longer and by the looks of both Ziggy and Clover's faces, they're completely dumbfounded.

It's A Losing Battle

Written by Rigby

It's a losing battle

All else is forgotten

All I see is her

As she dances

Round and round

So I'm falling

Falling to the floor

Right at her feet

It's a losing battle

It's a losing battle

She's already won the war

Lust & Lyrics

The cage doors rattle

She's finally made me her whore

It's a losing battle

It's a losing battle

She'll leave me all rotten

All I know is her

As she sings

On and on

So I'm falling

Falling from the sky

Right at her feet

It's a losing battle

It's a losing battle

She's already won the war

The cage doors rattle

She's finally made me her whore

Hanleigh Bradley

Made me her whore
Made me her whore

It's a losing battle

She's floating in the clouds
But the clouds hit me
Like the stone cold floor

It's a losing battle
She's already won the war
The cage doors rattle
She's finally made me her whore
My heart races, my soul cries
I'm a gonna, through and through

It's a losing battle
It's a losing battle
She's already won the war
She's smiling like she don't know

Lust & Lyrics

She don't know, she really don't know

It's a losing battle

She's already won the war

I'm a man defeated

A checkmated king

Before his Queen

It's a losing battle

I'm a man defeated

It's a losing battle

I'm a checkmated king

And you're my Queen

You're my Queen

CREED

It's early. Really fucking early.

Too early.

Everyone is standing around in the bloody freezing cold waiting to leave while Switch, the band's manager runs around doing fuck knows what.

We were supposed to leave thirty minutes ago but nothing is going to plan this morning.

The others are all stood together, talking animatedly. They're far too happy and it's far too early.

Not me though.

My mood is shitty and the last thing I want to do is stand around listening to the guys worry over how cold Clover is. Fuck that bullshit.

Instead, I'm already on the bus, eyes closed, headphones in my ears, pretending to sleep. My backpack is on the chair next to me. It's a totally intentional move.

I don't want anyone to sit next to me – especially not Crimson or Nona.

When the others begin to climb onboard, I keep my eyes closed, hoping that the others will just ignore me and leave me the fuck alone.

I hear Clover tell someone, although I don't know who to just leave me be. Apparently, I'm not a morning person. Or at least that's what she's telling them.

Silently, I thank my twin.

It's one of the best things about having a twin sister. The way she just knows what I need. Right now, she knows I just want to be left the hell alone.

I'm going to break up with Nona. I've already decided. Except it's easier to decide it than it is to actually do. I just can't bring myself to disappoint her.

Disappoint myself.

I only open my eyes once the bus is on the road. Glancing around, I locate the others, wanting to know where I need to avoid.

Nona and Crimson are sitting up front. I don't understand how Crimson can act like nothing happened. We fucking kissed and yet she's sitting there with Nona as if it never happened.

I don't know how I feel about it. Cross that I don't mean more to her?

I can barely look at either of them, I feel so fucking guilty.

Rigby is sitting opposite me. He's typing on his phone, probably playing a game. Ziggy and Jett are sitting a bit further back, one asleep while the other reads a book.

Then my eyes land on Clover and Nash sitting towards the back of the bus. She's giggling happily, a wide smile covering her face.

If it wasn't for the guys, Clover would still be backpacking around the world. I should thank them. Except if Clover wasn't with them I wouldn't be so fucking confused.

I wouldn't even consider other options. It's one or the other not both but she's got both.

In fact, she's got more than both. She's got four fucking boyfriends. It's bloody mental.

It's not that I want more. I don't. It's not that I want both of them. I really don't.

I just don't want to have to choose.

I keep thinking back over everything I've done, every mistake I've made. I shouldn't have kissed Crimson. That blasted conversation should never have happened, the one where I said far too much.

I shouldn't…

I stare out the window, my jaw tight, my shoulders tense.

I shouldn't have hit on Nona when I still liked Crimson.

This mess is all my fucking fault.

I need to hit reset, end everything before it gets out of hand, before someone gets hurt…

That's bullshit though. Crimson has already been hurt and Nona is bound to get hurt too. By putting it off, I'm being selfish. It's an act of self-preservation.

Frowning, I close my eyes again. We're going to be on the road forever. Switch drives slower than Jett's granny. I wish I could have brought my own car, at least then I could have avoided everyone easier.

Or even better we could have taken a flight.

We're kicking off the tour in Scotland, Edinburgh to be precise.

The list of venues is crazy long. So long in fact that I can't even remember all the places we'll be playing. Edinburgh, Glasgow, Belfast, Cardiff, Newcastle, Leeds, Liverpool, Manchester, Southampton, Brighton…

I don't even know where else.

It's going to be fucking busy. Just what I need. I'll be too busy to think about Crimson or Nona. Too busy to worry about how much of an arsehole I am.

Then once we're done with the UK, we'll be jumping on a plane for the international tour. Fingers crossed, mum will choose a different team for makeup and wardrobe on that tour.

I could ask her.

Except I don't want to.

Just like I don't want to dump Nona.

Or stop kissing Crimson.

NONA

Creed is being weird.

Either that or I'm being sensitive.

I'm not sure which.

The others have told me he's just not a morning person, but I'm not sure that's it. It's not like this is the first time I've seen him in the morning. Although it is by far the earliest.

I'm not daft enough to think anyone is particularly talkative at five in the morning, but by ten I'm beginning to think something is wrong.

He hasn't even looked at me once since we first all gathered outside the label building this morning, let alone speak to me.

It's been hours since we left London and we're now all sitting in a service station having breakfast. Well, everyone except Creed that is.

I don't know where he's gone off to.

He had rushed to get off the bus before the rest of us without saying anything to anyone. I'd been worried but Clover had smiled and told me just to give him some space.

I wanted to ask her then what she knew.

But I knew she'd never tell me.

I don't know what I'm supposed to think. He's been weird for days, avoiding me. It's like he's suddenly gone cold.

It doesn't help that Crimson refuses to talk about it. Every time I bring it up, she just goes quiet without giving me any advice the way she normally would.

It's so frustrating.

Standing to my feet, I tell the others that I'm going to go for a quick walk and that I'll meet them back on the bus. They just nod their heads before returning to their conversation.

I don't know what I want to do. Find Creed? Demand that he talk to me? Check that he's okay?

I can't decide if I'm angry or worried.

No. That's not true.

Two days ago, I was worried. Now I'm angry. Or at least I'm pretty sure I'm angry.

It's not like he's just been weird today. If it was just today, I'd feel differently.

I'm scared he's going to dump me before we've even really started. I'm tempted to avoid him, so he can't. Except, I don't want to put it off. If he's going to dump me, I want to get it over and done with.

Only days ago he was bringing me coffee every day and then suddenly he went cold.

I can even pin point when it went wrong – the night they finished the album – I just don't know why. I don't know what caused the change of heart.

I look everywhere inside the building but he's nowhere to be found. So I step outside into the blistering cold, thinking that he might have already returned to the bus.

Wrapping my coat around myself, I begin to make my way across the carpark.

But no one is there. The bus is still locked and definitely empty.

Turning, I look back towards the service station, leaning back against the side of the bus. That's when I see him. He's sitting outside on a bench off to one side of the building.

Sighing heavily, I wearily make my way towards him. I'm nervous he'll leave if he sees me.

When I'm standing directly in front of him, I take a deep breath. He's not even looking at me. It's as if I'm completely invisible as he sits there staring at the ground.

"Creed?"

My voice gives away my nervousness.

He doesn't look up as he replies, "yeah?"

That's it. That's all I get. He doesn't talk to me for days and when he finally says something its 'yeah.'

I don't know what to say now that I'm standing here. An awkward silence falls around us and he clearly has no intentions of helping me to start this conversation.

"What's wrong?" I ask.

"Nothing," he says unconvincingly.

I don't know what to say. He must think I'm stupid.

"You're lying."

"So what if I am?" he asks.

I hesitate to answer. What am I supposed to say? That if he's lying I'll dump him? But I don't want that. That I'll be angry?

Apparently, I don't answer quick enough.

"Let's break up," he says with a coldness I've never heard in his voice before.

JETT

There's a weird awkward tension when we all climb back on the bus. Nona looks like she's been crying, her eyes rimmed with red as she snivels.

If I have to hazard a guess, it would appear Creed has dumped her. But that doesn't make sense because I thought he liked her.

The stony look on his face confirms my suspicions.

Crimson tries to pull Nona into a hug but Nona pushes her away, surprising all of us.

"Go away," she says quietly.

Crimson looks hurt but then her eyes move to Creed and she frowns. Turning back to her friends, she tries again, "Nona."

"Just leave me alone, Crimson. I don't want to fight with you in front of everyone else."

Clover climbs out of the seat next to me and makes her way towards the two girls.

Damn it.

I was looking forward to sitting with her. Ziggy and Nash are grinning at me as if they're delighted that I'm missing out. *Dicks.*

"Nona, why don't you sit with me," Clover asks.

Switch gives her a grateful smile as she manages to coax the make up artist into a seat.

"Okay. Everyone ready?" he says before turning the key in the ignition and starting the engine.

The rest of the journey is uneventful except for the occasional sniffle from Nona. Creed ignores everyone, refusing to explain what happened when the other guys ask in hushed voices.

Rigby is unimpressed.

He hates that we've already got a bus load of drama before the tour has even started but he doesn't say it.

He's not that stupid.

Truth is Creed's drama has nothing on the chaos we've been causing for months and the potential ramifications if our relationships with Clover are exposed. Creed breaking up with his girlfriend wouldn't even make it into the tabloids but the four of us dating the same girl…

Well. That would be headline news.

Yup. Rigby has good reason to keep his mouth shut.

It's mid-afternoon before we arrive in Edinburgh. There's no time to check into our hotel or anything.

Switch ushers us straight onto the stage for a rehearsal, without even giving us five minutes to take a leak.

The girls are nowhere to be found. I'd been hoping that Clover would sit in on our rehearsal but no such luck. Instead she went off with Nona as soon as we arrived.

As soon as they were off the bus, Crimson had turned on Creed, suddenly livid.

"What the fuck did you tell her?"

"The truth," he had replied, before pushing past her, and climbing off the bus.

Crimson had rushed after him, clearly not content with his answer.

Clover had returned just as we were finishing up our rehearsal, but the other two girls had not been with her. Now several hours later, we're waiting backstage for them to return. They're supposed to be doing our make up. We're due to go on stage in less than an hour and neither Crimson nor Nona are here.

Clover is checking her watch and Rigby is huffing impatiently.

"They'll be here," Ziggy says as if he's completely oblivious to everything that happened earlier on the bus. I swear that boy only sees what he wants to see.

"I wouldn't bet on it," Creed mutters.

"And who's fault is that?" Rigby retorts.

Clover lays a hand on his arm, silently telling him to drop it.

"If they don't come in the next five minutes, I'll do your make up myself," Clover says.

I bulk at that idea. I've been on the unfortunate end of Clover's face painting skills before. Creed and I exchange glances before bursting out laughing.

"Hey," Clover grumbles. "I'm pretty good at make up."

"I seem to remember that's what you told Jett about face painting when we were ten."

"You turned me into an Oompa Loompa," I tease her.

The others are smirking, enjoying this new titbit of information about our girlfriend.

"Well, if you don't want my help, what are you going to do?" she asks when our laughter dies away.

I have no answer for her.

Nash smirks, stepping towards the mirror. "Learn how to apply mascara?" he suggests.

"It's not as easy as it looks," comes a voice from the door.

"Thank fuck," Nash exhales as Crimson makes her way into the room.

"Nona?" Clover asks but Crimson shakes her head.

I don't know what that small action means. She doesn't know where Nona is... Nona isn't coming... It could mean anything and yet Clover seems to understand perfectly.

"Right, who's first?"

NASH

Switch pops his head around the door of our dressing room to tell us it's time. He doesn't hover. It's almost like he doesn't want to give us enough time to ask for anything.

Lazy sod.

Although chances are, it's probably just habit. When we first started out, Ziggy used to chase him out of the room, begging for him to cancel everything. That boy had serious nerves.

With a smirk, I reach for Clover, pulling her into my arms. My lips smack against hers as I kiss her aggressively. It's all time will allow. It's brief but hot as her tongue twists around mine once before retreating back into her own mouth.

Then with my mouth still against hers, I say, "while you watch us up there, I want you to think of all the delicious things we're going to do to you later."

I move slightly so I can whisper in her ear, "I want you wet."

Then I'm pulling away and without another word, I head out the door. Climbing on stage, I grin knowing full well Clover isn't the only the one who will be thinking about later while we're playing our set.

No. I'm already half hard just from the thought of her sprawled out beneath me.

And I'm completely fucked. I'm a horny git at the best of times but knowing that Clover is just waiting to be fucked, I'm not just horny. I'm fucking tormented.

It's my own damn fault. I'm the one that put the thought into both our minds.

I play my base perfectly. No duh. No one would know my mind isn't in it. I'm playing by instinct or muscle memory or something, while I imagine plunging my dick into Clover.

She's the best fucking drug. I'm buzzed, high just on the thought of fucking her.

My eyes wander to where I know she is watching us but I can't see her. It doesn't matter though.

Instead, I push all my energy into playing my bass, plucking the strings the way I plan to play her body later.

The crowd is screaming, usually I dig that sound, live for it even, but not tonight. Tonight, I'm consumed by thoughts of Clover.

I wonder if she's screaming our names the same way all our fans do, or if she's acting cool somewhere off to the side.

Creed and Rigby are singing like there's no tomorrow, like this moment is all there is and the energy is infectious. I'm grinning like the fucking Cheshire Cat and I have to remind myself to school my expressions. I have a persona to maintain.

With every song, I grow more and more impatient and when it's finally all over I practically throw myself off stage. Clover is waiting just in the wings. I grab her hand, pulling her down the corridor and back into the dressing room.

Pushing her against the wall, I slam the door behind us and kiss her harshly. I'm so fucking hard. I'd fuck her right here if we had enough time.

But the others will be right behind us.

Which isn't really a problem except Creed will be with them and I don't think anyone wants Creed seeing me fuck his sister. He'd probably kill me. It's one thing to know I'm doing it and another thing seeing and hearing it.

I pull back just as the door opens behind us. We're both breathless but the others don't say anything.

It's been a long day. Holding Clover's hand, I sit myself down on a sofa that is against the wall, pulling her down with me.

Switch opens the door. I've never understood that nickname.

"Ready to go?" he asks.

I wish he was asking if we were ready to go to the hotel but I'm not delusional. We'll be here another hour or so, greeting VIP ticket holders.

With a sigh, I kiss Clover on the cheek quickly before standing to my feet.

"Let's get this over with," I say gruffly. "I want to go to my fucking bed."

Or Clovers, I finish in my head, before following Switch out into the hall.

To look at us, you'd have no idea that none of us want to do this. We're all smiling like we live for this shit. And usually we do. But we're all so bloody tired. The last thing we want to do is stand around, signing shit and being gawked at by teenage girls and their mothers alike.

ZIGGY

Over the next few days there is a horrible tension on the tour bus. Nona isn't talking to Crimson and neither girl is speaking to Creed.

Every day is the same. We spend our days rehearsing and being interviewed by the press. Then we play our set in front of a different crowd before going and checking into whatever hotel we're sleeping in where the four of us feast of Clover.

The days are the hardest. The press are everywhere. I have to continuously stop myself from touching Clover. All those little touches… Playing with her hair, massaging her neck, kissing her cheek… All the things I normally do without thinking, I can't do, not with them here.

Their eyes are on her, wondering who she is. In fact, they've asked several times. But we've refused to answer. Only saying that she's part of the production team. That's it. That's what we've been told to tell them.

But they don't drop it easily.

They can probably sense the sexual tension that follows Clover wherever she goes. They can probably see the way our eyes follow her wherever she goes.

We try our best to keep Clover out of the spotlight, but it's next to impossible with the press following us everywhere we go.

We're in Glasgow, our last stop in Scotland before we head over to Northern Ireland. It's frustrating because Clover will be leaving us tomorrow. We'll head over the Irish Sea after seeing her off at the airport so she can return to London.

I don't want her to go. But it's probably for the best if we don't want too many questions asked.

I talk Clover into accompanying me around the corner to a little coffee shop to order some much needed caffeine for everyone.

Mostly I just want five minutes alone with her.

I take her hand in my, ignoring the little voice in my head that tells me I shouldn't. It's not wise but I don't care. Not when she's leaving tomorrow.

We queue quietly, pretending that we're not who we are, pretending that she's not Clover Levon and I'm not Ziggy, the drummer that all the girls in this little café want to fuck.

They whisper. We hear them.

But we don't pay them any attention at all.

Clover tries to pull her hand back but I don't let her. I won't let her. I should let her.

It's only when I see them pull out their phones and start snapping photos that I finally allow her to drop my hand. I'm being selfish, exposing her to their scrutiny.

No doubt those photos will be on social media within seconds and then the reporters will ask more questions.

Grabbing the tray of coffees that the barista offers me, we head back out into the cold.

Earlier, I'd walked idly, making the most of our moment of freedom, but now I'm too aware that we've just had our picture taken, to enjoy our time together.

We barely speak as we make our way back to the venue. The others reach for the coffees as we enter the dressing room.

"Why are you all hiding in here?" I ask, although I think I already know.

"The reporters are out there," Jett tells me without looking up from his book.

Rigby doesn't look impressed. He's staring at his phone, his face scrunched up as if in pain.

"So… what happened to keeping your hands to yourself, Ziggy?" he asks sternly.

I bulk. I know I fucked up but I was hoping he wouldn't see the photos this quickly.

"It's not just his fault," Clover comes to my defence.

Rigs eyes turn to her, he's fucking livid. It's not jealousy though. It's worry. He's angry because he knows just how cruel the media and our fans can get.

"Be more careful," he says.

That's all he says and he doesn't wait for either of us to reply before leaving the room.

Creed sighs, stretching his arms above his head.

"Time to do it all again," he says before following after Rigby.

I haven't got time to dwell on this shit or worry that I've fucked up. It's time to rehearse.

RIGBY

Seeing Clover off at the airport is the hardest thing I've ever done. But it has to be done.

This morning the tabloids were full of articles about Clover. They had yet to find out that she was the other Levon child. Only because they were so focused on her relationship with the band.

The headlines all read things like 'Saving Creed's Mystery Girl' or 'Who's Girl Is She?'

I couldn't completely blame Ziggy though. The press had photos of all of us with her. A hug here, a kiss there, holding hands… You name it, they'd seen it.

We'd thought we were careful. Damn it.

I'm almost relieved. At least with Clover in London the reporters will leave her alone. Her parents on the other hand, not so much. They're going to have questions and I hate to think we won't be there to deal with it for her.

Hanleigh Bradley

I knew this would happen, but I had hoped we'd keep it quiet a little longer.

We'd even discussed what we would do if it came out. Tell the truth. That's what we decided but now faced with the reality of the world knowing, it's hard to do.

Not because I'm worried about what people will think about me. But because I want to protect Clover.

I'd hoped that when the time came, we'd tell them together. We'd tell her parents and fingers crossed they'd be cool about it. Everyone knew they'd been into some weird shit during their day.

Except that's probably just wishful thinking.

Ignoring my unease, I pull Clover into my arms. I don't care that people are watching us as I lift her chin up so I can kiss her goodbye.

"I love you," I whisper when I pull away.

"I love you too," she replies before turning to the others.

It's hard to ignore the scandalous intakes of breath that surround us as everyone around us witness the four of us take turns kissing our girlfriend goodbye.

There's no doubt about it now. We'll be making headlines tomorrow.

We stand in a huddle, all looking fucking downcast as we watch Clover walk through the doors to security.

There's no time to waste moping though.

"Time to go, boys," Switch comes up the escalator calling us over.

Glancing at my watch, I realise he's right. We've not got long before we need to get the ferry across to Northern Ireland.

I follow after him, in my head listing all the reasons why its good Clover has gone home.

There are reporters waiting for us at the bottom of the escalator. They start barking questions at us as soon as they deem we're close enough to hear them clearly.

"Who is she, Rigby?" One calls.

"Is she messing you guys around?" Another shouts out.

"Do you love her, Jett?"

"Nash, have you…"

I drown out their voices, humming myself a tune. I do my best to keep my eyes on the door of the terminal building. We just need to get out of here.

"Is she your girlfriend?"

"You're not sharing her, are you?"

That one causes me to pull up short. I tell myself not to react. It might be the truth but they make it sound dirty and sordid in a way it never has been. Not for us.

I can't tell them that though. Not now. I have to wait for Clover to tell her parents. That has to come first. Then we can answer their questions.

Hesitantly, I begin moving forward again, the others following behind me, the press quick on our tails.

Once we're safely on the bus, hidden away from the eagle eyes of the reporters, I pull out my phone.

Quickly, I type out a text to Clover.

I wish we were coming with you. I'm sorry.

I stare at my phone as those three little dots appear, the ones that tell me she's typing her response.

Don't be sorry. I'll see you soon.

With a sigh, I send her another text, reminding her that I love her before putting my phone in my jeans pocket. I tell myself that Clover is a big girl. She's more than capable of telling her parents about us. I don't like that she's doing it alone, I don't like that we're not going to be there to protect her, but I know she's perfectly capable of standing her ground.

I just hope she does.

CLOVER

I'm surprised to find Jasper waiting for me at the airport. I'd hoped to have at least a day to prepare myself before having to tell my parents everything.

"Why are you here?" I ask as he takes my bag.

"I'm here to take you home."

Damn it! I'd been hoping to curl up in bed in one of the guys' shirts for a long sleep. The last five days have been exhausting.

"Can't she wait?"

"It's not your mother."

That gets my attention, sending a shiver down my spine. It's not every day my dad demands to see me.

I'm left with very little choice.

"Fine," I say before following after him.

"Have you seen the news?" he asks as we get into the car.

When I shake my head, he passes back an iPad.

"It's only been a few hours and it's already everywhere. We can't block this," Jasper tells me, his tone lacking any emotion at all. If he has an opinion, he isn't going to share it. "You're parents are furious."

Well, that's hardly surprising.

Anything that could make Saving Creed look bad, anything that could affect their profit margins has to go.

I ready myself for the biggest fight of my life. This isn't about me. It's about Saving Creed and my parents fucking money.

Letting myself into the house, I ask the housekeeper Alice where my parents are. She informs me that they're waiting for me in my father's study.

This is the last thing I need right now but its out of my hands. With a quick rap of my knuckles against the door, I wait for them to answer.

"Come in," my father calls from within the room. His voice is icy cold. This isn't going to be fun.

I hesitate, breathing in a deep breath, before twisting the knob and pushing the door open. My face is set in a cool expression. I tell myself to keep calm, no matter what they say I can't react.

"Sit down, Clover," my father says sternly.

I don't say anything as I do what he says.

"I don't have time to waste on this," he begins immediately, before my arse even touches the cushion of the chair. "I don't want to hear anything about what you and those boys have been up to."

The way he says 'those boys' fucking hurts.

"Just know its not acceptable and it ends here!"

"No," I cut in.

"Excuse me?"

"I said no."

"Clover," my mother tries, "don't argue with your father."

"I'm not a child. You don't get to dictate who I date."

"Oh princess," my dad says snidely, "don't delude yourself that you're dating. What you're doing is fucking and nothing more."

His callous words shock my mum.

"Richie!"

"You'll give them up," he continues, completely ignoring my mum.

"And what if I don't?"

"I'll fuck them all over. I'll disband Saving Creed."

"You wouldn't," I gasp out.

He wouldn't. They're his money maker.

"I would."

"What and lose millions?" I retort angrily.

"Rather that than the world find out my daughter is a whore."

My mum is horrified. As if instinctively, she comes to my defence, slapping my father across the face.

"Leave," she tells me quietly.

I don't need to be told twice.

It's only when I reach the door that I hesitate.

"I won't end it. Not now. Not ever."

The words sound brave. They sound convincing. But I'm shaking with a mixture of rage and anxiety as I open the door and let myself out.

I push past Jasper and Alice, taking my bag from where it sits in the entrance hall. They both call after me, Jasper offering to drive me, but I ignore them.

I'm too angry to even try and be polite.

I just want to go home, back to the guys' place and curl up and cry. My phone buzzes but I ignore it. It's either my parents demanding that I come back to the house or one of the guys making sure I got back safely.

Either way, I don't want to answer.

I don't want to argue even more with my parents and I don't want to have to lie to the guys. I want them to enjoy their gig tonight, not worry about me and perhaps more importantly, I don't want them to worry about Saving Creed.

JETT

"Fuck sake," Rigby growls. "She's still not answering."

I try not to react. I need to keep calm. We're due on stage any minute now. If I'm not careful, I'll be walking out and heading straight to the airport.

We've all tried calling her.

It's been hours since she left, almost all fucking day. The papers are full of pictures of us all, especially Clover. I'm worried. I know exactly how awful her parents can be. I never wanted her to face this shit alone.

I'm cross that we weren't more careful. That it didn't all come out when we were all back in London together.

Rigby swears as he flings his phone down on the sofa.

"This is fucking shit," he barks out.

He looks ready to cancel the rest of the tour and he's not alone. I'd happily call quits right now, if it would mean being able to go home to Clover.

We have to do something. I'm restless.

Creed enters the room, his phone to his ear.

"He said that?" he demands.

His face contorts as he listens to the person on the other end of the line, growing more and more angry with every second.

"Fuck sake! He can't be serious?"

He begins pacing the length of the room.

"What about Clo?"

That one name has all of us staring at him. He nods his head after a moment.

"I've got to go. Keep me informed."

He hangs up, turning to look at us all.

"How attached to our label are you guys?"

His question surprises me. I thought the call was about his sister, not the band. But then it hits me. His parents are pissed.

"Not overly," I tell him.

"Good," he replies.

"I think we're about to be dropped."

"Why would they drop you?" Ziggy asks. "You're their son."

"Yeah and my band mates are all in a relationship with their daughter."

There's no venom, no bite to his words. He's just stating facts, not blaming us.

"Shit," Rigby says, kicking the wall in irritation. "What do we do?"

"We threaten to leave first," Creed replies with surprising calm. "We call their bluff."

"What if it's not a bluff?" Nash asks.

"Then we leave," Creed says, shrugging his shoulders. "We have no choice. It's either that or you all break up with Clover."

"That's not an option," Rigby tells us all.

It could have gone unsaid. Not even Creed would ever have agreed to his parents' demand, not when it would hurt his sister.

"Jett, get Switch to set up a press conference for tomorrow."

"Will he do it?"

"Probably not," Creed replies. Switch works for the Levons, not the band. "But he'll tell my parents our intentions. That's all we need."

I nod my head, understanding his meaning.

"Nash, make some calls. All the reporters you know… We need interviews and loads of them for tomorrow."

"Done," Nash replies, already pulling out his phone.

"Either way, with or without the label you guys are going public about Clover tomorrow."

Everyone nods their head in agreement.

"Rigby, we need to line up a new label, just in case."

"I'll reach out to a few," Rigby replies.

Relief floods me. Thank fuck for Creed. That boy always has a plan. He's exactly the guy you want with you when your life becomes a disaster movie.

Leaving the room, I type a quick text to Clover.

Don't worry. We've got this.

Then I make my way down the hall looking for Switch. I find him easily since he's on his way to our dressing room.

"What are you doing here, Jett? It's time to get out there."

"I need to speak to you."

"Can't it wait?" He's impatient. We're on a schedule and I'm fucking it up.

"No."

"Hurry up then," he says with a sigh.

"We want a press conference tomorrow."

His eyes narrow suspiciously.

"Why?"

"We've decided to leave the label."

"WHAT?" He practically shouts before looking up and down the corridor, probably checking that no one else heard what I said. He's caught off guard. He didn't expect me to say that.

"Saving Creed is dropping the label."

"Nah, man. That's a bad idea."

"We've decided. It's a done deal."

"What do you mean?"

"We've got a new label lined up," I lie.

I have to make this convincing if I want him to run and tell Mr and Mrs Levon. He has to be scared. Worried for his job.

His eyes wide, he shakes his head.

"Let's talk about this later."

"We won't change our minds."

"The compensation…" he begins.

"We don't need to worry about that. They said they'd pay for it."

It's another lie. I feel like a right shit for lying to Switch. He's a good guy. He's been a great manager. With us since day one. Since the moment we signed our contract.

But Clover is worth the lie.

NASH

Switch is nowhere to be found when we finish our set. He's left a note saying that we're to find our own way to the hotel and that he'll see us in the morning.

It's easy to imagine where he's gone.

He's run off back to London to tell Clover's mum and dad about the press conference. I'd call him a spineless git but I can't really blame him. If we leave the label, he'll lose his job.

He probably feels like we've betrayed him.

We're quiet as we walk around the corner to the hotel that we checked into earlier. It's weird not having Clover here with us. We've gotten ourselves into a bit of a routine. We'd have a couple of drinks in the bar together before heading upstairs for a massive fuck-fest.

But not tonight.

Tonight, Clover is miles away in London.

Sighing, I approach the bar to order a round of drinks while everyone else takes a seat in one of the booths.

Crimson and Nona don't stop or even say goodnight as they head straight up to their rooms.

I hope they sort their shit out soon. There's too much fucking drama going on.

None of us bother talking as we drink our beers. There's nothing really worth saying. Everything hinges on tomorrow.

"What do you think Switch will say?" Ziggy asks just as I'm finishing off my pint.

"Dunno," I say with a shrug. "Depends how pissed Mr Levon is."

"If I was him, I'd want to cut off all your balls," Creed tells us with a smirk.

"So, we're fucked, right?" Jett jokes.

"Pretty much," Rigby grins.

"Let's be real," Creed says. "Worst case scenario, we go independent or we get a new label."

"Best case?" I ask.

"You all get to tell the world you love Clover."

I could get behind that one.

"Either way, tomorrow we tell everyone everything. It's up to my parents whether they stand beside us or if we stand alone."

It's moments like this that it's easy to see why Creed is our leading man. He's a natural born leader. Bossy as shit but also damn good at getting us all on board.

***

The next morning, Switch is waiting for us just outside the hotel's restaurant.

"Mr Levon wants to speak to you guys. You're going to have to eat with him."

The last thing I want to do is eat my breaky with Clover's dad. Shit. I'm quaking in my boots.

Creed leads the way, stepping into the restaurant. He glances around before spotting his father off to one side. Approaching the table, he sits down directly opposite his father.

"Dad," he says, his tone giving nothing away.

"Creed," Mr Levon replies with a nod of his head. "Sit down boys."

He waves his hand to the other chairs and the four of us do as he says hesitantly.

"You want to leave the label?" Mr Levon isn't beating around the bush.

"You left us with no choice," Creed answers.

"I don't know why you'd think that."

"You threatened to disband us."

"Do you really think I'd do it?"

"I don't care. We won't be threatened."

"So, you're leaving the label?"

Neither Creed or his father want to lose face. It's pretty apparent neither of them want to give in.

"That really depends on you."

"What do you want?" his father asks, leaning forward in his seat.

"Back the fuck off. Let Clover and the guys be."

If Mr Levon is bothered that his son just swore at him, he doesn't let on.

"That's not going to happen, Creed."

"Well, then we've got nothing else to say," Creed replies, before standing to his feet, scraping his chair against the stone floor.

"Wait," Richie Levon says, sighing heavily. "Fine. I'll keep out of it. For now."

"That's all I ask." Creed smiles. "Clover has a pretty good head on her shoulders. You know? You should trust her judgment."

Mr Levon doesn't say anything, the twitch in his cheek the only sign that he's holding back what he really wants to say.

Standing to his feet, he buttons up his suit jacket.

"I presume you no longer need a press conference."

"No, thank you. We've already scheduled several interviews for today."

"About what?" He asks sceptically.

"Oh, you know. This and that. Mostly the new album."

With a nod, Mr Levon walks away from our table without another word.

CLOVER

My mum is calling me. Again.

She's been calling on and off all morning.

I don't know why she won't just leave me the hell alone. It's pretty obvious what she wants to say. She just wants to repeat what my father has already said.

Flipping through channels on the TV, I'm surprised when I see Rigby's face on the screen. I quickly unmute it so I can hear what he's saying.

It's then that I realise he's talking about me.

He's telling everyone about our relationship.

"I love her," he says without a second's hesitation. "It just so happens that three of my best mates do too."

That's how he describes it. He says it like it's the most natural thing in the world.

"So, you're all going to date her?"

"Date her... Love her... Live with her..." Nash says. "We're going to do it all."

"Are you not worried what your fans will think?"

"Not in the slightest," Ziggy replies. "Our fans love us, they want us to be happy. Clover makes us happy."

He says it so innocently as if he actually believes the words he's saying.

"Isn't that a little naïve?"

"Probably." Nash shrugs his shoulders. "But we have to believe the best of our fans."

"So, how did you meet her?"

The guys smirk at each other momentarily and I wonder if they're going to tell the reporter EVERYTHING. Are they really going to tell everyone that I pretended to be my twin brother.

"Well... anyone who knows my parents, knows they're absolutely bonkers," Creed says casually. "Clover is my twin sister."

That gets the reporter excited. They knew Creed had a twin but they never put two and two together.

"I was in an accident," Creed explains. "I was pretty hurt and my parents forced Clover to take my place. They were worried that we wouldn't get the album finished without a little help."

"So, Clover pretended to be a boy? She pretended to be you, Creed?"

"Yeah. For several weeks. Of course, it was all my parents crazy idea but it led to the guys getting pretty close to Clo."

The reporter can hardly believe her ears and neither can I. My mum barges into the living room. I didn't even realise she had a key to Saving Creed's place but then again it's probably owned by the label.

"What the fuck are they playing at?" She barks out angrily, staring at the TV before turning to me. "And you, why the hell aren't you answering your phone?"

"I didn't want to."

"Fuck sake, Clover," mum complains. "Saving Creed is safe. They won. So, stop being difficult."

"I'm not being difficult."

Now I sound like a petulant child.

Sighing, she flings a brown envelope down on the coffee table.

"Look that over. I think you'll like what you see. I'm fed up of fighting you on it. If you don't want to sign with the label then that's your call."

"What?"

I reach for the envelop.

"You might think it's love but trust me, it's not. Right now, it probably seems fun but it won't last."

"Whatever, mum."

"Just look that over." She points to the envelop. "It's everything you've ever wanted."

She then begins to walk away, preparing to leave.

I open the envelop, shocked out of my mind by what I find inside it. It's the sort of opportunity I'd die for.

"You're trying to manipulate me?" I demand to her back.

"No," she says as she turns back. "Just giving you what you want."

"And what do you want in return?"

"Nothing. I'll just be happy knowing your thousands of miles away from those boys."

With that she leaves without waiting for me to reply.

Looking down at the envelop again, I sit back down on the sofa. My eyes wander to the TV where Rigby is still talking about me.

My mum wants me to choose.

But it's impossible. More than that it's fucking cruel.

What mother would make her daughter choose between her dream and love?

Dropping the envelop onto the table, I close my eyes and try to settle my breathing. I won't do it. I won't leave them.

I choose them.

It doesn't matter that that envelop contains my dream job, the chance to write the score for a Hollywood movie. It doesn't matter because I choose Rigby.

I choose Jett.

I choose Nash.

I choose Ziggy.

Nothing else matters, not next to my boys.

CREED

"You're going to turn it down?" I ask down the phone, completely bewildered.

"Yeah. Of course, I will."

"Why?" I ask. It doesn't make sense. It's her fucking dream.

"I don't want to pick."

Does she not realise that by turning it down, that's exactly what she's doing?

"Who says you have to pick? Did mum say you couldn't do it unless…?"

"No but her intention was explicit. She wants me as far away from the guys as possible."

"Right," I reply.

I'm furious they've done this. Not so much that they've offered Clover this opportunity but that they're trying to control her with it.

"I think you should take it," I tell her.

"Why?"

"What do you mean? It's your dream. It's everything you've ever wanted."

"Not anymore."

I know what she means. Now her heart isn't just dreaming of writing the perfect movie score, it's filled with thoughts of the four guys that are waiting for me in our dressing room.

I'm standing just outside the door.

"The guys aren't going anywhere. You can make it work."

"Make long distance work?"

"Yeah."

"But I don't want to let mum and dad win."

"They're not. You get your dream and the guys. Two things our parents don't want to let you have. The way I see it it's a win win."

"I don't want to leave."

"Clo, we spend so much time on tour anyway. What are you going to do? Sit at home and wait for the guys to come home?"

"I just don't want to be so far away from them."

"Just think about it," I tell her. "I don't want you to regret your decision."

"Okay," she huffs. I can hear the stubbornness in her voice loud and clear. Her mind is already made up.

I say a quick goodbye before opening the door behind me and walking into the dressing room.

The boys are all laughing at some joke Nash is telling them, all the worries of the last few days gone.

"Guys, can we talk."

I'm overstepping and Clover will be pissed when she finds out. They turn to face me, their faces turning serious.

"My parents are proper shits," I tell them. "They think they've played their trump card."

"What have they done?" Jett asks hesitantly.

"There's a movie that needs a score. Clover has been offered the job."

"That's brilliant!" Ziggy is delighted by the news, completely unaware what it means for him.

"Hollywood?" Jett asks.

When I nod, Ziggy's face drops.

Jett and the others have forced smiles on their faces. They know they should be happy for Clover but it's hard to be happy when it means being apart.

"She's going to turn it down."

"Like hell she is!" Rigby jumps to his feet, pulling out his phone.

"Book a plane for Clover," he shouts down the line. "I want her here by the time I get off stage tonight."

I don't have to ask who he's talking to. It's clearly Switch.

"Thank you for telling us," he says, patting me on the back. "Don't worry. We'll fix this."

"Hang on, Rigs." Ziggy isn't happy. "What are you going to do?"

"I'm… No. We're going to tell her to accept the job, go make her movie and then come home to us."

"I… I don't want her to go," Ziggy replies with a pout.

"Do you think I do?" Rigby turns on him. "It doesn't matter what we want."

"But…"

"No, Ziggy. It's her fucking dream. We can't take that away from her."

Jett and Nash are both nodding their head in agreement.

"But, what if she doesn't come back?"

"You really think that's possible?" Nash asks with a grin. "She's ours. She belongs with us. She'll come home when she's ready."

"But…"

"Ziggy, it's not up for discussion. The decision has been made. We're not like her parents, we're not trying to cage her in. We want her to be free. Right?"

With a sigh, Ziggy nods his head.

"Yeah, I guess. I still don't like it though."

Chuckling, I sit down to get my makeup done. I love my friends and for the first time ever, I'm grateful that they all love my sister.

RIGBY

Got to give it to Switch. He can act quickly when you want him to. Clover is waiting for us in the wings when we make our way off stage.

She's smiling, eager to see us even though it's barely been a few days.

She doesn't know why I asked for her to come. If she did, she might have refused.

"Hello love," I say, pulling her into my arms.

Embracing her like this would normally fill me with warmth. Not tonight though. Tonight, it fills me with dread because if I convince her, if I do what I should, I won't get to hold her like this for a while.

I let the others greet her before taking her hand and leading her towards the bus. I don't say much, letting the others keep the conversation going all the way to the hotel.

It's only when it's just the five of us in my hotel room that I finally say what I must.

"I want you to take the job."

"What?"

Her eyes widen, her expression a mixture of hurt, probably at the fact I want her to go, fear, perhaps because she didn't want us to know and anger, most likely directed towards Creed.

"Creed told you?"

Yup, the anger is definitely directed towards Creed. For a moment, I feel sorry for landing him in it.

"It's your dream," I say, sidestepping her question. It sounds cheesy as hell but I don't care. I can't imagine giving up what I do. I'm living my dream every bloody day and I want the same for her.

"We'll be here waiting for you to come back."

Another cheesy line right out of some low-rate romance movie.

"You'll wait?"

"What else would we do?" I give her an incredulous expression. "We love you, Clover."

"Tell us you'll do it." Jett steps forward. "Please Clo."

"You really want me to?"

She almost looks like she wants us to say no and perhaps a part of her does. I don't do it though.

No matter how much I want to keep her by my side, I won't do it. I can't do it.

"We'll miss you like fucking crazy," Nash tells her, coming up behind her and kissing her neck, "but yeah, we really want you to do it."

She rests against him, closing her eyes as I take a step forward, just a fraction, so I can kiss her.

It's slow and languid and for a moment I completely forget all about Hollywood and the movie and the big ocean that will be between us.

Pulling back, I ask, "what do you say, Clover?"

I have to get her to agree before I allow myself to enjoy this moment. I can't get distracted until my task is complete, no matter how tempting she is.

My hands are under her shirt, unclasping her bra.

"Okay," she says with a gasp as I tweak one of her nipples between my fingers.

"Good girl," Nash says against her nape.

"Now we get to spend the whole night reminding you what will be at home waiting for you," I tell her.

The four of us begin to remove our clothes and Clover stands there enjoying the sight.

Then I pull her shirt over her head while Ziggy unbuttons her jeans before Nash picks her up and places her gently on the bed.

Licking my lips, it's easy to imagine just how amazing tonight will be.

Every night with Clover is the best night of my life until the next night and then the next. She always surprises me, always exceeds my expectations.

I come up behind her, picking her up so she's sitting between my legs. I'm in no rush. Not tonight. I'm going to take my time to enjoy every inch of her.

My hands go to her shoulders, easing all her tension away while Jett sheathes his cock in a condom and lines himself up to fuck her.

It's weird. A few weeks ago, just the idea of this, the idea of him fucking her had me losing my shit with jealousy. But not now. Now it's as if it's exactly how I want it. It's how our lives are meant to be. And I wouldn't change it for the world.

Even if I could have her all to myself, even if she'd give me that, I would never ask for it. Not now.

I kiss a trail along her neck before whispering in her ear, "you're so sexy when you're being fucked."

CRIMSON

I'm at a loss for how to fix things.

I never should have kissed him. He was off limits. If I wanted him, I should have laid my claim long before she started liking him.

Hindsight is a fucking pain in the arse.

This is the longest Nona has ever gone without talking to me and I have no idea how to put it right.

She's been avoiding me, spending most of her time alone so she can stay away from me and Creed.

I want to hate him for fucking up my friendship with Nona except this is not completely on him. And no matter how pissed I feel, I can't completely ignore the facts. I'm as responsible as he is.

The guys are at the airport seeing Clover off. Again. I swear that girl spends more time at the airport than anyone else I know.

Creed is in the venue hall checking over the set up for tonight with Switch, leaving me alone in the dressing room.

The door opens and I look up to see Nona just as she begins to walk straight back out again.

"Nona, wait," I call out to her, getting to my feet.

"Not now, Crimson."

I grab her arm. I want to fix this. I need to make it right.

"I'm sorry, Nona."

Huffing, she pulls her arm away and enters the room, coming to sit down on the sofa that I just got off of.

"Do you think this is something that can be fixed with a quick sorry?"

"No."

I want to explain. I want to tell her that I think I love him. That he was mine first. That I wasn't thinking. Except no matter how true those words might be, they're all just excuses and they'll never mend our friendship.

"How could you?" she whispers.

"I don't know," I admit. "Truth is I betrayed you a long time ago. The first time you told me you liked him... I should have been honest with you then."

"Yes. Yes, you should have."

"I never meant to hurt you, for what it's worth. Quite the opposite actually."

"But you did. You hurt me. More than he did."

I know how she feels. I've been hurting for months. Except I had no one else to blame but myself.

"I'm sorry."

"Well, it doesn't matter now. It's over. We broke up. You can..."

"No. I won't. I'm not doing that."

There's no way Creed and I will be getting together now. That is definitely not happening.

Sighing, Nona rests her head on the back of the sofa, looking up to the ceiling.

"Do you know, I don't know how they do it."

"Do what?" I'm completely lost. Not at all sure what she's talking about.

"The four of them... share her."

With a smirk, I sit beside her.

"Fuck me, if I know."

"The jealousy… I hated you for just kissing him."

"I guess they're used to it," I reply, trying not to allow her words to hurt.

"Maybe. Creed is a right arsehole."

Only Nona could say that so sweetly. It doesn't sound vulgar or cheap when she swears.

"Yup," I agree.

"Hey!"

We both turn our heads towards the door to find Creed standing there, smiling at us both.

"Since you're now all about hating me," he begins, making his way into the room, "does that mean you made up?"

I hesitate, waiting for Nona.

Creed grabs a chair and pulls it over to where we are sitting.

"Sure," Nona says quietly, taking my hand in hers. "You're not that special, Creed."

"Glad to hear it," Creed replies. "I was beginning to get a big head."

We all laugh momentarily before going quiet.

"I'm really sorry, you know," Creed says seriously after a moment. "I don't know what I was thinking."

I don't tell him it's okay and neither does Nona.

"I really fucked up," he tells us. "Friends?"

I don't know if it's possible to be Creed's friend. I still love him and I'm pretty sure Nona does too. But I'm not like the guys, there's no world in which I'd share him, not with Nona, not with anyone.

So, I'm not left with much choice. It's not like we can just stop talking. We work in the same damn building and see each other every day and then when we're working on the tours… we'll be practically on top of each other on that damn bus.

Yeah, not talking isn't an option.

"Friends," I agree while Nona nods her head.

I tell myself not to hope for more. That it can't happen, not now, not ever. But even though I tell myself that, my heart doesn't obey and I feel a little bit of hope that maybe one day, he'll be mine.

CLOVER

Six Months Later

I'm bored. This should be the best moment of my life, it's a fucking dream come true, seeing my score put to movie. I'm at the premier, wearing a sheer dress, surrounded by the cast and crew that have worked on this production.

I've received countless job offers in the last hour and a half since I first walked down the red carpet.

I'll accept them all if I can… My only requirement, that I can work on the score from London.

L.A. is amazing. I love it here but I don't want to stay, not for a moment longer. If I could, I'd leave before the movie ends.

The only thing that keeps me in my chair is the knowledge that even if I leave early, I can't get an earlier flight.

I'm glad that I came. Glad that I took the job. For the first time in my life, I don't feel like my parents are controlling me. I don't feel caged in.

And it's all thanks to my boys.

Without them, I'd probably be singing on a stage somewhere, doing exactly what my parents expected me to do. My dream would have been impossible.

But they make me brave, in a way I'll probably never understand.

I'm impatient. I want to go home and see them. I want to get on that damn plane and fly back to London right this second. Just so I can spend a little longer in their arms.

I spoke to Jett a few hours ago. He'd called to tell me how proud they all were of me. He's so flipping sweet sometimes. Usually he's the quiet one but occasionally he completely disarms me with his cuteness.

The movie is coming to an end and I can't fucking wait. I know the scenes like the back of my hand and I'm counting down he seconds until the credits roll.

I should be basking in this moment, not trying to rush it along.

That's when I hear a voice in my ear, "be patient, love."

I go to turn in my chair, my heart racing with excitement. I'd recognise that voice anywhere.

Two hands brush against my neck.

"Look forward," Rigby says with a roughness that is purely him.

I want to see him. I want to see his face, kiss him… I want to know if he's alone or if the others are here too.

"Babe, watch the movie," Nash whispers in my other ear, before sucking on my lobe.

There's no way I can focus on the movie now, not with them so close. Not when I can't see them or touch them. It's not fucking fair. I want to touch them.

I've missed them so damn much.

My eyes on the screen, I try to ignore the way Rigby is stroking my neck. Finally, it's the final scene. Not long now.

"I love you in this dress," Nash tells me. "So fucking hot."

I'm going to kill them for this. Make them suffer.

When the film finally finishes, the director stands up to speak, praising everyone for a job well done.

I want him to shut the fuck up.

My breathing is harsh as I turn slightly in my chair to try and catch a glimpse of my boys, but Rigby tuts.

"Focus," he says. "This is your moment."

"I can't believe you're here."

"Did you really think we'd miss it?"

Finally the director stops talking and everyone is standing to give him an ovation. I turn around and smile widely when my eyes land on my four perfect men, all wearing tuxes. They look fucking hot.

Like crazy hot.

I tell myself I'll have to take a photo of them dressed like that for all their crazy fans.

"Hello Clo," Jett says with a secretive smile.

"You could have told me."

"And ruin the surprise?"

Ziggy is the first to hug me.

"Congratulations! You did it."

I really did. It's amazing really. I've finally done what I thought was impossible and it's all because of them.

"Thank you," I whisper.

"For what?" Ziggy asks.

"Making this possible."

"Love, this is all you," Rigby tells me, before wrapping an arm around my shoulder. "Now, is there a party we need to attend or can we go straight to bed?"

Giggling, I smack his chest.

"I'm supposed to be catching a plane."

"Shame… We were hoping you'd show us the sights," Nash says, but from the way he looks me up and down, it's pretty clear the only 'sights' he's interested is me naked in his bed.

Smiling, I let them guide me out of the theatre and into a waiting limo.

This moment couldn't be any more perfect. I finally have everything I've ever wanted and then some. I've missed them so much, too much.

It might not be conventional. It might even be too much for my Rockstar, drug crazed parents but I love four men and no amount of time or distance can change that.

Caged

You leave the cage door open

Its an illusion, mocking me

Telling me that I am free

Telling me that I can escape

But, I'm caged in, confined

Restricted by words

Wrapped in someone else's dream

I'm caged in, confined

Restricted by words

Wrapped in someone else's dream

You let me fly free

There's a time limit, holding me

Living for those moments

Lust & Lyrics

When I feel finally free

But, I'm caged in, confined
Restricted by words
Wrapped in someone else's dream

When will I finally be free
Of this destiny you've forced on me
When will you finally see
That I'm not who you want me to be

'cause, I'm caged in, confined
Restricted by words
Wrapped in someone else's dream
Someone else's dream

Hanleigh's Reverse Harems

Reverse Harem books have one female main character with multiple male main characters. It is not just a 'Love Triangle'.

Lust & Lyrics – Celebrity Reverse Harem

His, His Or His?

All Mine

Less Than Conventional

Kumari's Kitsune – Fantasy Reverse Harem

Cursed by the Crown

Tainted by Prophecy

Standalone Reverse Harems

First Snow

Hanleigh's London Saga

All the books in this Contemporary British Saga have interwoven plotlines, returning characters and places.

The Rules Series

Broken Rules

Enforced Rules

Revised Rules

A Secret Melody

The History Series

Repeating History

Deleting History

Forging History

A History In Paris

The Intimacy Series

Damaged Intimacy

Entangled Intimacy

Forceful Intimacy

Call Me Doctor

The Fate Series

Inescapable Fate

Inexplicable Fate

Irreversible Fate

A Bleak December

Hanleigh's London Boxsets

RULES

HISTORY

INTIMACY

FATE

Hanleigh's Other Books

The Elite Series

INSTINCT

CRAVING

Utterly Betrayed Series

Flip A Coin

Printed in Poland
by Amazon Fulfillment
Poland Sp. z o.o., Wrocław